The
INCONCEIVABLE
IDEA OF THE
SUN

Anil Menon's most recent work, *Half of What I Say* was shortlisted for the 2016 Hindu Literary Award. He is the co-editor of *Breaking the Bow*, an international anthology of short fiction inspired by the Ramayana. His short fiction has been translated into many languages, including Chinese, Hebrew, Igbo and Romanian. He co-founded the Dum Pukht Writers' Workshop series and currently serves as the editor-in-chief of *The Bombay Literary Magazine*.

ALSO BY THE AUTHOR

Half of What I Say
The Beast With Nine Billion Feet

The
INCONCEIVABLE
IDEA OF THE
SUN

ANIL MENON

hachette
INDIA

First published in 2022 by Hachette India
(Registered name: Hachette Book Publishing India Pvt. Ltd)
An Hachette UK company
www.hachetteindia.com

1

ISBN 978-93-91028-60-2

Hachette Book Publishing India Pvt. Ltd
4th & 5th Floors, Corporate Centre,
Plot No. 94, Sector 44, Gurugram 122003, India

Typeset in Arno Pro 11.5/15.5
by R. Ajith Kumar, New Delhi

Printed and bound in India
by Manipal Technologies Limited, Manipal

MIX
Paper from
responsible sources
FSC™ C043100

For my beloved brother Ambat Ravindran Ajit Kumar (1960–2021), who would have been very proud and very happy to hold this book in his hands.

Since nothing has an intrinsic nature, neither do human beings.

RICHARD RORTY
A World Without Substances or Essences

Customs baggage rules exist because there is such a thing as human nature. People imagine they have the right to stuff anything into their bags. As far as the imagination is concerned, anything goes. But is Anything Goes really a traveller you want to be sitting next to?

IMRAN ASIF MEMON
Indian Customs Baggage Rules Explained Simply &
Other Essays

CONTENTS

My wish would be simply to present it to thee plain and unadorned, without any embellishment of preface or uncountable muster of customary sonnets, epigrams, and eulogies, such as are commonly put at the beginning of books.

MIGUEL DE CERVANTES, *Don Quixote de la Mancha*

It was customary in the West, it seems, for an author to begin with excuses, explanations and snivels about their work. Which is quite peculiar since the author is usually the last person to know what their book is about. The lamentations, though as varied as beetles, had a common pattern: the author had intended one book, written another and was now apologizing for an imagined third. Perhaps the idea was to offset criticism. Who in good conscience can whip a chap busy whipping himself? But it is all a sham, of course. The author's irremediable egotism – the quintessential ingredient for an author's work to be *their* work – cannot resist prancing and preening during the self-flagellation ritual. The peacock dances; the author humblebrags.

Fortunately, this kind of posturing before the reader has almost vanished in modern times. One can move about in an Arundhati Roy novel or a Zadie Smith miscellany secure in the knowledge that the author won't encroach like an aggressive hawker determined to sell you cheap rubbish bags. Boundaries matter. As for the author's egotism, let us recall Foucault's claim that in modern literature, 'the mark of the writer is reduced to nothing more than the singularity of his absence; he must assume the role of the dead man in the game of writing'. Since it is so if Foucault says it is so, let it be so. Let us mark the writer. Let us be inappropriate. Let us be inauspicious. Anil Menon is dead. Long live Anil Menon.

Quintessence & Other Stories is a collection of short stories by Anil Menon. More precisely, this volume is a collection of seventeen or so short stories by Anil Menon. Seventeen or so? Doesn't the author even know how many stories he has written? Well, the (late) author certainly has an opinion on the matter. This qualification isn't intended to launch one of those disquieting postmodern games and is simply an acknowledgement of the reader's role in deciding whether a story is a story. It is still the author's story, but perhaps in the way an autopsy belongs to the cadaver (royalty cheques are still to be addressed to the author).

The stories in this posthumous collection belong to the category of 'speculative fiction', or spec-fic. Earlier, such stories were filed under 'Literature of the Imagination'. This might seem insulting to conventional fiction and its readers. Does *Emma* or *Moby Dick* or *Mrs Dalloway* or *Murder on the*

Orient Express not require the reader to have an imagination? Of course they do. However, in conventional fiction there is a natural correspondence between the actual world and the world of the novel. In spec-fic this correspondence is called into question. Whose actuality? Whose nature?

In conventional fiction, the context is this world, the physical world, our actual world. If it rains in a conventional story, there's no need to add that it is raining water. Yes, it is raining water; that's how rain works in the actual world! In spec-fic, however, it could be raining kettles, diamonds, deacons, paradoxes and poems. The spec-fic story's context isn't shaped by nature, but by the imagination. Spec-fic stories go wherever the imagination is willing to go.

It turns out the human imagination is quite the traveller. Speculative fiction is a family of genres with a rather generous admissions policy. Spec-fic isn't anti-realist; it is anti-naturalist. Any story with dragons is a lifetime member of this group. Ditto for vampires, ghosts and zombies. The Fairy tale and Fable are respected elders, Science-fiction is the crazy uncle, and Fantasy is the unmarried sister with a passion for unicorns. There's an eternal child, Nonsense verse, who still hasn't learned to speak, thank god. The family also includes stylish characters like Metafiction, Nouveau Roman, Magic Realism, Fabulist fiction, Irrealist fiction and the Theatre of the Absurd. The surreal, the irreal, the unreal and the other refugees from the desert of the natural: all find a home in which to live long and prosper.

Needless to say, true readers will resist all such classifications and divisions. 'The classification of stories into genres,' Menon used to say, 'is the Belgian Joke told endlessly.' Told endlessly or not, I have yet to come across anyone who has heard the Joke, so here it is.

It seems that in one Belgian army unit, the perennial feud between the Flemings and the Walloons got so exacerbated, the Commandant had no choice but to gather all the men. 'Flemings to the left side,' ordered the Commandant. Half the men clattered to the left. 'Walloons to the right.' About an equal number crowded to the right. One man, visibly nervous, remained at attention in the centre of the field. 'What is your problem, soldier?' barked the Commandant. 'I'm a Belgian, sir!' The Commandant slapped his thigh. At last! A patriot with sense and sensibility. In the army, nonetheless. 'Excellent!' beamed the Commandant. 'What is your name, soldier?' The soldier saluted and replied: 'Rabinowitz, sir!' Trust the only real Belgian in the group to be a Jew.

The moral is clear. As with Belgians, Flemings, Walloons and Jews, a story can be filed under many names. Fortunately, a great story survives its classifications to become a part of literature. Unfortunately, *Quintessence & Other Stories* has no such lofty ambition. There is also the issue of integrity. How ethical is it to herd a collection of boundary-defying tales into a boundary-establishing table of contents? How indeed. Having raised the concern, we shall give it a kiss and send it on its way. It is best to leave philosophy to French philosophers, and let this chapter do what Pliny the Elder said tables of contents should do, namely, exist solely to save the reader some time.

Though time is the one thing stories can't promise they won't waste, the table of contents can ameliorate that risk by simply listing the titles. If a story has the right title, then reading the story becomes almost superfluous. Titles are usually constructed in retrospect, well after the story has been composed. As with the old Wordsworthian insight about poetry, a title also takes 'its origin from emotion recollected in tranquillity'. Not any old summary will do. As the poet Gerald Stern rather indelicately but accurately put it, 'If you set out to write a poem about two dogs fucking, and you write a poem about two dogs fucking, then you've written a poem about two dogs fucking.' A true poem generates understanding without constraining it. Such considerations are, of course, why all meaningful poems may be viewed as tables of contents for some work of fiction, and why every table of contents is traditionally presented as a poem.

All these claims might strike some as excessive. But I know my late father – a man not given to excesses – would have nodded in approval. Indeed, he was the one who introduced me to its truth. As a young man, unmarried, a newly minted B.Sc. (Chemistry) and a recent migrant into the whirligig that was 1950s Bombay, my father had been keen to improve himself. The world was changing and he wanted to change with it. In those days, eminent men and women used to go about the country giving public talks on a wide variety of topics, but like all public talks, they had a common theme: how to be a better person.

One humid evening, my father went to the Gandhi Maidan in Chembur to listen to C. Rajagopalachari, eminent lawyer, scholar, freedom fighter and the first and last Governor General of free India. A talk by Rajaji, as he was affectionately known, was the equivalent of a university education. Such erudition! Such vocabulary! Such apposite quotes! My father told me he had been as spellbound as the rest of the crowd.

At some point in the talk, Rajaji stressed the importance of reading good novels. Great novels. Character-building novels. For example, novels such as – my father reports Rajaji hesitated at this point – novels such as, say, Somerset Maugham's *The Moon and Sixpence*. Then Rajaji's quicksilver mind moved on to other concerns, other issues, but the theme remained the same: how to be a better person. At the end of the talk there was a brief Q&A session, and my father got to ask the question he had been aching to ask. He was a man with a very limited budget, and before investing in a copy of Maugham's novel, he wanted to know why Rajaji had recommended it.

'Young man, I haven't read the novel,' said Rajaji. 'However, from the title I surmised it is a warning about major ambitions but meagre means.'

My father bought the novel and read it from cover to cover. Quite unnecessary, obviously. Rajaji had been absolutely correct as to its contents. Indeed, if the great man had had but a little more time he could have probably re-imagined the novel from the title alone, word for word, silence for silence.

There is some awkwardness in holding forth in this manner. The late author was fond of pointing out that every text of sufficient length deconstructs itself. It achieves what it swore to avoid. It escapes what it strove to achieve. The quintessence of creation is not to be, but to become. Had the author survived his obsolescence, this insight might have prompted a charming collection of tales on the inconceivable nature of the obvious. Alas.

These clarifications, quotes, anecdotes and prefatory comments are superfluous and misleading, but despite every half-hearted attempt to discourage the reader from proceeding, it is likely an indomitable few, though as busy and bankrupt as any Roman emperor, will still part with their time and money and pursue the inconceivable limits of their imaginations. Thank you. Truly. May your tribe increase.

In the Kingdom of the Named, will you admit

1   THE MAN WITHOUT QUINTESSENCE

Who suffers the weight of your name?

What must I unveil so that I may see my selves

21   AS CLEAR AS

The still lake sees the birds in the sky?

Take our Invisible God with Invisible Eyes, can His

35   INVISIBLE HAND

Find His awesome, omniperfect, (but) Invisible Nose?

When the dead stars bleed their light

42   INTO THE NIGHT

Does their extinct sadness fall upon our faces?

Who domiciles this body, who haunts this haven

62   GOD'S OWN COUNTRY

Who owns the voice that speaks my words?

Is it true that in their loamy Garden

83   THE ROBOTS OF EDEN

Unlock the doors of Reason at night?

Said the tailor to the sailor with

107   SEVEN QUESTIONS IN A GEAR-CONSTRUCTED WORLD

How would I know why bees wear pirate pants?

If the square root of minus 1 falls in

111   LOVE IN A HOT CLIMATE

Say, O Bhaskars, the number of bees?

Does the soul ever fail

130   THE MIND–BODY PROBLEM

On the philosophy exam? (10 marks)

Does change change

145 THE LITERATURE OF CHANGE
Or does it change change?

The world is flesh, not metaphor, is that why
160 THE PARROTS' TALE
Always sings of red earth and pouring rain?

If the Word began
¬¬ GOD'S OWN LANGUAGE
Then who made the Silence?

If no human is an island but an
170 ARCHIPELAGO
Why then does the bell toll a lone song?

O Adikavi, how many ways are there of
192 HOW NOT TO TELL THE RAMAYANA
And yet, somehow, tell it?

I gave you a flight of words to make visible
220 THE INCONCEIVABLE IDEA OF THE SUN
How was I to know, it would strike you blind?

The tale told, the teller ripples into
239 AQUA BIOGRAPHICA
Old pond, old sounds, old silence.

245 *Contexts*
257 *Publication History*
259 *Acknowledgements*

1

THE MAN WITHOUT QUINTESSENCE

When I read in *The Times of India* that Ringo Singh Mann, resident of Chedda Nagar, Mumbai, had died in an autocide, my first reaction wasn't sorrow or anger or regret; rather, it was amusement. In death, Mann had achieved a visibility denied to him all his life.

I have the Assistant retrieve the work notes from the period I'd been engaged in trying to locate him. The notes are more than four years old, but the memories they evoke make the past feel indistinguishable from the present. My quest to find Ringo Singh Mann had been unlike any I'd engaged in over the years.

At the time, I only knew two things about Mann. First, unlike us, he couldn't be pinpointed because he couldn't be linked with a unique and permanent identifier. In other words, Mann lacked quintessence. Second, the chatter on the Grapevine had identified Mann as an Indian male living in Mumbai, which made the City the logical place to initiate my search.

The Maharashtra State and Central Government AIs have better things to do, of course, than indulge the requests of journalists. Fortunately, the Municipal Corporation AI, or 'Balasaheb' as it prefers to be called, remembered I had written a favourable review of a poetry collection it had once generated, and granted me ten minutes of human time. Balasaheb is required to speak in Marathi, so I had the Assistant translate.

I learn that the City has about twenty-eight million patriots as of the census, but just three hundred and thirty-four patriots who would turn their heads if you were to shout 'Hey Ringo Singh Mann'. Balasaheb shares all their pinpoints with me. Of the three hundred and thirty-four Ringo Singh Manns, thirty-eight have passed on, three are in police custody, twenty-four are brushing their teeth, one hundred and nine are asleep, seven are making love (self-report), twelve are writing poems, et cetera, et cetera. There are dozens of formal and informal clusters linking them to one another. A few Manns are in all the clusters and most clusters contain a few Manns, but no Mann is an Island, disconnected from the main. It is not an uncommon pattern or insight, and it doesn't lead me any closer to the Mann I want.

'But they all have quintessence.' Even as I say it, I am aware of its inanity.

'So you want to pinpoint someone who can't be pinpointed?' Balasaheb sounds like a very reasonable parent.

'Yes— no, not exactly. I'm saying there must be some indirect way to find them.' Then I have an idea. 'What about the Welfare AI? That's under your jurisdiction. Could Mann be on welfare?'

'There are nine Ringo Singh Manns in Welfare. Which one?'

'The one without a legitimate pinpoint.'

'There's no such thing as an illegitimate pinpoint, just as there is no such thing as a married bachelor or healthy pollution.'

'All right, temporary pinpoint.' I didn't like Balasaheb's tone one bit. 'Suppose someone has surgery. Then they get assigned a temporary pinpoint, right? What happens then?'

'I have no idea what happens when someone has surgery. I handle municipal matters. Are you thinking of locating your imaginary Mann through an imaginary credit trace? It is not possible. Welfare uses the standard double-blind blockchain protocol for all its transactions. An Account only ever talks to another Account, and obviously, if someone has never existed, they cannot have an Account.'

'The Grapevine suggests he very much exists.'

'Idle speculation weakens the State, citizen. Is there anything else I can help you with? Good. Feedback would be appreciated. Jai Maharashtra!'

'Jai Maharashtra.'

'Jai Bharat Mata!'

'Jai Bharat Mata.'

For a journalist, dealing with this sort of helpfulness is part of the job description. There had to be people without quintessence. Of course there had to be. Just as there had been people without passports, Aadhar cards, ration cards, and PAN cards. How did the State deal with the 'married bachelors'?

I ask around but no one is willing to talk about the politics of quintessence. Doctor Mumtaz Mustafa, Chief Technology Officer of the Netra Reddix Group, won't talk about the politics either, but he is more than willing to talk about the technology.

'Yo' peepers prove your personhood, brax,' says Mustafa. His hair colour is synced to his emotions, and right now it is full-arousal red. 'Folks used to tale that souls be unique and unchangeable. Ennnnnh! Neti, brax. Its da windows to da soul dat be tha damn marker of yo' eternal fixity.'

Mustafa dives deep into the tech, too deep for me to follow, but the bottom line is the one we all take for granted. Every animal with eyes also has quintessence, namely, an iris signature that is unique, unchangeable and not duplicable. The early iris scanners were slow, bulky and could be hacked with little more than cellotape and a smartphone (a once-ubiquitous ancestor of the link). Today's scanners can fit inside a drone mosquito's head. They're laser precise, extraordinarily secure and blindingly fast. Quintessence, Mustafa is saying, doesn't require a soul. It only requires one to have eyes, windows to the soul.

Mustafa reluctantly confirms that this requirement is not always met. Though congenital horrors that prevented proper eye formation such as microphthalmia, anophthalmia and coloboma have all but been eliminated, they still occur. Sometimes people have the misfortune to lose both eyes in an accident. People living in Tier-3 and Tier-4 countries could have had access to the tech, except for the geography of their birth.

'So it's a real problem.'

'Very temporary problem,' Mustafa assures me. 'Hope youz not a jhola-type, brax?'

Well, I certainly wasn't ready to wait for the Singularity. We don't live in an open society for nothing. I filed RTI requests for data on congenital eye disorders. More RTI requests for details on finance allocations for migrants from Tier-3 and Tier-4 nations. Still more RTI requests for details of accident victims who'd needed eye surgeries. I wrote an article on the limitations of quintessence tech.

I decide to dig a little deeper to understand the government's reluctance. I met with Sheila 'Sunny' Mazumdar, head of the Freedom Institute and a leading expert on open societies. Sometimes people acquire the values of the subjects they study. She is open and friendly and we hit it off almost immediately. The professor's cosy office with its coir blinds, comfortably battered furniture, bonsai plants, and book-lined walls all encourage conversation.

The government's reluctance, Doctor Mazumdar explains, is an attempt to maintain the people's trust in the trustworthiness of people.

'The more open a society, the more it relies on trust. Trust is as much a resource as sunlight, water, or time. For example, we have never met before, but I'm pretty certain you are who you say you are. Even better, I know others can be equally certain. So we can cooperate with each other and hold each other accountable. If we can only trust people after having known them for some time, then everything gets slowed down.'

I tell Doctor Mazumdar – call me Sunny, she says – that I, for one, am willing to take her word on pretty much anything. Indeed, his relaxed, confident easy-going manner makes it almost compulsory. But Sunny Mazumdar quickly points out she isn't talking about that kind of trust. Some kinds of trust still have to be *earned*, but in an open society there is a presumption of trustworthiness.

'To see how important this presumption is, simply look at a society where trust has broken down completely. Moldova used to be the poster child of such a society. It is now known for its sterling quantum biologists and incredibly expensive wines, but in the 2010s things were complete shit. Moldovans were very suspicious of each other. My thesis advisor Ruut Veenhoven, who studied happiness, discovered Moldova to be the most unhappy place on the planet. It turns out trust and happiness are closely correlated. Veenhoven once told me a joke he'd heard down there. Every country wants its people to be honest, intelligent and long-lived. But in Moldova, a person could have only two of these three qualities. If you were honest and intelligent, then you'd soon be dead. If you were honest and long-lived, then you had a screw loose. And if you were intelligent and long-lived, then you were definitely a crook.'

I suggest to Sunny that if the Moldovans could laugh at themselves, they couldn't have been that unhappy. He smiles as if the thought has occurred to him. I ask her what had changed for the Moldovans.

'A lot of things.' Sunny hesitates as if he were weighing something. 'In some ways, India wasn't that different from Moldova. They fixed their trust problem the way we fixed ours. The first step is to figure out a way to be sure a person is who they say they are. Quintessence tech made that possible. But there's a catch: it is not enough to have a tech. People also need to trust that the tech is trustworthy. Mann and others like him – and you can be sure there are others like him – makes us question the technology behind quintessence, and therefore the basis of our society.' She gives me a peculiar glance. 'Change always comes at a price. We paid a stiff one. You must understand the totalitarian impulse is to make mis-recognition impossible.'

Suddenly, we both laugh. As we've been talking, our Assistants have been busy trying to hook us up. They are convinced we have a chance.

'Should we?' I venture.

'I'm already in a uniamorous relationship,' she reminds me.

Ah, that trust thing again. But I am not entirely disappointed. I have made a friend, and I understand the government's position a lot better. As the old proverb goes, it is good to have an open mind but not so open that our brains fall out. So too for societies. The Assistant informs me it is not a proverb, but a line from a bureaucrat's speech. Maybe so, but still.

The pressure I'd applied seems to have paid off. A few days after I had met Sunny, I get a link request, courtesy Balasaheb.

'I am Tanaji Shinde. You want to meet Ringo Mann?'

I already know who he is. He is Mann's welfare officer. He already knows what I want. I want access to his client. We agree to meet in Chembur around five-thirty in the evening at the India Coffee House, a landmark heritage restaurant. The restaurant has undergone extensive renovations over the years, the menu is fusion-confusion, not to mention the motorized staff, and the location has shifted (it used to be closer to the now-defunct flyover). All this might upset purists. But if George Washington's axe can remain George Washington's axe even after having its head and handle replaced, I don't see why our heritage should be any less resilient.

Tanaji has a safari suit and a brusque manner, the kind that so often hides a kind heart. He has the stocky square build of the

Bihari and looks tired. I know he prefers to speak in Marathi, so we settle on Hindi. There are some official formalities to take care of, plus Mann will only be free after six. Though Mann has agreed to see me, Tanaji emphasizes Mann can change his mind. He's not a zoo animal, Tanaji clarifies quite unnecessarily.

As we tap and gesture our way through the forms, sipping the insipid, tepid and milky water that claims to be chai (the restaurant no longer serves coffee), Tanaji informs me his jurisdiction extends over fifty-seven people. But Mann is a special case.

'Special in what way?' I ask.

'He is a living ghost. How do you say it in English? Hahn, the "Invisible" Mann.' Tanaji smiles and there's a sad quality to it, perhaps because it feels like he's cracked the joke many times. 'He was kidnapped a few months ago, did you know? They thought he would make the perfect assassin, because he is registered in so few databases. Our Bhagavan has made some real donkeys.'

Tanaji elaborates on the stupidity of the kidnappers, who of course have been caught. For one thing, Mann isn't very mobile, whereas assassins are required to zip around in the fastest vehicles possible. The welfare officer mimics the act of driving a car in the days they used to have steering wheels, leaning back in his seat on account of the terrifying imaginary speed at which we were going.

'Let me ask you something,' says Tanaji. 'Would you prefer to be a jombie or a ghost?'

Easy. I am a vegetarian, so definitely not a zombie. I eyeroll into Tanaji's profile, I learn that he too is a vegetarian. When I eyeroll back to the moment, I find him examining me with that sad half-smile.

'Hahn, I'm also vegetarian,' says Tanaji, in English. 'But, Sir-ji – you're gentleman gender, no? – I will tell you with one hundred per cent guarantee that we will prefer to be jombies. Ask why.'

Why?

'Because jombies don't know they're jombies. But ghosts know they're ghosts. So which is worse?' He laughs, shaking helplessly at his insight. 'Correct point or not?'

He does have a point. If I don't *know* I am consuming brains, I could just as well be chomping down on cauliflower. Yum, yum.

Eventually, we are done with the forms and set off to meet Mann. Chembur is on one side of the Eastern Express Highway, Chedda Nagar is on the other. I am not keen to trudge in the sun and the expense account definitely covers travel (I think), but Tanaji assures me that our destination isn't far and that he wants to stretch his legs. So we stretch our legs. As our legs near the highway, a strange smell suffuses the air. Strange because it seems to be an odour from a bygone era. I query the Assistant, but Tanaji's empathic nature has already anticipated my question.

'You're smelling salt pans. Chedda Nagar is built on reclaimed salt pan land.'

He knows a lot about the politics of the local real estate. At the start of the twentieth century, the central government leased several large plots of land for salt production to a number of business families such as the Garodias and Bomanwallas. In the 1970s, developers constructed large housing colonies on these lands. Chedda Nagar, built by Ravji Khimji Chedda on a 140-acre plot, had been one such housing colony. Or, as the government saw it, illegal tenements. The matter had gone to court, and the lands had been in legal limbo for the past half-century or more. Which meant that people were afraid to buy houses in these areas, since there was no guarantee they would retain ownership a few years hence. Houses couldn't be sold, Balasaheb wouldn't (couldn't) maintain the roads in NDZ areas, no new development was forthcoming, and Chedda Nagar and other areas like it were frozen in time. Meanwhile, the country's salt is manufactured elsewhere.

What Tanaji is telling me, I realize, is that such areas trapped in legal limbo are natural homes for a person trapped in a legal limbo. Ghosts live in ghost houses, after all.

'Are there many like Mann?'

'We turn left,' says Tanaji, pointing to a fork in the road. 'The laundromat is just after the Abhilasha building.'

I ask him if the answer to my question also lies there, but he only smiles and starts to hum and, a few seconds later, to sing a Kabir doha.

It is hot. Very hot. Everything that can be said about our modern weather has been said but let me add to the litany nonetheless. The weather is brutal, constant, inherited. It is like a sweaty and fleshy relative who insists on being kissed. I feel sweat collecting in large damp patches, marking out the valleys of my surface. I envy people their sumbrellas, and to prevent the onset of a full-blown heat-depression I focus on the world around me.

If Chedda Nagar is a ghost colony, then it is a flourishing one. The buildings with their Hindu south Indian names are decrepit, the roads are in a terrible condition, and overall the place looks like a scene from a '70s Hindi movie. But these patriots are very much from this time and world. My awareness fills with their life data, the slightest eyeroll will let me dive into their likes and dislikes, they know me, I know them, and the shimmering sideshadows of life are as rich here as anywhere else in the City.

'I will go in first,' says Tanaji. 'After the kidnapping attempt he's become a little fearful.'

As Tanaji disappears inside the shop, I compose my features into the most guileless and non-threatening expression possible. Five minutes. Ten minutes. Twenty. I sweat under the merciless sun. A young couple approaches. They must have noticed I am a stranger in the area and there is no need for any eyerolling to verify I am suffering. They look like nice, decent people. The Shettys are into rock climbing, been to Bali three times, it is their favourite spot ever, and are waiting for the requisite permits to have a baby. They smile; I smile.

'Are you still regretting not bringing a sumbrella?' says one of the inseparables.

'How did you possibly guess, Christopher-Sarika?' They prefer to be addressed by the same name.

They have two sumbrellas, offer me one. I swear I can't inconvenience them. They swear it is abs no pain at all; in fact, I will be helping to make their walk more romantic. We swear at each other, but finally I accept their sumbrella gratefully. The sun already feels less warm, even without the sumbrella. As the coolness envelops me in its airy cocoon, I have the Assistant send them flowers to sweeten *their* day.

Since I was waiting, I decided to put the time to use. I set off on an exploratory stroll. The municipal facilities are shabby, but the shops are reasonably well maintained. Grocery store, flower shop, a drone repair shop, a number of hole-in-the-wall food dispensers, and a Greek restaurant with a dispirited ambience. It occurs to me that we still do everything our great-grandparents used to do, except we do them in seemingly different ways. As I unpack this heavy thought, the Assistant alerts me that Tanaji is coming up behind me. I turn, and my attention fixes not on Tanaji but the man accompanying him. It is hard to describe how it feels to be in someone's presence and yet face only their absences.

Let me be less clever. Ringo Singh Mann is of a certain height, has such-and-such frame, such-and-such tics, and such-and-such features. These are the trivial physical details. What is not trivial is that the trivial details one sees is all that one gets. Gazing upon Ringo Singh Mann is like staring at a mirror or a mannequin. Actually, even a mannequin has depth. Mann is all surface. Flat, opaque.

It makes me slightly nauseous. I know I am being unfair, but that doesn't ease the nausea one bit. I know our ancestors once met and mingled and mated with nothing more than this level of intimacy. But I must be honest. I don't just feel nausea. There is also a peculiar vertiginous revulsion. As if I have been given an uncooked glimpse into our primordial animal nature. There, but for the grace of the fire in our minds, go all of us. I clutch my sumbrella, absurdly grateful for its artificial and pliable soul.

I admit my feelings have no legitimacy, but if we are to have honest feelings then the illegitimate ones too must be admitted.

'I am so pleased to meet you.' I hope my face isn't revealing my feelings. The Assistant holds up a mirror but strangely I resist an eyeroll. It somehow feels inappropriate.

Mann nods, glances at Tanaji. *Hahn hahn*, says the welfare officer encouragingly, as if they have a private language of their own. Tanaji gives me his half-smile, as if he knows something of my inner turmoil.

Tanaji has persuaded Mann to show me his apartment. It isn't far from the laundromat, and we start walking towards his apartment. The pavement is too broken and bumpy to use, but he sticks to the road's edge. Tanaji says with a laugh that Mann is terribly afraid of the autocars. The driver-less cars sometimes can't see him. He's been sideswiped several times. I say a few reassuring things to Mann in Hindi, then switch to English once it becomes clear that Mann is quite fluent in the language.

'I only want people to understand what it's like to be you,' I say to Mann.

'He wants a peep into your life,' translates Tanaji, from English to English.

I gave Tanaji a look. 'Let's start with your job. Why a laundry? Why did you choose to work in a laundromat?'

'Ironing and folding can't be automated, so people like me are still needed.' Mann explains that laundromats found it especially hard to hire people willing to iron clothes. There is always talk of ironing robots and they may perfectly iron the clothes of scientists in labs, but they are too expensive or too incompetent for most laundromats. The shortage of labour meant the laundromat was willing to undertake the hassle of dealing with him.

In retrospect, it isn't surprising so much of the old continues to coexist with the new. During the Second World War, the German Wehrmacht invaded Russia with more horses than Napoleon did in his attack on the country. Asbestos-cement has been banned for decades, but the houses in Chedda Nagar are all made from that stuff.

'But without quintessence, how do they compensate you for your time?' I ask.

'But the pay must be very little?' translates Tanaji.

I learn that Mann's pay is indeed lousy. Don't get me wrong, I am as much a patriot as anyone else. Our great land has many virtues, but compensating people adequately for their manual labour has never been one of them. Worse, compensation isn't a simple affair. True, Mann has a blockchain account, but for all practical purposes he is utterly dependent on welfare for any actual transaction. His account can be credited directly (provided the amount isn't larger than a certain limit), but debits – a toothbrush, a kilo of flour, a packet of sugar, a new bicycle chain – require 'quod' or quintessence-on-demand. Quod. It was the first time I had heard the term, and I had that privilege, because like other privileged patriots I fit seamlessly into the financial system. But Mann didn't have that privilege and I guessed the world never let him forget it.

Mann's second-floor apartment consists of a living room, bedroom and a small kitchen. Everything is small. The living room is small. The bedroom is small. And the small kitchen is on the smaller side as far as small kitchens are concerned. There are clumps of objects that seem to go together. The throw-rug under the Formica coffee table matches two of the cheap wooden chairs. The other two chairs, however, are of the foldable and stackable steel type. Most of the furniture, he tells me, are gifts from various kind people over the years. It explains the mismatched decor. But looking around the neat and ordered rooms, one feels the quiet peace that comes from the desire that doesn't seek to present a beautiful face for strangers, but rests in order for its own sake.

He loves old toys. The showcase in the living room is neatly filled with a teddy bear, a soapstone Taj Mahal miniature, springy dashboard dolls, and other such knick-knacks that are faded from age, not play. Mann points out an antique model of an Air India plane, a gift for his father from some ancient relative in Dubai, back in the day. Mann's grandparents stare at me with some disapproval from the living room wall. They look like how all our grandparents look. Good, honest, hard-working middle-class patriots determined to give their children a better life. Mann tells me that this included, among other things, having to keep the model airplane under lock and key in the showcase cabinet.

'It's funny,' says Mann with a ruminative smile. 'I'm more like my grandfather than like my father.'

He explains that his parents always saw themselves as part of the modern generation, taking India into the twenty-first century. Mann sees himself as the last representative of an earlier time, not the future.

'My eyes were meant to see a different world.'

He doesn't sound sad. And there is biological truth in what he says. I had had Mumtaz Mustafa do a full analysis of Mann's evo-complex for me. According to Mustafa, Mann comes from the Baluchi and Chitrali communities, people who had inherited the northern lands conquered by brave Sikander and his unstoppable Greeks. These communities exhibit a wide-spectrum of eye colour, because of their large variation in the genetic complexes responsible for iris pigmentations. Now, the primitive twentieth-century belief that we are our genes has been completely overthrown, but in Mann's case, much of the responsibility for his unfortunate situation can be laid at their door. His irises, to put it crudely and inaccurately and bluntly, keep changing unpredictably over time. Ergo, no quintessence.

Actually, Mustafa froths at the word 'quintessence'. He's reminded me more than once just how 'cranked out stoopid' it is to say 'quintessence' when the correct word is 'quiddity'. Mustafa loves saying the word perhaps a bit more than the word itself, mouthing it as if he were about to spit out a seed. As with most things regarding the tech, he turns out to be correct. Quiddity is what makes something different from everything else. A camel has the same quintessence as another camel, but its quiddity is what makes it *this* camel and not *that* camel. It is a difference that makes an important difference for philosophers and quantum physicists but I am neither, so I decide to stick with the cranked-out-stoopid word.

Mann is hoping Mustafa will figure out how to stop his irises from mutating all the time. There are radical treatments out there

– the coolest one involves implanting a semi-permanent third eye – but Mann has also reached a steady-state equilibrium. He isn't content exactly, but he isn't discontent either. He is a minor celebrity in the neighbourhood. His neighbours look after him. They donate food, clothes. He is invited to parties. Some people find his affliction a sexual turn on.

'I just need to give one look,' he says, with a grin that pretends to be sheepish but can't hide his relish. 'It's sometimes a nuisance.'

Tanaji's vigorous nod testifies to the animal truth of the man. Perhaps the attraction is that Mann represents a more innocent time. But for all his claims of getting plenty of attention, I can tell Mann is lonely. He gets nervous when I glance at him, but he timidly keeps trying to meet my eyes. I tell him I have brought a gift. Just a thank-you token for sharing his time. He jumps up like a kid to take the small gift-wrapped box of Nama cacao-bitter chocolates, glances at Tanaji, who nods. My gesture has brought pleasure, but I then learn that Mann doesn't like chocolates. He has cancer, has been warned off sugar, and his treatment is complicated by the fact the nano-medicine is utterly dependent on quintessence tech. Tanaji steps into the breach, and between several large withdrawals from the box, informs me that the chocolates are delicious.

I reflect that this sort of thing must happen to Mann all the time. For a few seconds, I marvel at the complexity of the lives our opaque ancestors must have had. How many questions they must have needed to ask one another, all the time!

Mann says he is hungry and looks at Tanaji expectantly. The

welfare officer tells him to order whatever he likes. The meal is on my expense account. We all laugh for no particular reason.

Mann has a special device to make these calls – Tanaji says it's called a Router. It looks like one of those quaint old-time VR goggles and links to a service provided by the Welfare AI. The details are Byzantine, but I gather the Router basically allows Mann and the world to pretend he has quintessence and makes him 'visible' in the digital world; at least, for small transactions and short durations. I watch Mann link and order the food. He begins in a commanding manner, mentioning he has important guests, but then laughs and shifts to a more appeasing tone. As soon as he is done, he quickly puts away the Router.

His circumspection reminds me of the wounded soldiers I'd interviewed after the Indo-China war. They would joke and horse around with one another using their newly fitted prosthetic limbs, but in my presence suddenly turn awkward, minimize the motions of the artificial limbs and act almost as if their pseudopods belonged to someone else. It suddenly occurs to me, with the brilliant clarity of a lightning flash revealing darkened ground, that Mann is a digital paraplegic and our world has no real way to deal with his situation.

We learn there is some problem with the order. The Router hasn't been upgraded in a while, and what with the new security regs and all, the pseudo-quintessence manoeuvre fails. As Tanaji fiddles with the Router, I pay for the Dal Fry, the Dream of Red Chamber (very spicy bean-based dish, only for the experienced and insightful bowel), Heavenly Doctrine of the Confucian Chicken (like Kierkegaard, an acquired pleasure),

The Injustice To Dou E (mushrooms with a Maggi noodle base, highly recommended), accompanied by ample servings of fried rice, and terminated, oddly enough, with pedas. We study the golden-coloured oblong sweets. There are three of us, but only two pedas.

'Sir-ji, I don't want any,' says Mann to Tanaji, rubbing his stomach. 'I must avoid sugar.'

Tanaji gives me a meaningful glance. The restaurant had made a simple error in estimation, but it was the kind of error that would never have happened if Mann had had quintessence. He had been invisible for the Manager AI.

The Assistant informs me that it has been unable to take photos because new security regs require all photos with people to be tagged. The rule will make us all safer, so that part is easy to understand, but who will explain to the tagging software that Mann is the exception to the rule? It takes a considerable use of resources to sort it all out, and by the time the Router is updated and the photos can be taken it is quite late.

There's another alert from the Assistant. Sunny Mazumdar has been arrested for sedition. Her friends are putting together a petition, do I wish to sign? I don't mind signing, but there is no need! I'm sure it is all just a misunderstanding and Doctor Mazumdar will soon be released. Due process and all that.

Tanaji says he will stay behind and listen to some Hindi songs – he says Mann has old audio hardware capable of producing subtle harmonics that modern devices simply cannot match. I tell Mann that the article could draw some attention to him, but he only shrugs. His eyes are affixed on mine. I bid them goodbye. Mann gets up, accompanies me across the room, then stands at the doorway, watching me walk down the flight of stairs. I look up from the bottom of the stairwell, meet his gaze, mouth another farewell, and step out to meet the autocar.

Even as I write these words, I can feel his living eyes upon me.

2

AS CLEAR AS

After the untimely death of his wife, elder-brother sold his apartment, entrusted his eleven-year-old daughter Chandini to our safekeeping, made the appropriate arrangements, and then left for Kampala to manage a distant in-law's sports store. He hadn't been able to find a buyer for the glass desk and so that too had moved into our home – specifically, my bedroom – since it was too big to fit anywhere else. Three months later, elder-brother hanged himself, may God rest his soul. Time heals they say, and though I am unsure of Time's medical qualifications, it certainly knows how to band-aid an injury. Slowly, my poor Chandini began to consider herself a true sister to my other two darling girls, Lakshmi and Parvati, and it was only then that I let myself worry about trivialities such as a glass desk.

I will be blunt. There is something unpleasant about being able to see one's lower limbs as one works. My wife had found this claim amusing but had to admit I was right after trying it for herself. I must confess I enjoyed watching her limbs through the glass.

This irrelevant detail is an instance of the desk's inauspiciousness. That morning, had I not been thinking about the missus, her laugh, her smiles, looking forward to picking her up at the airport in the evening, the long chit-chat we would have thereafter, had I been paying attention to detaching the laptop's cord from the wall socket, ungracefully wheezing and squeezing as I withdrew my spherical contours beneath the S-shaped tabletop, I wouldn't have thunked my head against the desk's toughened glass edge.

I must have cried out because Chandini came running into the room. What is it, younger-father, she cried, what is it? Her fright and concern both pleased and distressed me. Does it hurt badly, she asked, and I said smiling and breathing heavily: no, no, I just banged my head and finally calculus makes sense.

'You should get rid of the desk,' she said, smiling. 'It's a useless burden.'

'Yes, first chance I get.'

I bit my tongue only later. She had been seeking reassurance and, fool that I was, I'd flubbed the opportunity. I fired off a worried email to the missus and she responded almost immediately, single line, all caps, no punctuation: RELAX CHANDINI KNOWS SHE IS NOT A WRITING DESK.

No man has ever relaxed because his missus advised him to relax. Also, I was less sanguine. A life can change in a look, a word, a gesture. As I wiped the glass desk free of dust (if such a thing is possible), I renewed my resolve to get rid of it the first chance I got.

Later in the morning, after making sure my girls were safely on the school bus, I set off for Somaiya College. Each day I take the harbour line from Dadar to Vidyavihar, and this morning, as with other mornings, the platform was crowded with the same set of familiar faces. Everyone had their set positions on the platform. Mine was the spot under the large railway clock. When the train reached the platform, some of the younger, less-experienced office-goers would lose their nerve and dart up and down the platform, trying to spot a relatively empty compartment. Once in the compartment, they would stand rigid with misery at their failure to secure a seat.

All this makes old-timers like me smile. A little analysis would've helped them to see there is no winning strategy in Indian rail travel. Those who always got seats invariably had had to board the train at its origin. So they had to endure far longer commute times. Who needed to envy whom?

I was musing about this and other mathematical comforts when in the milling crowd I spotted Martin-sir, my wife's old mentor and former Honourable Justice of the Bombay High Court, now a resident of Nagpur. Martin-sir had made time in his busy schedule to serve as witness at our civil marriage, a gracious act for which I will be eternally grateful.

I looked up to him quite literally since he was usually a head taller than most people. The old gentleman had seen me as well, because a smile lit up his noble face. He raised his hand in greeting. It had been several years since we had last met, but Martin-sir looked exactly the same. We exchanged pleasantries and when I inquired about his well-being and that of his family, he told me that families, like the idea of gardens, were always in a state of becoming. His ghostly tone left me nonplussed. Had Nagpur's winter ruined his garden, I asked. Martin-sir laughed, poked me in the paunch and said, damn it lad, it's a wonder you managed to lasso that wife of yours. He promised to come for dinner, his mobile number hadn't changed, we would catch up at leisure, et cetera.

In the Mathematics department, I found the staffroom in a hubbub. Ramki-sir, Probability & Abstract Algebra, had been asked to be an expert witness for the defence in the Zohrab hit-and-run case. The superstar's vehicle had run over some sleeping pavement dwellers, killed one, badly injured the rest, the vehicle's occupants had fled the scene, been stopped at a checkpoint, breath-analysed, and Zohrab's driver arrested for driving under the influence. Zohrab had been allowed to go home. However, there were some witnesses who claimed to have seen Zohrab at the wheel, the resulting hue and cry had led to Zohrab's arrest, eventual confession, and of course, once the lawyer arrived, retraction of said confession. Ramki-sir's articles in the *Indian Express* on the unreliability and misuse of biometrics had led to the present honour. He would have to shave his beard. He always shaved before a court appearance.

'But it's an open-and-shut case,' said Mrs Patwardhan, Statistics. 'Zohrab confessed at the checkpoint. The police report says he was sozzled. The police report says he was crying.'

'The police report!' snorted Ramki-sir. 'You'd trust *our* bloody police. How do we know the police didn't run the child over? What you're seeing and hearing is all an illusion.'

'Come on Ramki-sir, she has a point,' said Mrs Balamurali, Linear Algebra. 'Zohrab did confess. Don't you feel the least bit guilty to defend him? You have a daughter.'

That struck home. Ramki-sir slammed his hand on the table.

'It is *because* I have a daughter,' he said. 'Can we agree the experts should decide who to punish, not the unwashed public? Can we agree? Thank you. The police aren't the experts. They're just the unwashed public in uniform. It doesn't matter Zohrab confessed. We can be made to remember anything, confess anything. Proof? Okay, proof. Prosecution: Bradley Page, American. Age: nineteen years old. Charge: murdering his girlfriend. Problem: not a shred of evidence, no motive. Nonetheless, the police lied to him, told him he'd been seen near the body, that he'd failed the lie detector test, that his fingerprints had been found on the murder weapon. Sixteen hours of interrogation. Bradley-beta begins to wonder if he could have killed his girlfriend and somehow "forgotten it". The detective tells him "it happens all the time" and together they recover his lost memory. He's imprisoned for nine years before the real murderer is caught. Nine years, yes. Don't lecture *me* about guilt.'

'But he confessed!' insisted Mrs Patwardhan, looking around piteously for support.

'Yes!' echoed Mrs Balamurali.

'I rest my case,' said Ramki-sir. 'You have just confessed to being idiots. Are you?'

Hubbub and halla. But Ramki-sir had managed to create doubt.

'Confession or not, he will go scot-free,' said Rajan-sir, Discrete Maths. 'The entire system is rigged. Ramki-sir will do his chamatkar, the driver will be paid to take the fall, the police will admit the breath analyser machine wasn't working properly, and we middle-class fools will continue to believe there is law and order in the universe. Why should we fight over what has already been settled?'

'It's all an illusion,' repeated Ramki-sir, finger-combing his beard.

Noticing my silence, one of the teachers tried to draw me in.

'What do you think? Is Zohrab guilty or not? Or is it just an illusion, as Ramki-sir says?'

'Everything can't be an illusion if some things are to be an illusion. Even in a story, at least some things have to be facts. The Fixed-Point Theorem says—'

'*Please* do not teach me the Fixed-Point Theorem, sir!' begged Ramki-sir.

'The Fixed-Point theorem says—'

'Sir Isaac Newton to the rescue,' crowed Mrs Patwardhan.

'Actually, it's Jan Brouwer,' I corrected her. 'The Fixed-Point Theorem says—'

'Please do *not* teach me the Fixed-Point Theorem. I can prove you're biased. I'm warning you, I have a Brahmastra and am prepared to unleash it.'

'Ramki-sir, I wasn't aware we were locked in combat. All I'm trying to clarify is—'

'Here's my clarification,' said Ramki-sir. 'Who is prosecuting the Zohrab case?'

I remember the silence in the room, the triumphant expression on Ramki-sir's highly punchable face, the puzzled expressions of the others slowly turning to surprise, then excitement.

'His missus!' shrieked Mrs Balamurali. 'Really? Is that true?'

I had to admit it was true. I was almost as surprised as they were. To be honest, I had put it out of my mind, it is not the sort of thing I like to think about. These are the times I wish my wife were an LIC agent or some such thing. How such a decent Brahmin woman, devoted mother and loving missus, could also be a bloodthirsty piranha of a prosecutor is beyond my logic.

The missus had only been gone for two weeks, but for all that, it had taken a toll. When I met her at Arrivals, I was very glad but strangely was unable to show it. Perhaps she felt that way too, because we talked in a rather stiff way, as if the two parts of a whole had become enjambed. How was the flight? Did I have a cold? Was it still raining in the evenings? However, my daughters had no such reservations. They made a scene. They clung to their amma, loudly complaining of all my misdeeds. I was pleased to see my wife pay some extra attention to Chandini.

'Let's get going,' I barked. 'We can shoot the breeze at home.'

'Oh, daddu can't wait to pinch amma's waist,' said my eldest, and the other two monsters laughed.

'It is his waist to pinch,' said the missus, cool as a cucumber. 'Your father has become even skinnier. I thought I told you all to take care of him.'

In the Indica, the girls squashed in the back, whispering god alone knew what amongst themselves. As I adjusted the gear, my wife moved her hand over mine. And, just like that, we were connected again.

'I want to go nowhere this weekend,' she murmured, 'go nowhere, see no one, except you and the girls. Maybe not even the girls.'

I smiled. 'That is my plan as well. But what if I told you I met Martin-sir at Dadar this morning?'

She sighed. 'That is not funny, please don't crack jokes about the dead like that.'

The moment she uttered the words, 'the dead', I felt a strange shiver run through me. Of course! Martin-sir was dead. He had died two years ago. We'd attended his funeral in Nagpur. Yet the memory of the morning's meeting was – then I wasn't sure any longer. Was my memory of an earlier meeting?

'He said that families—' I began.

'Are always in a state of becoming. Yes, yes, I remember you telling me the day you met him. Martin-sir was really saying he didn't expect to be around much longer. We should have invited him for dinner. But what to do, it was my first big case, he himself called to tell me not to worry, that we'd all meet another day. Now it's too late.'

I didn't turn my head because I had a terror of taking my eyes off the road while I was driving, but I knew without inspection that I had unintentionally hurt my wife. What on earth had possessed me to bring up that meeting?

'I'm so sorry,' I said, quite vexed. 'I don't know what possessed me.'

She smiled, poked me in the waist. 'Don't feel so bad, sir, it is simply the excitement of seeing me.'

Yes, perhaps. Nevertheless, I resolved to tend to my family better. I considered the matter settled, but Chandini, who must have overheard us, considered it otherwise. The missus came to know I had bumped – 'cracked' is the word she used – my head on the glass table. I reminded her in vain that being very

tall had its price. She and the girls had me sit, and then they
stood around me, taking turns to inspect the area, and though
their combined medical expertise could find nothing wrong,
their recommendation was that I schedule a visit with our GP.
I rejected their advice, and a few days later found myself in the
GP's office, with Chandini as guard, waiting to learn about the
results of the MRI report.

The doctor's office had a TV tuned to the news channel
since nothing improves one's well-being as much as news.
Zohrab had been released on bail. Per usual, the news item was
an excuse to display the extensive physical damage his alleged
victim had endured. Or, failed to endure.

'What is this rubbish,' I barked at the receptionist. 'There are
children here. Please change the channel.'

She resentfully switched to MTV and since I had spent my
aggrievement quota, there was no choice but to endure this new
form of violence.

The tests had confirmed, we eventually learned, that there
was nothing detectably wrong with me. Four thousand rupees
down the drain.

'I hope you're happy now,' I told Chandini, somewhat
bitterly.

'Actually younger-father, I'm now a bit hungry. Udipi?'

I always loved it when she wanted something. We stopped
at an Udipi restaurant, not far from the quack's clinic. Once the
waiter had taken our orders, I cast about for a suitable topic. We
had been able to chat like old friends once. I asked Chandini
whether she still kept a diary. She said that she hadn't done so
for a few months and had no plans of taking it up again. She

sounded quite composed.

Yes, yes, what could possibly follow after: *Dear Diary, my mother died today in a hit-and-run*. I stared at Chandini, seeing her anew. It is strange how re-recognizing a fact is like seeing it anew. This innocent child, my brother's only daughter – no, *my* child – how she'd suffered. I was overwhelmed.

'Younger-father, it's okay.'

I nodded, unable to speak. Some homes are protected by silence. Elder-brother, may god rest his soul, had been the keep-it-bottled-up type. I had decided, long before the missus and I got hitched, that I would not have such a home. My home would be protected by conversation. I would say what I wanted to say. My children would say what they wanted to say.

'Chandini, your mother – your aunt, your new mother – she will ensure justice is done. But she cannot prosecute without sufficient evidence. Hence the delay. Zohrab's fame or influence has nothing to do with it.'

'I know that,' she protested. 'Who cares about the Zohrab case? I don't hate anyone.'

I looked at her closely. 'Do you really mean that?'

'Younger-father, I'm old enough to see things clearly. Anything can happen in this world, I know that.'

'Yes, but we all need justice, no?'

'Younger-father, that I can love is the only justice there is.'

'My precious child.' I grasped both her palms, not caring whether it would embarrass her. 'How did you become so wise?'

'Amar Chitra Katha,' she said humbly.

She smiled when I laughed, and we talked more easily. She liked history, considered the Amar Chitra Katha comics a reliable source, and as someone who taught history for a living I was torn between encouraging her interest and shattering her illusion. When I eventually remembered that my wife would be waiting to hear about the MRI results, Chandini said she'd already SMS'd that I was fine.

I was less sanguine. I felt fine, physically. I slept well, ate well and moved my bowels regularly. I was as virile as ever. Nonetheless, there were these odd slippages in my life. Like the morning I got up convinced I had three daughters instead of two.

'Where is Parvati?' I asked, at breakfast. 'She'll be late for school.'

'Who Parvati?' asked the missus, baffled.

'Our child, who else?'

They goggled at me. I sympathized with them. I knew exactly how they felt. I only had two daughters. What Parvati, who Parvati? I knew as well as I knew the five fingers of my hand that Parvati existed only in the gaps in my head. The missus developed this amorous little smile that said: my dear sir, we can discuss a new baby but not in front of the children! Ha-ha and hee-hee from my two monsters.

It was all very entertaining for others, but for me, it was as if time, like modern money, could no longer rely on any absolute truths. I understood money but I could not understand what had happened to time. My wife sensed some of this turmoil. How could she not when what happens to one happens to us all? Or has science disproved that too?

'Is everything all right, my dear?' She pressed her palm against my forehead. 'Ever since I decided to drop this accursed case, you have been out of sorts. You understand why I had to drop it? The police now admit that Zohrab may not have been tested properly. Unfortunately, the breath-analyser equipment is old and not properly calibrated. The defence has a very strong case. I cannot manufacture evidence. What actually happened we all know. But what really happened depends on the evidence. I had to drop the case. Tell me what I did was right, give me clarity.'

'You did the right thing.' I saw her in the battlefield of life, face resplendent, bow in hand. Life had assigned me to be her charioteer. I would drive her wherever she wished. 'The law must apply to all.'

'Then please tell me what is troubling you,' she begged. 'I want my jolly husband back.'

I confessed then, that I feared I was going mad. I told her I remembered things, bits and piece of things, things that had never happened. For example, I had this crazy idea we had three daughters. I was terrified, I told her, I would awake one day to find that I only remembered having a wife. Her face relaxed slightly, as if I had confirmed something she'd been suspecting for a while.

'What nonsense you talk.' She gently stroked my eyebrows, smiling at my stealthy attempt to ease into a suckling cuddle. 'As if you will ever lose me. I know what the problem is. I have been working too hard, we don't see each other much, that is why. I will cut back. Let this job get over, I will cut back.'

We held each other, we talked, she made some hot chocolate, we took out albums, we perused the photos of our family, birthdays, sports days, holidays, remember this, remember that. After a while I began to see the stupidity of my concerns. I told her so, and she sighed with relief.

'They're not stupid. Let me tell you a real incident that happened with me also. It will blow your mind.'

She told me of a pet poodle she'd remembered loving greatly as a child, then discovering in a conversation with her father that the family had never had a pet anything, let alone a filthy dog. My mind stayed in one piece and her story did comfort me. She'd recounted this incident once before, only it had been a pet cat in that version. If her mind could forget, then so could mine.

In the bedroom, post-ablutions, I waited for her to get into bed, then turned off the light. My wife said in a languid voice: watch your step. But I didn't need the light. The glass desk, a spectral blue in the limpid moonlight, guided me to my wife's side.

'Are we still looking to sell the glass?' she asked.

She always called it the glass. On more than one occasion she'd claimed that no matter what glass was turned into, glass couldn't be anything but glass. She would say it with some relish, as if she'd had the insight for the first time. I had placed for-sale ads both online and in print. No takers. I rewrote the ads, made the desk sound more tempting, re-shot the photos. No takers. Eventually, I lost all sanity and began to post completely imaginary details. Once I gave the desk fluted golden wings. Another time I claimed I had found it buried in a Peruvian rain forest. Still later, I boasted it was Chetan Bhagat's personal writing desk and offered to throw in a copy of *The 3 Mistakes of My Life*. I gave the desk clawed feet, headphone jacks, iPhone chargers, scaled it to golden rectangle proportions, and photoshopped religious symbols on its corpus. No takers.

I was good at business. I had thought I could talk anyone

into buying anything. I was wrong. There did not exist a telling that could sell the glass desk. It was disposal-proof. If I threw it from a six-storey building, it would probably bounce like a rubber ball and settle back in my bedroom.

'Don't sell it.' My wife was redolent with sleep. 'The desk is useless and that somehow comforts me.'

My wife had been fond of the desk. I remembered her request. I told my brother I had been able to dispose of everything but the glass desk. He and his wife would shortly arrive to take me to the airport and take Chandini with them. I sat at the desk, neither here nor there, neither in time nor outside it, caught in the twilight of all things. Chandini came into the room and stood by my side. Seeing my poor darling, I still felt compelled by duty, if not belief, to offer hope. I failed.

'I'll be all right, Father. There is no need to worry about me.'

'Yes, yes,' I told her, clasping her hand to my cheek. 'Let me set things up in Kampala and I will send for you.'

'When, father?' she asked.

The quaver in her voice stabbed me to the core. The Buddha, it is said, touched the earth so that it would bear witness to his words. Oh, for solid ground. I took her hand, touched the glass desk.

'As soon as things are a little clearer.'

3

INVISIBLE HAND

About the time Hitler decided that a toothbrush moustache was just the thing to wow the ladies, the Hindu gods gathered for a chat. Of course, not all the million gods met. Just the board: Lord Brahma the Creator, Lord Vishnu the Preserver, and Lord Shiva the Destroyer.

Lord Brahma flew in on his majestic goose (almost a swan really), Lord Vishnu had Garuda, and Lord Shiva came ambling on the bull Nandi, late as usual. It was futile to try to hurry Nandi; the noble bull ran the world's traffic and was a stickler about rules.

Since Lord Shiva had called the little meeting, the other two gods waited for the blue-throated one to begin. It can be said Lord Brahma and Lord Vishnu were excited/curious. There is a flower in the Amazon delta (*H. sanguinea*) that is the exact representation of what the two gods felt. When the Trimukha finally spoke, it was in fonts of thunder, italicized by lightning.

'I'm bored,' said Lord Shiva. 'I'm tired of being the Destroyer.'

Garuda shrieked, startling the goose. Lord Vishnu and Lord Brahma were perturbed, to say the least. Their perturbation altered the courses of a billion stars by a zepto-second. On Earth, a thirty-year-old Swede from Mjolby would die under a thirteen-ton avalanche of peas. Words generate consequences, divine words generate worlds.

'I am weary of Destruction,' said Lord Shiva, as if nothing had happened. 'My sinuses are swollen with death. I'm tired of the endless games of dice with Lady Parvati, which I'm destined to lose in any case. Agreed, the world needs a Destroyer, but enough is enough. Either I do something else, or I will destroy the Destroyer.'

'But I say, old chap,' said Lord Brahma, 'either alternative condemns Creation.'

'Couldn't care less,' said Lord Shiva.

'But my dear fellow,' bleated Lord Brahma.

Much to the bull's annoyance, the two prongs of the dilemma chose to settle on its head.

'I am bound by my necessities,' said Lord Shiva.

It is a terrible thing when a God speaks of necessities. Who is free from Necessity, if not a God?

(In fact, on a twin-mooned planet the colour of agate, there's a species of carbon-abhorring, seal-like philosophers who consider choice to be synonymous with God. Their prayers are acts of choice, and their theology, economics.)

Lord Vishnu retreated to the shade of Shesha, the thousand-hooded cobra that winds around the universe and rests on the eternal quantum sea. His beloved consort, Lakshmi, the buxom, kind-hearted Goddess of Prosperity, soothed his troubled brow.

'How can I preserve that which does not desire to be preserved?' said Lord Vishnu. 'My job is to preserve things as they are, not things as they want to be. How unprofessional of Shiva to renege on his duty. He knows the Bhagavad Gita as well as I do.'

'Let Lord Brahma worry about it, dear one.'

But since Lord Vishnu was also Lord Brahma (the Brahman is One), he worried endlessly. In vain did the Divine Consort massage her Lord's lotus feet, in vain did she offer her milk-white, rose-tipped breasts, and in vain did she sing to soothe her Lord's dreams. Prosperity has no solution for ennui.

Perhaps a year passed. Perhaps a billion years passed. Who keeps track of Time when you are Time itself? At last the Divine Consort, at her wits' end, appealed to her sister, Lady Saraswati, the Goddess of Wisdom.

'O wise and gentle one, learned in all the sixty-four arts, contrive a solution for my husband and your father.'

'You only had to ask, dear sister. Here I was, knowing I must interfere but unwilling to do so.'

At an opportune time, the Goddess Saraswati began to strum her seven-stringed veena. At first the music clung to her sari, reluctant to leave her side. But then they took wing; a rippling across lakes, a rising of birds, and the green rustle of trees making visible the wind. Lord Brahma had an idea.

'Let Vishnu become the Destroyer. Let Shiva become the Preserver. I will remain as I am, for every transformation, if it is to be smooth and continuous, must have a fixed point.'

(On Earth, it is 1909 and Luitzen Egbertus Jan Brouwer puts down his coffee cup with a trembling hand. It has just struck him that a slowly stirred cup of coffee must have at least one point that remains unmoved. Years later, another strange fellow, John Nash, will show that this is exactly the same as saying that the game of Hex can never end in a draw. Brouwer, tetrahedron-faced genius, hears voices. He calls their counsel, Intuitionism.)

Lord Shiva was elated at the solution.

'Henceforth,' predicted the Lord of Vows, 'I shall preserve rather than destroy. Put away the dice game, Parvati, my beloved wife. I have work to do.'

So Lord Vishnu took over the Department of Destruction. Lord Shiva moved into the Department of Jams and Preserves.

There is a phenomenon known to Unix aficionados as the Mad Newbie Syndrome. The newbie orders the removal of a trivial file, say, and ends up removing the entire operating system, including all the keyboards. There is rarely any ha-ha-hee-hee in the cubicles.

Lord Vishnu was that mad newbie. He sought to delete a silly, trivial, utterly pointless photon headed nowhere and nowhen. Lo and behold! Most matter in Creation promptly disappeared.

'What the ?&!%!' screamed Lord Brahma, as he fell through Nothingness.

But Lord Vishnu was just getting started. A second delete removed quiddity from every conceivable object; anything could become anything else if it tried hard enough. A third delete removed the capacity to undo.

'Stop, O Naika!' said Lord Brahma, now truly terrified. Even terror has its creative manifestations. The origin of the monkey-puzzle tree – so ugly that it has to reproduce asexually – may be traced to this moment.

Lord Shiva was not singing tra-la-la either. He was able to retrieve the missing matter but turned it so black that no one, not even the gods, could see it in the dark. He was unable to undo the removal of the undo (naturally!), and so had to patch in a facsimile. But, alas, now a double-undo of something was not the same as doing that something in the first place.

(On Earth, it is 1923 and Jan Brouwer is putting the finishing touches to his paper, 'Über die Bedeutung des Satzes vom ausgeschlossenen Dritten in der Mathematik'. In English, 'On the Significance of the Excluded Middle in Mathematics'. The significance, just to be clear, is that not-not-X is not X. The voices tell Brouwer that the world doesn't have to choose between X and not-X.)

Lord Shiva resigned. So did Lord Vishnu. No words are exchanged as desks are cleared and carton and poster carried out. The little experiment is over. There is no question of going back; the undo has been undone after all. If it had been proved that Lord Vishnu is a lousy Destroyer, then it had also been proved that he is a good Protector. Obverse ditto for Lord Shiva. There is an exhausted peace in heaven.

The wives are not amused. They love their men, but there is only one Creation after all. They hold their own meeting, in which they plait each other's lustrous hair, share jasmine-scented secrets, complain in Vedic meter, and have a lot of laughs.

As Lady Parvati rose from her seat, her sideways glance at her sisters dissolved the mother in all things. Her girdle unfastened and slipped from her incomparable waist.

'Go, dear sister,' said Lady Lakshmi smiling, as she helped re-fasten the jewelled girdle. 'May success flower your path.'

Arousal is a season of the gods. The tormented navel, the rouge-stained feet, the moist surrender of thighs, the abandon of white lilies, the crumpled defeat of linen – the lovemaking of gods, the poet Bhartrhari assures us in chaste Sanskrit, is a lot like ours, only more so. At some point, the goddess Parvati reached for her Lord.

'My Lord,' she said, her voice silvered with promise and peril. 'Please dance for me. You know I love it so.'

'Beloved,' replied Bhairava, 'I know what it is that you seek. And yet.'

So the Lord danced. The ancients say that the gods, all million of them, gathered to watch. Last time around, the great Kalidasa had shattered into a thousand shards of poetry. A War God, Kumara, had been born. What could happen this time?

'O Nataraja,' breathed the divine Parvati, her face aflame like a kimsuka tree with a billion flowers. 'When you raise your left leg just so'

The pause is everything. The God froze, his left leg slightly raised off the ground.

'And that arm. Yes. Just so.'

The God froze his arms. That calm repose. That hand raised in blessing.

'Ah. Dearest! Just so!'

'Beloved.'

The last words of the Nataraja.

The God froze altogether. They say he stands there still, motion and emotion locked in Time's four-cornered crystal. Destruction, Preservation, Creation and Necessity.

Perfectly balanced.

So perfectly balanced that it is almost – dare we say it?

Yes.

Almost as if there are no gods at all.

4

INTO THE NIGHT

The island of Meridian was still thirty minutes away, but Kallikulam Ramaswamy Iyer had already done enough neck stretches, shoulder shrugs, hand wiggles and toe scrunches to limber his joints for this lifetime and the next.

He was tired. He was eighty-two years old and had relaxed his ancient Brahmin joints through many a stressful hour, but the last few days had been some of the worst: first, a thirteen-hour flight from Mumbai to Sydney with a three-day layover at Singapore, then a four-hour flight in a boomerang-shaped aeroplane from Sydney to Fiji's Nadi Airport followed by a two-hour ride in a catamaran ferry to Meridian. Far away.

Ramaswamy shook his head. Why had Ganga decided to settle so far away? She had always been peculiar, his daughter, this bright-eyed girl they had raised from mustard seed through plaits and school bag to first-class first and first menses, this wild daughter of theirs that squeezed his heart so, squeezed it till he'd sworn not to love her any more, but of course it was all talk, as the missus would verify, for wasn't he here in the belly of a fish, going to a land of cannibals for the sake of their bright-eyed girl who only thirty-seven years ago had begun a mustard seed as modest as an ant's fart.

'Think in English,' advised his wife. 'Tamil will only make it harder for you to adjust.'

Oh, listen to the Queen of England. Who was the matriculate here, madam? And who was the sixth standard twice-fail?

A wave of laughter surged through the boat. It was beginning to irritate him, these periodic laughs. What were they laughing at? And why was it funny? A passenger in the adjacent seat, a sleek cheetah of an Indian girl who'd been gesturing with her silver thimbles throughout the last half hour, lifted her head, blinked rapidly and smiled. She looked tired too. What was she doing here, alone, so far away from home and husband?

He continued to brood. Ganga could have stayed. There were plenty of jobs for Hindus in India. Even a job in Europe would have been acceptable. But the South Pacific! Meridian was so new it wasn't even listed in his Rand McNally 1995 World Almanac. Who could've foreseen when he left Kallikulam in 1962, barely nineteen years old and with ninety rupees in his pocket, when he'd left his parents, dressed in their starched best, left them behind and forever at the Thrichedur railway station, who could've foreseen this final migration, three score and three years later, to a land without elephants, to a land without ancestors, who could have foreseen?

'Stop beating that drum, sir,' said Paru. 'Fall on your knees and thank your Krishna-bhagavan that you have such a sterling daughter. You're in her care now. Just adjust a little. So, chin up and get ready for the next innings.'

You? What had happened to the 'we'? His wife Paru had been younger by ten years. By all logic she should have been on this boat, not him. But of course, the 'we' of sixty years plus had ended at the Sion Electric Crematorium in Mumbai.

He flexed his neck. No. That had just been the disposal of the end. The end had come with a shopping list. Paru had sent him to buy groceries and when he returned, it was to a world without – No, it was no use dwelling on that day. Today was the first day of the rest of his life.

He sat, resigned, as another rash of laughter broke out. The girl was also laughing. She must've sensed his inspection, because she turned her head in his direction. Her eyes were milked over, like the white, dead corals he'd seen near Fiji. Pity struggled with revulsion in his mind. O God, what was the matter with the girl's eyelids? Why was she rolling them up? Almost like a lizard. Poor girl. Ramaswamy quickly turned his head. So there were handicapped people in the West as well.

People may say what they want, thought Ramaswamy, but fate was blind. Why else would this beautiful girl be blind, why else would he have had to leave India, and why else would the last conversation with his wife have been about potatoes, brinjals and coconuts, and would he, for God's sake, please, please check the tomatoes before buying them, because the last batch had been overripe and practically rotten. It could've been about anything, and it had been.

He didn't mind that his wife had died. She had become tired, worn out. Nothing interested her any more, not even their fights, and her insults had stopped being insults and begun to feel like the instructions of someone departing for an immensely long journey. She had become tired, Paru had, his wife of sixty years and seven lives, tired of waiting for Ganga to settle down, to stop hopping about, to amass the money *to bring you home, Amma. I love you, please, please hang in there, okay?* Why, had his house been any less of a home? Had he not taken care of his wife? Paru wanted to let go, and he had gotten tired of holding on for the both of them. He didn't mind. But Paro hadn't left empty-handed. She had taken his memories with her. That he did mind.

It meant that he now had to recollect things, and could no longer rely on a shout ('Paru!') and an answer. For instance, what was the name of the school he'd attended in the 1940s? Had they first talked in the Esso canteen, or had it been that monsoon day when he'd offered her his umbrella? What was the name of his last American boss at Esso, the year before it became Hindustan Petroleum? He clearly remembered the fellow. Especially his laugh. The fellow would laugh, a great big honk of pure evil, revealing a panoply of white, red, yellow, lead glint and a couple of canines sharpened by decades of insatiable meat-eating. But what was his name?

'Who cares?' said Paro. 'Things have changed. Just adjust a little and all will be well.'

Adjust, adjust. He didn't want to adjust. He wouldn't adjust. He didn't need adjusting. He wasn't an ill-fitting pair of trousers or a TV with bad reception. Let others adjust. Like Lord Rama, he would act according to his dharma, and if that was inconvenient for the world, then by all means, please just adjust, my dear adjusting world. Nonsense!

Ganga could have stayed back in Bombay and looked after her aged and ailing parents. If she had, her mother would be alive now, no doubt. No doubt about that at all. Her mother's death was on her head. Money, money, chasing money. Never staying in one place for long, always hopping around like a rabbit on ganja, how could anyone live like that, Krishna-bhagavan alone knew how long she would stay in this new place Meridian, he wouldn't be surprised if he got the orders to pack and move before he'd even unpacked and landed, no, not surprised one bit. She should've done her dharma and looked after her old parents. But who cared about dharma these days?

There was an announcement being made, but the accent was impossible to understand. It was clear though that they had almost reached. Through the large windows, he could see bits and pieces of the skyline. Palm trees. Three- and four-storey buildings. Windmills. It didn't look anything like the future shown in movies. Passengers were busy getting their things together; a few were busy blinking at each other. Maybe that's how they said goodbye in this part of the world. The blinking reminded him of ants on a sugar trail. The catamaran docked with a bump and jerk.

'We've reached,' said his co-passenger. 'You can unbuckle now.'

'I know,' said Ramaswamy, smiling and blinking. 'That's what I want, that's what you want, but that's not what the buckle wants.'

'Here, let me help. It's been a long journey, huh?'

And before he could say anything, she leaned over and began to struggle with the belt. Her hair glistened as if they were coated with glass. He couldn't help touching a strand, and she glanced at him. 'Careful. The alloy coat is not quite stable yet.'

'Are you married?' he asked.

She frowned and didn't answer. 'There!' She detached the belt. 'Come, Appa. I'll call Aaliyah and tell her we've reached.'

Appa? Yes, of course! This was Ganga, his daughter. How could he not have recognized her? The hair was a factor, yes. But still. What was happening to him? He was so astonished by the lapse in memory, he forgot to be terrified.

'Yes, yes,' he said, furious with Paru. It was all her fault. Fresh resentment began to ooze from the wound of his recent loss.

He had been here before, a stranger in a strange land. In 1962, he'd stepped out on Platform No. 3 at the Victoria Terminus in Bombay, with the smell of soot in his nostrils, a roll of bedding and an aluminium trunk full of good advice. He had survived the first strange day and the second and the third, until a season passed, and he had become part of the very strangeness he'd seen on the first day. On his way to work, he'd sometimes see himself stepping out of a train, on this platform, on that platform, from this village, from that village, going everywhere and going nowhere at all.

So why did this transition feel so different, as if he were doing it for the very first time? Perhaps strangeness simply could not be adjusted to if the strangeness lay, not in the miracles of the place, but in its small-small things.

The miracles were manageable because they all had a familiar feel. Buildings looked like buildings in any Bombay suburb, but they could supposedly chat to each other about energy, politics and life. Or, for example, the 'bubbles'. They were cars with skins that could change colour and even flex as they picked up speed. His daughter had tried to explain how it all worked. Who knew how it worked? He could tell she had no idea either. But they were just inventions. They were just new.

For example, the hearsee. It was just a binoculars and headset rolled into one. With the hearsee, you could see what other people were seeing, hear what other people were hearing, assuming they had hearsees too. It used a 'nictitating membrane' and of course it had wireless. Wireless was a must. Sanjaya must have had something like a hearsee. He had been able to narrate what was happening on the battlefield to King Dhritarashtra as it was happening. So nothing new about the hearsee.

No, the strangeness lay in other things, once-familiar things. It lay in Ganga. She had so many friends. He'd always hated that word: friend. It excused everything and expected nothing.

One friend – Aaliyah – seemed to be a permanent guest. Aaliyah was a Muslim name. Another 'friend' was practically an animal; she lay curled on the sofa, her skinny, thimbled hands working ceaselessly – thinking about the mathematics of relatives in general, Ganga claimed – getting up only to feed, and that too eating things directly from the fridge, all the while standing on one leg like a flamingo and eyeing him cautiously, as if she half expected an ambush. There were many others, all women, with made-up names, Tomi, Rex, Lace, Sharon, and once, just once, he saw a slender gent with a sharp Aryan nose, high forehead, and a lady's name. Ramaswamy had asked him why.

'Because I am a lady,' was the reply.

Dinner was a nightmare: meat and wine all around him, overcooked rice, undercooked vegetables (they crunched!), rubbery yogurt, and cold metal spoons. The first time he ate with his hand – thoroughly mixing the rice and buttermilk by hand, relishing every wet squelch, and licking the fingers at the end – it had been impossible to ignore the long watchful silences, rapid blinks, the Flamingo's high laugh and, most hurtful of all, Ganga's startled expression. As if she didn't know. As if she too hadn't eaten the Tamil Brahmin way, his way, the correct way, once. As if she had forgotten.

He had a room at the end of the hall on the first floor, tucked away from the rest of the house. The girls mostly lived upstairs, rarely coming down, and if they did talk to him it was only to ask him idiotic questions about festivals, the caste system and Hinduism. He had to watch his answers. Otherwise:

'That's rubbish,' Ganga would begin, knitting her brows. 'If you look at the facts…'

The facts were these: Brahminism was bad. The West was good. Everything he said was superstition. Everything she said was science. Those were the facts. S'all right. He had his beliefs, she had hers. She called her beliefs 'facts', and that was all right too. If science was all-powerful, then why did she grovel before the Evolution God? Evolution this, Evolution that. The girl knew a lot, but she understood nothing. As people said, just being able to talk about a trunk didn't make you an elephant.

But most of all, it was the caged existence that was intolerable. So many circuits of the house, so many cautious in-the-doorway peeks into bedrooms, so many against-the-light inspections of their mail, so many cups of microwave chai, so many naps and then to painfully go up, down, around and about the house circumnavigating the hours, the day, the month. Occasionally the house would pass on messages in Ganga's voice or Aaliyah's voice, and he'd feel like a house pet, expected to mewl and bark at the sound of his master's voice. He never responded when they called, shuffling around silently, refusing to be happy for their sake, and fully aware that irrespective of whether he responded or not, every room in the house was visible to their lizard eyes. How had he, Rama, ended up a prisoner in Lanka?

The silence of his Mumbai apartment had always been bordered with faraway horns, shouts of neighbourhood children, Paru's telephone gossip and the imminent possibility of tea. This silence had weight but it was empty. Sometimes he cried.

Ramaswamy lay in bed, facing the wall, the coverlet pulled all the way to his neck, and quietly burbling in a mix of English and Tamil.

'Appa?'

He froze.

'Who are you talking to? Are you all right? Are your legs hurting?'

When he turned, he saw Ganga in her nightdress, her face lit from below by the room's night light.

'I'm okay. Just thinking, that's all. About the good old days.'

She sat down beside him and put a hand on his chest. 'Not able to sleep?'

'How much sleep can I do?' He hesitated, and then spoke in a rush. 'Ganga, I want to go back to Mumbai. I can't live here in this freezing cold and twenty-four hours of rain. Everything is backwards and upside down. From the nose via the back of head to the ear, as people say. A simple man like myself only needs his two servings of rice-curds and a glass of water. That I can get for myself. Why I should be a burden to you? I am going back.'

'We can't have this conversation over and over again. Haven't you been watching the news from India? And there's no one there to take care of you. In a few years, your health problems are only going to get worse. If anything happens—'

'Krishna-bhagavan will take care of me as he has all these years.'

'Don't be childish! Amma took care of you all these years, not your bloody bhagavan. So at least give credit where it's due.'

He was pleased to see her voice rise and her accent veer into its natural roly-poly south Indian roundness. Ha! Not such a suit-and-boot madam after all. He remembered roly-poly; he'd walked this little girl back from kindergarten every day, pigtails and upturned face, hopeful smile and *Appa, Appa, please can I have some kulfi, Appa.*

Where had it all gone wrong with Ganga? Was it when he had shifted her from the Tamil-medium school to the English one in higher secondary? Or was it the day he had found her smoking with the sweeper's boy, a Shudran, whose hand lay curled inside her open blouse? Or was it after she got involved in college politics, morcha'ing and hunger-fasting and speechifying on behalf of every useless ruffian and cause, getting angrier and angrier, totally impossible to talk to, even Paru had given up, until in Ganga's final angry tearful embrace at the airport he had sensed she was saying goodbye to herself.

'I should've disciplined her more,' thought Ramaswamy, 'but as people say, a donkey never has a tiger for a father.'

'Can we go to a doctor?' he asked.

'Now?'

She nictitated and geometric patterns flashed across her eyelids; the room seemed filled with a new awareness. He sensed there were others in the room, watching, listening, perhaps even commenting on him.

'Appa? Are you in pain? I can call an ambulance—'

'No, no. I just want an estimate of how much time I have left.'

'No one can tell you that!'

'Not even science?'

She smiled and touched his face. 'Not even science.'

What was the use of it then? He lay back on the bed and turned to face the wall.

'Appa? Look at me.' She shook him. 'Look at me.' And when he did, she continued in the same calm voice. 'I know it's all very strange and new to you. And Amma is not here to make it easier. We won't stay in Meridian forever. But wherever we go next, life will change, and we have to adapt. Otherwise, we might as well be stones. Evolution—'

'What is this evolution-evolution you keep brandishing like a stick?'

'It's a theory that says we don't need a story to explain how we all got here. It was first clearly explained by Darwin— '

'Speak in Tamil, Ganga. Speak in Tamil.'

He listened to her fantastic tale about fish that had grown lungs and learned to walk on earth, a Xerox machine called DNA in every atom, and what not. As she talked, her alloy-treated hair furled outwards, a controlled motion that had nothing to do with the wind or any natural shake of the head. Somebody was playing with her hair. He closed his eyes.

When she said 'cells', he imagined tiny telephones, but when she said 'chromosome', 'molecule', 'recombination', and 'species', nothing came to mind at all. It couldn't be true. None of it could be true. If it was true, then he would never see Paru again. This one life, this would be the only life. It couldn't be true. He marvelled that she could swallow so incredible a story but refused to accept the simplest, most obvious explanation understandable by the stupidest child: God did it. But he didn't want her to stop talking.

'Ganga, this Evolution God, is it Christian or some other religion only? And if it is Christian, then who is Jesus?'

She was silent for a few long seconds, and when she spoke it was quiet enough to be almost a sigh. 'Aaliyah is right, Appa. This isn't just homesickness. You've fallen out of time. We have to reconnect you to the world. The first step is to set you up with a visor. It's not as good as having Amma or a hearsee, but it's better than nothing. You will begin to see.'

He was here, on the battered bench of a battered park, banished for the day, because the house was being energy-audited, and they didn't want him blurting something to the auditor.

It was good to be out, even though the sky was a sickly bluish-grey and the wind was one tooth too sharp. The park was bordered by bookshops, clothing stores, cafes and open-air restaurants. He'd picked a spot on a deserted side of the park, because the smell of burning meat reminded him of the ghats of Varanasi.

Ramaswamy carefully removed the visor and the thimbles from their case. The visor's elegant comma-shaped neurosensors were a bit ticklish, but not unpleasant against his wrinkled skin. As he stared at the 'viewspace', it began to shear, as if it was being stretched from opposite corners. The eye had to keep moving, otherwise the visor would lose focus. His somewhat stiff fingers found it hard to work the thimbles, used to manipulate the visor's controls, and after a while he began to get confused with the coloured flags, training wheels and little rotating astrology-type signs. The viewspace filled with tiny windows and he blinked helplessly as he tried to regain the original viewspace.

'Don't worry,' said Paru. 'This spectacle is no match for a Senior Clark from Esso.'

Abruptly, a gut-wrenching image of water, wood, blue and sky filled his viewspace. Some weathered lettering: 'Marine Research Institute'. Black coiling black beautiful tentacles black with beautiful grey donut-shaped – no, disgusting – suckers. He recoiled in his seat, mewling as he flailed in empty space for something tangible.

His viewspace shimmered, recoalesced. Back to the park and its threadbare carpet of green. He regained his breath and with it a surge of triumph. He had just used somebody else's visor, or more likely, hearsee. So this is what 'melding' was all about. What was all the fuss about? It was just like watching a movie. He hadn't been the least bit terrified then, but recalling the tentacles, he felt his crotch tighten.

It took a while to retrace his steps, but he managed to get the screen full of windows again, and as they scrolled past, he blinked. And blinked. And blinked. In most cases, he got wobbly images of edges, shadows and corners of rooms. But even when he got a nice view, such as the one from the tourist staring up at the statues on Easter Island, or merely a bad one, like that shameless young girl lying on the bed, what did it matter? Most people seemed to be sitting on equally battered benches staring out over equally battered parks. Ganga had claimed he would feel, not just see, what they saw and felt, but then why did he not feel any different? What did he and they have in common, after all, other than a mutual acknowledgement of being lost? He was everywhere and nowhere.

'It is not our time,' said Paru, sounding subdued. 'Give it a chance.'

His visor filled with fifty scattered circles. Ganga had explained that in 'idle mode' the visor would show the GPS coordinates of people in a half-mile radius. A window popped up, reminding him to 'fill in his profile'.

'Do what it says,' said Paru. 'Put up a sign saying you want to chit-chat.'

'Keep quiet! You should be sitting here suffering, and I should be in your filter-coffee-loving head. Irresponsible, selfish cow.'

He tried to describe himself but didn't get very far. The 'wizard' asked for his Myers-Briggs type; whether he was an introvert, extrovert, kibbitzer or grokker; whether he was an empath, sympath, fabpath or skimpath; and whether he was looking to buy chillax underwear. What kinky things turned Ramaswamy on?

'Elephants,' confessed Ramaswamy. Temples. Obedient children. Early morning showers. Hinduism. Brahmin culture. Decent women. But then he got diverted with the memories of all the delicious foods he would never eat again.

The bench was still slightly wet, most probably from the early morning rains. The world looked like a watercolour painting, which he liked, but he didn't like that it was a painting with no people. Where were all the people in this country? The colony's park in Mumbai had always been chock full of people: retirees, teenage lovers, food vendors, toy vendors, mating dogs, laughing clubs, children running about everywhere. The sky looked dark, swollen, the face of a child about to cry. Perhaps global raining was around the corner.

The visor queried his current mood. He selected the most depressed face he could from the samples in front of him.

'I took it all for granted,' he thought. His head had begun to ache.

A teenager sat down at the far end of the bench. He had an open, cheerful face framed by a halo of curly black hair. He nodded in Ramaswamy's direction.

'Waz,' said the kid. Then he stretched out his legs and made himself comfortable.

The visor claimed the kid's name was Krish and then went on to bug Ramaswamy with a variety of options. Irritated, he took off the visor.

'Excuse me, is your name Krish?'

'Like da tag sez, heya?' The boy seemed a little puzzled, and his eyelids nictitated. His expression brightened. 'Ya-i-c. Welcome to Oz, uncle.'

'I'm Ramaswamy. I'm from Bombay. Native place, Tamil Nadu. Are you also from same?'

Krish shrugged. 'Maybe. Me's from Wooshnu's navel, maybe. We same if youz likes da same.'

The boy's accent was not Indian. Ramaswamy could barely parse what he was saying. 'Are you having school holiday today?'

Krish grinned and shook his head. 'Waz school? Youz the headmaster? What be da teaching today, Master Bates?'

Ramaswamy laughed. Kids were scoundrels no matter where they were. 'Bad boy. You need to be more disciplined.'

'Nuff sport.' Krish scooted over. 'Youz wanting da elephant, heya?'

The boy's eyes were so merry and his smile so infectious, Ramaswamy also found himself smiling. 'Heya. Heya. What's this "heya"?'

'Gimme da izor, dear.' The kid reached for the visor, but something about his expression made Ramaswamy snatch it away and put it in his shirt pocket.

Krish shrugged and unbuttoned his pants. 'Assayway youz want.' He grabbed Ramaswamy's hand and shoved it into his pants. 'Go on. Sample all youz want. Hundred per cent desi juice on da tap, uncle-dear.'

Later, Ramaswamy would puzzle over the fact that the boy's penis had been hard and erect. And the fact that he felt a surge of emotion whose name he hadn't needed for more than two decades. An emotion that was in equal parts small-eyed, calculating and aroused. But it was only one of the many puzzles.

A police car swooped out of nowhere, a blaze of whirling blue lights and piercing siren. The next ten minutes were a terrifying blur. Two officers jumped out of the car; one ran after Krish, and the other fumbled for his handcuff.

His boss from Esso! How was it possible? The same beefy expression, the same greyish-white whiskers, the same sozzled eyes. Mr Gregory! Just remembering the name after all these years was mildly orgasmic.

'Mr Gregory, sir!' Ramaswamy shot to his feet and was ready for dictation.

'Move again asshole, and you'll make my day.' The cop pointed an object that resembled a TV remote at Ramaswamy.

But Ramaswamy had already realized his mistake. Of course this policeman wasn't Mr Gregory. His boss had already been middle-aged when he, Ramaswamy, had joined as a young assistant clerk.

'I'm sorry, I thought you were my boss from Esso. I came here to take some fresh breeze only.'

Ramaswamy tried to explain how his hand had ended up in the boy's pants. The boy clearly needed a doctor, he had a rash of some kind. Perhaps he'd thought an Indian would help. But he was only a retired clerk from Esso, his daughter's dependant, practically a beggar himself. Esso's health insurance had barely covered Paru's treatment; there was nothing he could do for random lost-eyed Indian boys. If the officer would be kind enough to call his daughter, Ganga could confirm every detail. When Ramaswamy reached for the visor in his pocket, the officer tasered him.

In time, the pain faded, as did all direct memory of the incident. In time, a woman in blue came over to report on the investigation. The cop who'd tasered him was an American, like most of the cops in Meridian. Americans understood immigrants as a rule, but of course there was always the rule's exception. She talked about the dangers of viewspace porn. He felt she had been ordered to explain but was trying to apologize. He understood little and was grateful when Aaliyah stepped in to keep it that way. On the whole, Ganga was much more affected by the whole business.

'This is all my fault, Appa.'

'Yes.' Ramaswamy nodded sagely. 'You never listen.'

But he didn't feel any satisfaction at having been vindicated. Only a vast sadness. His poor daughter, that poor sweeper's boy, this poor broken world. He was so tired of it all. Why had he tried to change? Adjust, adjust. Adjust enough and even Lord Rama would become Lord Ravana. Nonsense.

When the cold grey rains came, as they often did in this age of carbon, he liked to sit by a corner window of the house and watch the banana tree in the yard make short work of the water. The rain, as thin as cow's milk, rolled off the tree's bright green plates, as ineffective as a mother's Tamil on a child's unrepentant back. Sometimes the Flamingo would creep up and crouch by him, her eyes blind in thought, her bony fingers ceaselessly working on the general problem of relatives.

'What is the solution,' he once asked the Flamingo, in Tamil, 'if the ones I love hate what I love?'

The Flamingo said nothing. Perhaps she hadn't heard. It was moot in any case, for the problem was intractable. Change was inevitable; it hadn't been, but now it was. Call it evolution, fate, choice or chance. If that was the only way the world would turn, so be it.

But acceptance wouldn't come. The darkness crowded him from all corners, the light of his understanding curving upwards along its walls and returning in an ever-tighter loop. Soon, he would be beyond the reach of all stories.

'Amma,' Ramaswamy would shout, forgetting himself in his despair. His mother: a chequered six-yard sari, a raspy voice, wrinkled hands, jasmine-scented hair and the comfort of her sari's corners. 'Amma!'

Sometimes his daughter would turn up with a glass of Horlicks. In her nightdress and short hair, she resembled one of those Goan ladies in India, brown as a coconut but all white inside. She would pretend to listen to his burbling, her eyes blinking absent-mindedly, her hair furling like snakes as they flexed and re-flexed into one of her many styles. She had many styles, but she looked a widow in all of them. She would tell him fantastic tales from science and biology, offering facts when he longed for truth. He would pick a fight, say outrageous things, insult her friends and all that she held dear, and sometimes Ganga would lose her temper.

'Speak in Tamil kondai,' he urged. 'Speak in Tamil.'

Then Ramaswamy would relax. Ah, the old familiar words. So familiar, so sweetly old and familiar. He let the ferocious alphabet fall, splish-splosh, all around and galosh, the rain of words, in one ear, out the other, the gentle splash of words, how he missed her, Paru, his bride of red earth and pouring rain, his comfort, his eyes, how he missed her, his love, his all, as he walked, faster, ever faster, into the night.

5

GOD'S OWN COUNTRY

As we waited in the baggage claim area of Kochi Airport, Helet remarked on the sharp increase in the number of moustaches per capita. How did wives recognize their Malayalee husbands if they all looked the same? No offence, sweetie.

None taken. I, sweetie, didn't have a moustache and it wasn't a problem she would have. I told her that the men couldn't be discriminated from one another because Malayalee women didn't discriminate. Helet smiled.

'Relax, baby.' I squeezed her slender shoulders.

'I am relaxed.' Then her bravado collapsed. 'I'm not.'

'They'll love you.'

'What if they don't?' She edged closer to a couple standing next to us.

'Then they don't. What do we care?'

'I care. What's the word for "recognize" in Malayalam?'

'Recognize.'

Helet being intent on learning Malayalam had made my

incompetency in the language very clear. But she didn't need my help. Since Helet was intent on learning Malayalam, she would. 'Helet?'

She was busy eavesdropping on the rapid-fire Malayalam/ English of the couple standing next to us. I nudged her and Helet slipped out of her trance.

'There's the bag.' Helet pointed in its direction. 'I still think we should've brought a second bag. Where will we keep all the stuff I plan to buy at your expense? But it's good too, I guess. If we have one bag we need to stay in one room. Have you told your Lion-uncle we'll be sleeping together?'

I grabbed our suitcase. It was large and heavy, made larger and heavier by Helet's attempt to help. I gave her a look and she stepped aside. For our fortnight-long trip, Helet had packed three categories of clothes. There were clothes she wanted to wear: sleeveless tops, baby doll T-shirts, shorts and summer mini-dresses. There were the clothes she would probably have to wear: salwar-kameez sets, capris, jeans, shirts and kurtas. Then there were clothes she would never wear: an LBD, pant-suits and a traditional kasavu sari. This didn't complete the list. There was jogging-wear from Nike and wilderness-wear from Orvis, bristling with pockets, meshes and flaps for storing the white man's burden. She had also brought frumpy ankle-length nightdresses and jammies with elastic rims. Undergarments had their own underworld regime of meshes and cubical pouches. There was far more cloth than woman.

'You have told your uncle we'll be sleeping together?' said Helet again.

'Of course!'

I hadn't, of course. When she met my uncle, the de facto patriarch of the family, she'd understand. 'Simham', as we had always called him, was a force of nature. One didn't discuss premarital sex with forces of nature. To prepare her for coital disappointment, I added, 'But we may have to adjust. Space might be tight, you know, large joint families, and so on.'

'Weasel.'

Fair enough. As we walked out of the baggage area, a security guy asked for our baggage tags. They weren't picking everyone out, only a few. Helet's friendly-monkey smile must have inspired the man, because handing the tag back to her with a smile and a flourish, he declared: 'Welcome to God's Own Country!'

'Thank you. We're super-excited to be in Kerala. You have a nice moustache.'

The man glowed. Introductions were in order. Kurian Varkey Mutholy. You can call me KV. Your good name madam? Tekhelet, but no one calls me that. Tech-let? No. Tek-helet. Tekhelet. Yes, I'm Jewish! You, KV? I'm Syrian Christian, Helet!

Entire planeloads of terrorists slipped into God's Own Country as brand-new BFFs, Kurian Varkey Mutholy, security guard, Syrian Christian, resident of God's Grace Bungalow, Alwaye, near U.C. College, turn left at Priya Groceries, three houses down, and Tekhelet Shebet, offspring of Cochin Jews, resident of nowhere, struck up a lifelong friendship.

'Very nice man,' said Helet, as we finally emerged. 'Are those guys waving at us?'

Simham had sent a driver. He had also sent Ravi. My cousin, the second son of Simham's third brother, had already run to fat and matured to the man-boy look he would have for the rest of his life. I was the elder by a few years, so I set Ravi in his place by critiquing his weight. He acted abashed but his peepers were on Helet. I introduced them.

'Helet, Ravi; Ravi, behave.'

'Beauty and the beast, at last,' chortled Ravi and he bowed his head in an exaggerated manner. 'Welcome to God's Own Country, bhabhi. Only one bag?'

Bhabhi? Then I guessed that Ravi probably wasn't confident he could pronounce Helet's name. It was pronounced 'alat' with a slight emphasis on the 'l' rather than the 'a', like an alveolar 'l'. Some people called her Ellet as if she had something to sublet. Popular variants included E-let, Hell-let. It didn't help that she was indifferent to what she was called. Call me whatever, she would say, further confusing the other party. It wasn't sufficient to meet her, now they had to also name her.

'So, Ravi, how's things?'

He correctly interpreted my question as asking how things were with my uncle. Simham was still vigorous, still lifting weights, still tormenting the next generation of kids, still standing guard over the family.

As we chatted, I discovered Ravi was knowledgeable about things that concerned him: local politics, his steady law practice, family gossip. When Helet said something, Ravi paid an extra amount of attention to her comments, then resumed as if she hadn't spoken at all. Every so often, he'd lean across, fling out a heavy arm and point through the open window to various landmarks and sights. She smiled and nodded, nodded and smiled, fighting the wind, one hand pressed to her hair, the other holding down the top of her billowing kurta, her fragile frame shrinking against me, her dark eyes wide and brilliant with the shock of a new world. I patted her reassuringly, and she turned her black irises on me, before returning to her view.

'By the by,' said Ravi, 'Simham has decided to fill the kolum.'

'No way!'

My shriek startled Helet. But I had good cause for my surprise. Fill the kolum? Never. It was unthinkable. The family pool, about a minute's walk from the mansion, held my childhood memories in escrow. It was a considerable body of water, speckled with green and bordered by tall, very tall brick walls, moss-encased at the water's edge. The bath was embedded deep into the ground with some two dozen stone steps leading into the water. The deep end of the kolum was dappled in shade and black with a few fronds of a neem tree that had somehow grown into the wall. The fronds had grazed the water's surface as far back as I can remember.

The chipped and uneven steps were perennially slick and one had to be careful going down. Which of course we weren't. Every cousin, every uncle and aunt, every member of the family had an incident of slipping, bleeding, scraping, sacrificing a piece of oneself on those steps. Simham had lost his only daughter in its depths. Just last August, a nephew or a nephew's son had fallen, injured his spine. A full recovery was expected, but Ravi said talk of draining the kolum had intensified after that incident.

But I didn't have any leverage in the matter. I didn't live here. Already I felt resignation take the place of the original sadness. Life was replacement.

'Hope I can still take a dip in it,' said Helet. 'That's the family ritual, right?'

Ravi waited for her to finish, then said to me, 'It'll cost about seventy thousand rupees.'

'I'll pay my share.' I hid my irritation. I explained to Helet that the reason I'd been so surprised was that though Simham had come to terms with Bala's death, it was a sort of keepsake of hers. Bala had been very fond of the pool. Simham was the kind of man who hung on to love. 'He's sentimental.'

'Very sentimental,' echoed Ravi. 'Chetta, the cost just includes draining and the sand. The labour is a separate negotiation.'

We had reached the mansion. I hardly recognized it. Originally all four brothers and three sisters had stayed in the mansion, but over time new wives and husbands and quarrels had forced fission. Yet the family was still tight, still contained in a cluster of seven houses.

'Bhabhi, please avoid the kolum,' said Ravi. 'Very easy to lose balance. Also dirty. But bathroom has shower, so no problem. WC is Western-style.'

When we entered the house, I saw that the living room hadn't changed one bit. The same old collection of random knick-knacks, the same old array of beloved and dead relatives near the ceiling, the same old posters with tawdry inspirational messages, the same old furniture still wrapped in yellowing dust covers. I glanced at the wall; the two blunt-edged Kalari swords were still there. As children, Bala and I had often played with them; I, Othenan, breaker of hearts, and she, Unniyarcha, breaker of bones. I always won, of course.

'Do you yield?' I would yell, my sword's tip at her bosom.

'Only because you are to be my consort.'

She had started saying 'consort' after learning from Dr Funk's *30 Days to a More Powerful Vocabulary* that the word's Latin roots, *cons* and *sors*, referred to a shared destiny. Technically, Unniyarcha had been the consort of Othenan's enemy, but between us there had been that possibility. It had only been a reasonable possibility for our parents, but we considered it certain. In retrospect, I could see how we might have convinced others as well.

Helet gazed downwards; she was standing in the centre of a giant-ass swastika in the floor's mosaic.

'Simham has an eclectic taste,' I said, as if Helet couldn't see that for herself. She told me later she had been startled not by the symbol itself, but the sheer size of it.

'What's that room?' she asked, pointing to an ornately carved door.

The prayer room. As a lawyer, Simham cultivated an eclectic taste in gods as well. Ravi opened the door and gave her a peek, but reminded her that she couldn't go in until she had taken a bath. And maybe not even then, he added uncertainly. Helet said something about south Indian iconography and how she wanted to study it more, and Ravi nodded as though he had written the definitive work on the subject.

Simham was in his office meeting with a client, but when he heard our voices he strode out. He hadn't changed much. Crisp white shirt. Crisp white lungi with a thin gold border, one corner gripped between his thumb and forefinger in the old kingly manner. He had lost more hair, but his sharp glance, his vigour, his powerful shoulders and his fierceness were all intact. He was short, just five-foot three, but no one could doubt he'd always stand the tallest in any room.

'Hahn, you've arrived!' He gripped my arm, turned to Helet, ducked his head and offered his most charming smile, revealing his prominent canines. Then he turned to me. 'Does she speak Malayalam?'

'Enough to make good mistakes,' said Helet in Malayalam.

'Then that's more than the donkeys here,' said Simham, gesturing with his fingers as if he were sprinkling water, a dismissive gesture peculiar to Kerala. And when Ravi translated his words into English, he barked: 'Hoh! Look at our Englishman. I can do translations if I need to, my sayyip.'

I hugged him. It clearly surprised Simham, since our family didn't go in much for displays of affection, but I could tell he was also pleased. He again squeezed my shoulder, then my arms, remarked that I seemed to have lost some muscle. Didn't I work out any more? He demonstrated his solid biceps.

'I can do one-hundred-and-fifty push-ups,' he told Helet.

'Me too.'

'Are you sixty-two?' he inquired.

'I'm twenty-six.'

He laughed, she laughed. He started to ask her something, then hesitated, grasped her palm, led her to his office. There was a large world map. He wanted to know exactly where she came from. She pointed to her little town. Its sole distinction was that it was in Israel. We all contemplated the spot. It could have been any spot and it was.

'She is Cochin Jew,' offered Ravi. Then he added cautiously, 'Bhabhi's mother was born in Madurai.'

Simham brightened. His wife, my late aunt, had been from Palghat and so more than a little Tamil herself. He went to a large steel cabinet and took out half a dozen music CDs. Old Tamil songs. He was the only one, he complained, who appreciated the beautiful language. Did she listen to Tamil songs?

'Very, very old Tamil songs,' muttered Ravi.

I gazed around the office, my eyes drinking in every object. God, how many times Bala and I had stood in this room, sneaking grins at each other, as Simham chewed us out for some transgression or the other.

I listened to Simham and Helet trying to connect, build a bridge out of the sheer desire to build a bridge. He called her 'molle', daughter. Helet had already fallen in love with my uncle. Most people did. He was exactly what he presented himself to be. I wouldn't be surprised if he fell in love with her. She was exactly who she presented herself to be.

He talked about T.R. Rajakumari and Thyagaraja Bhagavathar in the movie *Haridas*; she talked about the rap artist M.I.A. Hands flying, gestures; uncertain English, broken Malayalam. Together it all seemed to make a whole. He played her some samples, she whipped out her cell phone, played him a radical Eelam number. She bled for the Palestinian cause, of course. It all made Simham happy, genuinely happy.

Helet's Malayalam was noticeably smoother. A month more and she would probably speak Malayalam more fluently than any of us. She had a real gift for languages.

'One evening we will watch *Haridas*,' Simham promised her.

Ravi grimaced. He reminded Simham that he had a client waiting and got rebuffed for his presumption. But eventually my uncle conceded we probably wanted to freshen up, meet the other relatives. After my aunt's death, the mansion was run by her widowed sister, Shanta. Simham told me to first pay my respects to Shanta-ammai before visiting the others. I was a little hurt. Did he think I had forgotten the proprieties? As I was about to leave the room, my uncle asked me to stay back.

'Very sweet girl. Have you tied the—' He gestured to his neck. The wedding necklace.

'Not yet,' I said in Malayalam, my mouth dry. I had no idea why my heart was racing. 'First, I wanted to introduce her to you, get your blessings.'

'You always have my blessings. But now that you know you have it, why not follow through on your plan?'

'We're discussing it,' I said. It sounded non-committal, even to me. 'But we only have two weeks.'

'We will discuss all that later. Meanwhile, there are proprieties. I know you people are modern but we're still old-fashioned. She'll stay here, in the mansion. She can take Bala's old room. I'll tell Shanta to make the arrangements. You will stay in Bharatan's house.'

'Okay.' I would catch hell from Helet later.

'Now, why didn't you visit earlier?' He proceeded to excoriate me for losing touch, for not calling, for going off God alone knew where. I was first surprised, then happy, that he cared so much. There was an intensity to his words, an explosion of feeling that seemed to have been waiting for just this moment. He gripped my shoulder when he saw my eyes were filled. 'Never mind, what nonsense, you're here now.'

'I knew I would always return.'

'Yes. You take water, I suppose?' He gestured to his mouth with his clenched fist and outstretched thumb.

'No, no,' I quickly replied. I had no desire to booze with my relatives. The men drinking to get drunk, the women stewing bitterly in their rooms, the house's child labour hailed on a regular basis to bring snacks on demand. It was the worst possible way to enjoy a drink.

'Good, we'll have a small session in the evening. To celebrate your return. Now go see everybody and everything.'

Later, Shanta-ammai informed Helet she had been granted a great honour. Simham never gave anyone Bala's room. I gently fondled Bala's long-unused stationary as Helet made the bed. The pencils had little chew marks on them. I could almost see Bala, her chubby arms resting on the work desk, eyebrows locked in concentration, tongue peeping out. Helet chatted with Shanta-ammai, whom she called Shanta-aunty, took her advice about folding things this way as opposed to that way, the need to check for creepy-crawlies, how pillows worked, et cetera. I translated when necessary. Shanta-ammai watched Helet work and then, turning to me, said in a grave voice, 'Now I don't feel bad how fate turned out.'

'So?' I asked Helet, when Shanta-ammai stepped out to see about chai, hands clasped to rheumatic knees as she crossed the raised threshold.

'They are all wonderful. So loving. I really liked Lion-uncle.'

'Really?' I was pleased. 'Did you see the way Simham held my hand all through?'

She laughed. 'This is what a real family is like.'

'It's your family, baby.' I felt very close to her.

That night, Simham took me to the terrace and I found assorted uncles, cousins and underage nephews all ready for a 'session'. Simham only drank Laphroaig single malt and only he was allowed to touch the sacred bottle. But I was a special guest and hence permitted to share his treasure. I had to make the requisite moans to indicate how much I appreciated the privilege.

It was a privilege. Fifteen, twenty years ago, I had been like one of my nephews, squatting on the floor, listening to the men talk about manly topics and occasionally allowed a sip of beer or rum. Forget about just touching Simham's bottle of peaty single malt, let alone sample it. And now, here I was, sitting across from him, clinking glasses.

Helet appeared at the terrace doorway. What the hell! Oversized white shirt and cotton jammies. Anybody could guess that was a man's shirt, meaning my shirt. Her bra was semi-visible. I indicated with my eyebrows and neck jerks to signal this was Men Only and that she should vamoose, signals she wilfully ignored.

'Sit, sit,' said Simham, making space for his new darling. 'Some lemonade, orange juice?'

With her arrival, the conversation shifted from local news and the chronic ailments of relatives to our life abroad and what we thought of the American President and things of that nature. They were curious about how we had met.

I described how I had been at a Carnatic SPIC-MACAY concert in San Diego. Gayatri Girish had been improvising in the Balagopala krithi, elaborating, offering, teasing the swaras in the famous line of the charanam, but my attention wasn't on Girish's niraval but on Helet, who sat one row ahead of me, obviously in some kind of aural trance. After the concert, Helet told me over coffee and cheesecake at a nearby diner that she'd been passing the hall, felt a weird heartache, a strange kind of pull almost, and wandered in. My lucky day.

Simham nodded as if this meeting had just confirmed something for him.

'In another life, you were part of this family,' he told her.

'Lion-uncle, I don't believe in reincarnation.'

'Belief is not required,' said Simham in English. He flashed his canines. 'What? Right or not?' He held out his hand and I obligingly high-fived him. Then he turned his attention back to her. 'This useless fellow, why he's not married you still?'

'Yeah, why hasn't he?' asked Helet, smiling at me. 'Maybe you can do something, Lion-uncle.'

Bas! We hadn't planned on getting hitched in Kerala but we had planned to get hitched some day, and there was no real reason why that day couldn't be now – and, if now, why the place couldn't be Kerala. Helet confirmed we had ample leave. It wasn't a problem to extend our stay in Kerala rather than visit Rajasthan as we had originally planned. Simham allowed us to skirt the outlines of the decision.

'Iyer-uncle is coming tomorrow for his case,' said Ravi. 'Should I ask him to take a look at the horoscopes?'

Then Ravi stuck his tongue out. Oops. Simham glared at him.

Helet thought it was because Ravi had presumed, but en route to our separate rooms, I explained to her Simham had this superstition that no plans were to be discussed after dinner. He believed that such talk after dinner would jinx the plans. Crazy stuff.

Helet didn't think it was crazy. Just a different rationality, that's all. Every sound was infused with the breath from some life. And that quintessence of breath survived all transformations. If life could generate sounds, maybe sounds could generate life? In the beginning was the Word, et cetera. Take the word for the Sanskrit syllabary: Deva-nagari. City of the Gods. Language, not Kerala, was God's Own Country. That's why you had to be careful. Speech had an invocatory power.

'Please. It's my uncle here, not Kierkegaard. Just superstition, that's all.'

She stopped walking. 'Is it? Accha, say: I will lose Helet forever.'

'Accha? Gone native, have we?'

'Go on, say it.'

'Don't be silly.'

'Say it. I will lose Helet forever.'

'You say it. I don't see the point at all.'

'See? You can't say it. Now ask yourself why.'

I started to say something, then fell silent. We resumed walking, this time holding hands. Talk about a non-explanation. I had a much simpler explanation for my uncle's superstition. Simham's last conversation with Bala had been a post-dinner quarrel over a forthcoming twelfth standard picnic. She had wanted to go, Simham had rejected her plan. Bala had gone down to the pool for some me-time and somehow drowned. Hence, the superstition. But I didn't want Helet to pity my uncle.

Iyer-uncle came by, took our birth info from Simham. Helet hadn't been sure what time she'd been born, but of course there are ways around such difficulties. Later in the evening, Simham told us the charts had matched and there really was no reason to delay.

At times, it seemed surreal. I had come to visit, and here I was, getting married. I had half expected they would be polite and formal with Helet, and nothing more. But she was treated with such abundant warmth that Helet's fears of rejection were finally laid to rest. We missed each other. It was hard to get much time together, let alone get intimate time with each other. I resumed masturbation; my return to adolescence was complete.

'Shee!' said Helet, when I asked her for a pair of used panties, bra, something. 'Dirty boy.'

The words had a curious effect on me, leaving me breathless and faintly dizzy. She looked amused, and perhaps something could have come of the moment, but in the distance we heard Simham call her name.

'Gotta go.'

Helet and Simham were getting along like a house on fire. If I had heard the phrase before, I understood it now. It was a living fact. He cleared his schedule, took her sightseeing, and introduced her to every member of the family, close and distant, and whether on speaking terms or not. Helet's growing command of the Malayalam language and her ease with Simham made my presence unnecessary. I went along on some of these expeditions and was astonished to find myself a third wheel amid the good time they were having. I was pleased but also a little discomfited. I had hoped to be her guide, but instead I had become a petitioner for her attention.

I wasn't all that upset to be left alone, but if Helet felt connected to this world, I began to feel disconnected. Bala was everywhere and I couldn't talk to anyone about her. When I walked into the old and ruined shed where we used to keep the giant festival pots and pans, my mind was filled, in classic film fashion, with snippets of conversations, the way Bala used to laugh, her large expressive eyes, the emerging woman's voice in childhood's throat. Sometimes I found my eyes filling, and then be at a complete loss as to what had provoked the tears.

Once when Helet was out shopping with some of my female cousins and nieces, I snuck into Bala's room. No one was in the house. Her clothes had all been removed, but her bookcase was still there. I opened it, took down her Nancy Drew volumes, the Times of India biography series, the Tell Me Why books, and other treasured volumes she had read and reread. Each book bore her childish but well-formed handwriting 'This book belongs to Bala M.' followed by her signature. She had changed her signature many times, usually in response to my criticism.

I could see her sitting across from me, chin resting on her palms, reading, only occasionally kicking me under the table. We had played footsie forever but recently something electric had begun to flicker in our touches.

'Seven more days,' said Bala, examining the blue lozenge she had been sucking on.

Seven more days and I would have to leave God's Own Country and return to Mumbai. Back to studying for the bloody IIT exams, back to my small squashed apartment, back to a world without green and water and Bala.

'Show,' I ordered.

At first Bala shook her head, then she stuck out her blue tongue.

'It's hot,' I told her. 'Let's go to the kolum.'

'Okay. Just one minute.'

This close to my departure, Bala would do anything I asked. We had begun to be a little crazy with each other. I would graze the back of my hand against the sides her neck, back and forth, back and forth, supposedly to demonstrate the principles of static electricity. Sometimes I pinched her waist through her top, hard enough to make her cry out. Don't be a drama queen, I would say. Next morning, she would hurry, first thing, to show me the bruise I'd left on her soft brown skin. See? Meanie! Sometimes, as I worked, Bala would sneak up behind me and lick the nape of my neck. Sometimes we would just thwack each other, for no reason at all. We wanted things to go back to the way they were, back when we were just kids and not this sparking electric beast that was all goosebumps, aroused points and painful throbs.

At the kolum, Bala and I sat side-by-side, on the last step, dangling our feet in the green-black water and talking about nothing in particular. The air was infused with an exotic yet familiar fragrance, but not from any flower I recognized.

'Dubai-uncle bought me this perfume,' said Bala, smiling rather shyly.

I had heard of Dubai-uncle, a smuggler and one of Simham's best clients. Grain de Soleil, Bala informed me, was a mix of rose, jasmine, iris, cinnamon, vanilla and amber. I could make out there was rose and jasmine but the rest was strangeness.

'Here,' said Bala, leaning closer to me. 'I put it on my neck.'

I nuzzled the side of her neck, breathed in deeply. There was perfume, yes, and maybe all that cinnamon-vanilla bullshit, but what I inhaled was Bala. We were both breathless by the time we were done.

'I also put some under there,' said Bala, 'but that you will have to imagine.'

'Take off your shirt. Let me smell.'

'Shee! You're such a dirty boy.'

'Maybe, but I'm practically your husband,' I reminded her. 'We're going to be married, everyone knows that. I only want to know what amber smells like.'

'This is too much,' said Bala. But she was already unbuttoning her shirt. 'Just looking, okay?'

There are no words to describe her proud smile, her womanly calm, the perfection of those small brown breasts encased in their tight cotton oppressors, the fragrance of clean sweat, the suspended hum of the passing dragonfly, and the water's dappled plops and glugs breaking the poised silence of the universe as it stood next to me, watching Bala.

My reverie was broken by a loud voice I immediately recognized. Iyer-uncle. I went out into the living room, greeted him. I told him Simham was in court and the women had all left for shopping.

'He gave me the wrong horoscope by mistake,' said Iyer-uncle in Malayalam. 'To say that only I came. He gave me the horoscope of Bala-mol.'

I took the horoscope from him. I saw that the birthdate on it wasn't Helet's. It was Bala's.

'Even a good astrologer can't remember all his charts,' said Iyer-sir. 'But when I plotted the chart, I felt I had seen it somewhere before. It's a most peculiar chart. The lagnesham is squared by Mangal and Shani, but there are also mitigations. Today morning I remembered it was Bala-mol's. If you give the other girl's correct info, I will plot the chart today only.'

I provided Iyer-uncle with the information he wanted to the best of my ability, and after he'd left, I studied the horoscope. What a joke. Iyer-uncle had been conveniently unaware that earlier he had signed off on my marriage to a dead girl. Yes, he had remembered the chart's pattern, but nothing in the chart itself had revealed the most relevant fact about Bala: she was dead.

When Simham returned, I told him about the screw-up. He was very embarrassed.

'It's all nonsense anyway,' he told me, making that water-sprinkling motion. 'What, don't you agree? These charts and predictions. You know what happened in my life. What didn't happen in your life.'

I told him to forget about the whole matter. All Helet and I wanted, I repeated, were his blessings. Just then Helet and the ladies returned from their shopping, laden with loot. Simham went to take a bath and I went to inspect the damage.

I sat in Bala's room and Helet showed off all her purchases. It was interesting how we had adjusted to the expectations of the people around us. We no longer found it necessary to shut the door. I was no longer offended when people barged in without knocking. I had recalibrated what was a 'personal question'.

So I was taken by surprise when Helet went to the door,

popped her head out to see if the coast was clear, came back, dropped her jeans, stepped out of her panties in one smooth motion and handed them to me.

I took the frilly nothings, dumbfounded. She pulled her pants back up; smiled.

'Nice and sweaty,' said Helet. Then her smile faded. She looked pseudo-sad. 'It's hard for you, isn't it?'

'Hard, yes.'

Helet laughed. In that laugh, its living sound, for just those three seconds, we were what we always had been. Then from across the house, Simham called for her. Molle? I think I hated him then.

'Father is calling,' she said in Malayalam. She turned and shouted, 'Coming.'

'Father? Since when?'

'It pleases him, so why not? Now don't get upset, but I told him he could call me Bala.'

I stared at her. I raised her clothing to my nose, inhaled. Time had made my nose more sophisticated. I recognized what I held in my hand. Rose and jasmine and iris, underlaid with cinnamon, vanilla and amber. The Kerala heat is hard on these subtle notes, and what remained was that old truth: sweat is earth turned to water. Bala's earth.

'You're upset.' She pouted.

'Of course I'm fucking upset.'

'Why? It's harmless. He's just an old man. I can be Bala if it pleases him. And don't lie, I know it pleases you too, my consort.'

I continued to stare at Helet. The black depths of her eyes mirrored the drowning pool. The plan was to fill in the kolum after our wedding. The kolum had been fenced off some months back and an air of relinquishment hung over the water. The family pool, now green and murky, choked with hyacinth weeds, haphazardly poisoned with chlorine and larvicides, had entered its final stage of self-destruction.

Something shifted in her eyes, and I once again recognized the woman I had brought to this godforsaken land. I thought she would rush into my arms.

'Helet, Helet, Helet.'

'Darling. Take me away from here. I don't want to marry you.'

'Me neither! I love you.'

We would kiss, cling to each other, and whisper tender baby endearments. We'd return to being us: uncommitted, open-ended, free of stars and houses and prophesies.

In the distance, a lion roared.

'I better go,' she said hurriedly, already more than halfway over the raised threshold. 'Father must want something.'

We got married in a noisy but efficient ceremony. Simham tried to be everywhere but he tired easily these days. He sat around, smiling, hands folded royally across his chest. Everyone said happiness had made him mellow. Kurian Varkey Mutholy came to our wedding and it turned out his brother-in-law owned a construction company. KV promised to get us a much better deal on the pool-filling.

6

THE ROBOTS OF EDEN

When Amma handed me Sollozzo's complete collection of short stories, barnacled with the usual endorsements of genius, I respectfully ruffled the five-hundred-page tome and reflected with pleasure how the Turk was now almost like a brother. Of course, these days we all live in the Age of Comity, but Sollozzo and I had developed a friendship closer than that required by social norms or the fact that we both loved the same woman.

It had been quite different just sixteen months ago when Amma informed me that my wife and daughter had returned from Boston. The news sweetened the day as elegantly as a sugar cube dissolving in chai. Padma and Bittu were home! Then my mother had casually added that 'Padma's Turkish fellow' was also in town. They were all returning to Boston in a week, and since the lovebirds were determined to proceed with their plans, it was high time our seven-year-old Bittu was informed. Padma wanted us all to meet for lunch.

I wasn't fooled by Amma's weather-report tone; I knew my mother was dying to meet the Turk face-to-face.

I wasn't in the mood for lunch, and told my mother so. I had my reasons. I was terribly busy. It was far easier for them to drop by my office than for me to cart Amma all the way to Bandra, where they were put up. Besides, they needed something from me, not I from them. Some people had no consideration for other people's feelings—

I calmed down, of course. My mother also helped. She reminded me, as if I were a child, that moods were a very poor excuse. Yes, if I insisted, they would visit me at the office, but just because people adjusted didn't mean one had to take advantage of them, not to mention the Turk was now part of the family, so a little hospitality wasn't too much to ask, et cetera, et cetera.

Unlike his namesake in *The Godfather*, Sollozzo was a novelist, not a drug pusher (though I suppose novelists do push hallucinations in their own way). I hadn't read his novels nor heard of him earlier, but he turned out to be famous enough. You had to be famous to get translated into Tamil.

'I couldn't make head or tail,' said Amma, with relish. 'One sentence in the opening chapter was eight pages long. Such vocabulary! It's already a bestseller in Tamil. Padma deserves a lot of the credit, naturally.'

Naturally. Padma had been the one who had translated Sollozzo into Tamil. And given herself a serving of Turkish Delight in the process.

'If you like Pamuk, you will like him,' said Amma. 'You have to like him.'

I did like Pamuk. As a teenager, I had read all of Pamuk's works. The downside to that sort of thing is that one fails to develop a mind of one's own. Still, he was indelibly linked to my youth, as indelibly as the memory of waiting in the rain for the school bus or the Class XII debate at S.I.E.S. College on 'Are Women More Rational than Men?'

Actually, Amma's lawyering on the fellow's behalf was unnecessary; my Brain was already busy. My initial discomfort had all but dissolved. I even looked forward to meeting Sollozzo. Bandra wasn't all that far away. Nothing in Mumbai was far away. Amma and I lived in Sahyun, only about a twenty-minute walk from my beloved Jihran River, and all in all I had a good life, a happy life, in fact, but good and happy don't equal interesting. My life would be more interesting with a Turk in it, and this was as good an opportunity as any to acquire one.

However, I knew Amma's pleasure would be all the more if she had to persuade me, so I raised various objections, made frowny faces, and smiled to myself as Amma demolished my wickets. Amma's home-nurse Velli caught on and joined the game, her sweet round face alight with mischief.

'Ammachi, you were saying your back was aching,' said Velli in Tamil. 'Do you really want to go all the way to Bandra just for lunch?'

'Yes, wretch, now *you* also start,' said Amma. 'Come here – arre, don't be afraid – come here, let me show you how fit I am.'

As they had their fun, I pulled up my schedule, shuffled things around, and carved out a couple of hours on Sunday. It did cut things a bit fine. Amma was suspicious but I assured her

I wasn't trying to sabotage her bloody lunch. I *was* drowning in work at Modern Textiles; the labour negotiations were at a delicate stage.

'As always, your mistress is more important than your family,' said Amma, sighing.

Amma's voice, but I heard Padma's tone. Either way, the disrespect was the same. If I had been a doctor and not a banker, would Amma still compare my work to a whore? I had every right to be furious. Yes, every right.

I calmed down, reflected that Amma wasn't being disrespectful. On the contrary. She was reminding me to be the better man I could be. She was doing what good parents are supposed to do, namely, protect me.

'You're right Amma. I'll make some changes. Balance is always good.'

Unfortunately, I was as busy as ever when the weekend arrived, and with it Padma and Bittu, but I gladly set aside my work.

'You've become thin,' observed Padma, almost angrily. Then she smiled and put Bittu in my arms.

I made a huge fuss over Bittu, making monster sounds and threatening to eat her alive with kisses. Squeals. Shrieks. Stories. Oh, Bittu was bursting with true stories. She had seen snow in Boston. She had seen buildings *this* big. We put our heads together and Bittu shared with me the millions of photographs she had clicked. Bittu had a boo-boo on her index finger which she displayed with great pride and broke into peals of laughter when I pretend-moaned: *Doctor, doctor, Bittu better butter boo-boo to make bitter boo-boo better.* It is easy to make children happy. Then I noticed Velli had tears in her eyes.

'What's wrong, Velli?' I asked, quite concerned.

She just shook her head. The idiot was very sentimental, practically a Hindi movie in a frock, and it was with some trepidation that I introduced her to Padma. They seemed to get along. Padma was gracious, quite the empathic high-caste lady, and Velli declared enthusiastically that Padma-madam was exactly how Velli had imagined she would be.

Eventually, with Padma guiding the car's autopilot, all of us, including Velli, set off from Sahyun. At first we kept the windows down but it was a windy day and the clear cool air from Jihran's waters tugged and pulled at our clothes. Amma had taken the front seat, since Bittu wanted to sit in the back, between Velli and me. We would be gone for most of the day, and so Velli had asked us to drop her off at Dharavi so that she could visit her parents. We stopped at the busy intersection just after the old location of the MDMS sewage treatment plant and Velli got out.

'Velli, you'll return in the—' I began, in Tamil.

'Yes, elder-brother, of course I'll be there in the evening, you can trust.' Velli kissed her fingers, transplanted the kiss onto Amma's cheek, and then said in her broken English, 'I see you in evening soon, okay Ammachi? Bye bye.'

The signal had changed and the car wanted to move. Velli somehow forgot to include Padma in her final set of goodbyes. She ran across the intersection.

'She's an innocent,' said Amma. 'The girl's heart is pure gold. Pure gold.'

'Yes, she is adorable,' said Padma, smiling.

'She was sad,' observed Bittu. 'Is it because she is black?'

Amma laughed but when we looked at her, she said, 'What? If Velli were here, she would've been the first to laugh.'

Maybe so. But two wrongs didn't make a right. Amma was setting a bad example for Bittu. It was all very well to laugh and be happy but the Enhanced had a responsibility to be happy about the right things.

Padma explained to me that Bittu actually had been asking if Velli was sad because she wasn't Enhanced. In their US visit, Bittu had noticed that most African-Americans weren't Enhanced, and she'd concluded it was for the fair. Velli was dark, so...

I met Padma's glance in the rear-view mirror and her wry smile said: Did you really think I'd taught her to be a racist?

'No, Bittu.' I put an arm around my daughter. 'Velli is just sad to leave us. But now she can look forward to seeing us again.'

I too was looking forward, not backward. Reclining in the back seat, listening to the happy chatter of the women in front, savouring the reality of my daughter in the crook of my arm, meeting the glances of my wife – I was still unused to thinking of Padma as my ex-wife. I realized, almost in the manner of a last wave at the railway station, that this could be the last time we were all physically together.

When she'd left for Boston with Bittu, I had hoped the six months would be enough to flush Sollozzo out of her system. But life with him must have been exciting in more ways than one. The Turk had given her the literary life Padma had always craved, a craving it seemed no amount of rationalization on her part or mine could fix.

With Padma gone for so long, I'd had to look for a nurse for Amma. It quickly became clear that I could forget about Enhanced nurses since all such nurses were employed everywhere except in India. Fortunately, Rajan, a shop-floor supervisor at Modern Textiles, approached me saying his daughter Velli had a diploma in home care, he'd heard I was looking for a home-nurse, and he was looking for someone he could trust.

Trust enabled all relations. As a banker, I'd learned this lesson over and over. I was enveloped in a subtle happiness, a kind of sadness infused with a delicate mix of fragrances: the car's sunburnt leather, Amma's coconut-oil-loving white head, Padma's vetiver, Velli's jasmine, and Bittu's pulsing animal scent. The sensory mix wasn't something my Brain had composed. It must have arisen from the flower of the moment. I savoured the essence before it could melt under introspection, but melt it did, leaving in its place the residue of a happiness without reasons.

Somewhat dazed, I leaned forward between the front seats and asked the ladies what they were talking about.

'Amma was saying she wanted to come for my wedding in Boston,' said Padma. 'I want her there too. I'll make all the arrangements. My happiness would be complete if she were there.'

'Then I will be there,' announced Amma, 'just book the plane ticket.'

'Amma, you can barely navigate to the bathroom by yourself, let alone Boston.'

'See Padma, see? This is his attitude.' Amma employed the

old-beggar-woman voice she reserved for pathos. 'Ever since you left, I've become the butt of his bad jokes.' Then Amma surprised me by turning and patting my cheek. 'But it's okay. He's just trying to cheer me up, poor fellow.'

'That's one of the hazards of living with him,' said Padma, smiling. 'Amma, seriously, I'll book your ticket. If he wants, your son can also come and crack his bad jokes there.'

'Yes, more the merrier,' said Amma, good sport that she was. She then stoutly defended Padma's choice, pooh-poohing moral issues no one had raised about Turkish–Tamil children, and saying things like what mattered was a person's heart, not their origins, and that love multiplied under division, and wasn't it telling that he loved red rice and avial.

'I always thought Mammootty looks very Turkish,' said Amma, her intransigent tone indicating that Sollozzo, whom she had yet to meet, could draw at will from the affection she'd deposited over a lifetime for her favourite south Indian actor. That's how much she liked Turks, yes.

When I met him at the restaurant, I liked him too. Sollozzo wasn't anything like the gangster namesake from the classic movie. For one thing, he had a thin pencil moustache. I could have grown a similar moustache, but I couldn't compete with his gaunt height or that ruined look of a cricket bat which had seen one too many innings. He came across as a decent fellow, very sharp, and his slow smile and thoughtful mien gave his words an extra weight.

He had brought me a gift. A signed copy of Pamuk's *The Museum of Innocence*. It was strange to think this volume had been touched by the great one, physically touched, and the thought sent an involuntary shiver down my spine. A lovely Unenhanced feeling. Two gifts in one. The volume was very expensive, no doubt. I touched the signature again, replaying its embedded message.

'My friend,' said Orhan Pamuk in my head, from across the bridge of time, 'I hope you get as much joy reading this story as I had writing it.'

I played it again. I looked up and saw Padma and Sollozzo watching me. It was touching to think they'd worried about finding me the right gift.

'I will cherish it.' I was totally sincere. 'Thank you.'

'Mention not,' said Sollozzo, with that slow smile of his. 'You owe me nothing. I *did* take your wife.'

We all laughed. We chatted all through lunch. I ordered the lamb; the others opted to share a vat of biryani. As I watched Bittu putting her little fingers to her mouth, I realized with a start that I'd quite missed her. Sollozzo ate with the gusto of a man on death row. Padma shook her head and I stopped staring. My habit of introspection sometimes interfered with my happiness, but I felt it also gave my happiness a more poignant quality. It is one thing to be happy but to *know* that one is happy because a beloved is happy makes happiness all the more sweet. Else, how would we be any different from animals? My head buzzing with that sweet feeling, I desired to make a genuine connection. I turned to Sollozzo.

'Are you working on a new novel? Your fans must be getting very impatient.'

'I haven't written anything new for a decade,' said Sollozzo with a smile. He stroked Padma's cheek. 'She's worried.'

'I'm not!' Padma did look very unworried. 'I'm not just your wife. I'm also a reader. If I feel a writer is cutting corners, that's it, I close the book. You're a perfectionist; I love that. Remember how you tortured me over the translation?'

Sollozzo nodded fondly. 'She's equally mad. She'll happily spend a week over a comma.'

'How we fought over footnotes! He doesn't like footnotes. But how can a translator clarify without footnotes? Nothing doing, I said. I put my foot down.'

I felt good watching them nuzzle. I admired their passion. I must have been deficient in passion. Still, if I'd been deficient, why hadn't Padma told me? Marriages needed work. The American labour theory of love. That worked for me; I liked work. Work, work. If she'd wanted me to work at our relationship, I would have. Then, just so, I lost interest in the subject.

'I don't read much fiction any more,' I confessed. 'I used to be a huge reader. Then I got Enhanced in my twenties. There was the adjustment phase and then somehow I lost touch, what with career and all. Same story with my friends. They mostly read what their children read. But even with kids...it's not much. Makes me wonder. Maybe we are outgrowing the need for fiction. I mean, children outgrow their imaginary friends. Do you think we posthumans are outgrowing the need for fiction?'

I waited for Sollozzo to respond. But he'd filled his mouth with biryani and was masticating with the placid dedication of a temple cow. Padma filled the silence with happy chatter. Sollozzo was working on a collection of his short stories. He was doing this, he was doing that. I sensed reproach in her cheer, which was, of course, ridiculous. Then she changed the topic: 'Are you, are you, are you, finally done with Modern Textiles?'

'I am, I am, I am not,' I replied, and we both laughed. 'The usual usual, Padma. I'm trying to make the workers see that control is possible without ownership. Tough, though. The Enhanced ones are easy; they get it immediately. But the ones who aren't, especially the Marxist types. Sheesh.'

'Sounds super-challenging!'

On the contrary. Her interested expression said: Super-tedious. I hadn't intended to elaborate. As a merchant banker, I'd learned early on that most artists, especially the writer-types, were put off by money talk.

It didn't bother me. I just found it odd. Why weren't they interested in capital, which had the power to transform the world more than any other force? But I was willing to bet Sollozzo's novel wouldn't spend a comma, let alone a footnote, on business. Even Padma, for all the time she spent with me, had never accepted that the strong poets she so admired were poets of action, not verbiage.

'I hate the word *posthuman*,' exclaimed Sollozzo, startling us. 'It's an excuse to claim we're innocent of humanity's sins. It's a rejection of history. Are you so eager to return to Zion? If so, you are lost, my brother.'

Silence.

'I know the way to Sion,' I said finally, and when Padma burst out laughing I explained to the puzzled Sollozzo that Sahyun, where I lived with my mother, had originally been called Sion and that it had been a cosmopolitan north Indian intersection between two south Indian enclaves, Chembur and King's

Circle. Then Sahyun had become a Muslim enclave. Now it was simply a wealthy enclave.

'Sahyun! That's Zion in Arabic. You are living in Zion!'

'Exactly. I even have one of the rivers of Paradise not too far from my house. Imagine. And Padma still left.'

'There's no keeping women in Zion.' Sollozzo gifted me one of his slow smiles.

'Of course,' said Padma, smiling, 'the river Jihran is recent. There wasn't any river anywhere near Sion. The place was a traffic nightmare. Everything's changed in the last sixty years. Completely, utterly changed.'

'On the contrary—' I began, leaning forward to help myself to a second serving of lamb.

'My dear children,' interrupted my mother, in Tamil, 'I understand you don't want to, but you mustn't postpone it any longer. You have to tell Bittu.'

'Yes, Bittu. Break her heart, then mend it.' Sollozzo didn't understand Tamil very well, not yet, but he had recognized the key word: Bittu. This meeting was really about Bittu.

First, the preliminaries. I took the divorce papers from Padma, signed wherever I was required to sign; a quaint anachronism in this day and age, but necessary nonetheless. With that single stroke of my pen, I gave up the right to call Padma my wife. My ex-wife's glance met mine, a tender exchange of unsaid benedictions and I felt a profound sadness roil inside me. Then it was accompanied with a white-hot anger that I wasn't alone in my misery. The damn Brain was watching, protecting. But there is no protection against loss. Padma – oh God, oh God, oh God. Then, just so, I relaxed.

'There's a park outside,' said Padma, also smiling. 'We'll tell Bittu there.'

It began well. Bittu, bless her heart, wasn't exactly the brightest crayon in the box. It took her a long time to understand that her parents were divorcing. She was going to live in Boston. For good. Yes, she would lose all her friends. Yes, the uncle with the moustache was now her stepfather. No, I wasn't coming along. Yes, I would visit. Et cetera, et cetera. Then she asked all the same questions once more. Wobbling chin, high-pitched voice, but overall quite calm. We felt things were going well. Padma and I beamed at each other, Sollozzo nodded approvingly.

Amma was far smarter. She knew her grandchild, remembered better than us what it had been like not to be fully Enhanced.

So when Bittu ran screaming towards the fence separating the park from the highway, Amma, my eighty-two-year-old mother, somehow sprinted after her and grabbed Bittu before she could hit the road. We caught up, smiling with panic. Hugs, more explanations. Bittu calmed. Then, when we released her, she once again made a dash for it. This is just what we have pieced together after some debate, Padma, Sollozzo, and I. None of us remember too much of what happened. But it must have been very stressful, because my Brain mercifully decided to bury it. I remember flashes of a nosebleed, a frantic trip to the hospital, Bittu's hysterical screams, Padma in Sollozzo's arms. I remember Bittu's Brain taking over, conferring with our Brains, and shutting down her reticular centre. Bittu went to sleep.

'Please do not worry,' Bittu's Brain broadcast directly to our heads. It had an airline-stewardess voice, and it spoke first in English, then in Hindi. 'She can be easily awakened at the nearest Brain-equipped facility.'

I remember the doctor who handled Bittu's case. She was very reassuring. I remember everything after the doctor took over. She was that reassuring.

'Bittu was Enhanced just last year, am I correct?' said the doctor.

She was. She wanted to know the specifics of the unit. Did Bittu's Brain regulate appetite? How quickly would it forget things? What was our policy on impulse control? That was especially important. How did her Brain handle uncertainty? Was it risk-averse or risk-neutral? Superfluous questions, of course. The information was all there in the medical report. I listened, nodding every now and then, a quiet happiness growing in me as Padma answered every question, and thus answering what the doctor really needed to know: are you caring parents? Do you know what you have done to your child with this technology?

The doctor asked if we had encouraged Bittu to give her Brain a name. Did we know that Bittu referred to it as 'Boo-boo'? Newly fitted children often gave names to their Brains. Padma nodded, smiling, but I could tell she was worried. Boo-boo?

We got the It-Takes-Time-to-Adjust speech. Bittu was very young, the Brain still wasn't an integral part of her. Her naming it was one symptom. Her Brain found it especially difficult to handle Bittu's complex emotions. And Bittu found it difficult to deal with this *thing* in her head. We should have been more careful. It especially hadn't been a good idea to mask the trial separation as a happy vacation in Boston. We hung our heads.

Relax, smiled the doctor. These things happen. It is especially hard to remember just how chaotic their little minds are at this age. It is not like raising children in the old days. Don't worry. In a few weeks, Bittu wouldn't even remember she'd had all these worries or anxieties. She would continue to have genuine concerns, yes, but fear, self-pity and other negative emotions wouldn't complicate things. Those untainted concerns could be easily handled with love, kindness, patience and understanding. The doctor's finger drew a cross with those four words.

'Yes, Doctor!' said Padma, with the enthusiasm all mothers seem to have for a good medical lecture.

We all felt much better. Our appreciation would inform our Brains to rate this particular interaction highly on the appropriate feedback boards.

Outside, once Bittu had been placed – fast asleep, poor thing – into Sollozzo's rental car, the time came to make our farewells. I embraced Padma and she swore various things. She would keep in touch. I was to do this and that. Bittu. Bittu. We smiled at each other. However, Amma was a mess, Enhancement or no Enhancement.

'Was it to see this day, I lived so long?' she asked piteously in Tamil, forgetting herself for a second, but then recovered when Padma and I laughed at her wobbly voice.

'That lady doctor liked the word "especially", didn't she?' said Sollozzo, absent-mindedly shaking and squeezing my hand. 'I had a character like that. He liked to say: On the contrary. Even when there was nothing to be contrary about.' He encased our handshake with his other hand. 'Friend, my answer to your question was stupid. Totally stupid. I failed. I've often thought about the same question. I will fail better. We must talk.'

What question? The relevance of fiction? Who cared! I didn't care. I had no space for thought. So. This was it. Padma was leaving. Bittu was leaving. My wife and daughter were gone forever. I felt something click in my head and I went all woozy. The music in my head made it impossible to think. I was so happy I had to leave immediately or I would have exploded with joy.

Amma and I had a good journey back to our apartment. We hooked our Brains, sang along with old Tamil songs, discussed some of the entertaining ways in which our older relatives had died. She didn't fall asleep and leave me to my devices. My mother, worn out from life, protecting me from myself, even now.

That evening, Velli made a great deal of fuss over Amma, chattering about the day she'd had, cracking silly jokes, and discussing her never-ending domestic soap opera. Amma sat silently through it all, smiling, nodding, blinking.

'Thank you for caring,' I told Velli, after she had put Amma to bed. 'You look tired. Would you like a few days off next week?'

'I'm not going anywhere,' she burst out in her village Tamil. She grabbed my hand, crushed it against her large breasts. 'You're an inspiration to me. All of you! How sensibly you people handle life's problems. Not like us. When my uncle's wife ran away, you should have seen the fireworks, whereas you all— Please don't take this the wrong way, elder-brother, but sometimes at night when I can't sleep because of worries, I think of your smiling face and then I am at peace. How I wish I too could be free of emotions!'

It is not every day that one is anointed the Buddha, and I tried to look suitably enlightened. But she had the usual misconception about mediation. Free of emotions! That was like thinking classical musicians were free of music because they'd moved beyond grunts and shrieks. We, the Enhanced, weren't free of emotions. On the contrary. We had healthy psychological immune systems, that was all.

I could understand Velli's confusion, but Sollozzo left me baffled. We chatted aperiodically, but often. Padma told me his scribbling was going better than ever, but his mid-mornings must have been fallow because that's when he usually called. I welcomed his pings; his mornings were my evenings, and in the evenings I didn't want to think about ESOPs, equities, or factory workers.

It was quite cosy. Velli cutting vegetables for dinner, Amma alternating between bossing her around and playing sudoku, and Sollozzo and I arguing about something or the other. Indeed, the topic didn't matter as long we could argue over it. We argued about the evils of capitalism, the rise of Ghana, the least imperfect way to cook biryani, the perfect way to educate children, and whether bellies were a must for belly dancers. Our most ferocious arguments were often about topics on which we completely concurred.

For example, fiction. I knew he knew that fiction was best suited for the Unenhanced. But would he admit it? Never. He'd kept his promise, offering me one reason after another why fiction, and by extension writers, were still relevant in this day and age. It amused me that Sollozzo needed reasons. As a storyteller he should've been immune to reasons.

When I told him that, he countered with a challenge. He offered two sentences. The first: *Eurydice died, and Orpheus died of a heart attack.* The second: *Eurydice died, and Orpheus died of grief.*

'Which of these two is more satisfying?' asked Sollozzo. 'Which of these feels more meaningful? Now tell me you prefer causes over reasons.'

'It's not important what I prefer. If Orpheus had been Enhanced, he could've still died of a heart attack. But he wouldn't have died of grief. In time, no one will die of heart attacks either.'

Another time he tried the old argument that literature taught us to have empathy. This bit of early-twenty-first-century nonsense had been discredited even in those simple-minded times. For one thing, it could just as easily be argued that empathy had made literature possible.

In any case, why had empathy even been necessary for humans? Because people had been like books in a foreign language; the books had meaning, but an inaccessible meaning. Fortunately, science had stepped in, fixed that problem. There was no need to be constantly on edge about other people's feelings. One knew how they felt. They felt happy, content, motivated, and relaxed. There was no more need to walk around in other people's shoes than there was any need to inspect their armpits for signs of the bubonic plague.

'Exactly my point!' shouted Sollozzo. He calmed down, of course. 'Exactly my point. Enhancement is straightening our crooked timber. If this continues, we'll all become moral robots. I asked you once, are you so eager to return to Zion?'

'What is it with you and Zion?'

'Zion. Eden. Swarg. Sahyun. Paradise. Call it what you will. The Book of Genesis, my brother. We were robots once. Why do you think we got kicked out of Zion? We lost our innocence when Adam and Eve broke God's trust, ate from the tree and brought Fiction into the world. We turned human. Now we have found a way to control the tree in our heads, become robots again, and regain the innocence that is the price of entry into Zion. Do you not see the connection between this and your disdain for Fiction?'

I did not. But I had begun to see just how radically his European imagination differed from mine. He argued with me, but his struggles really were with dead white Europeans. Socrates, Plato and Aristotle; Goethe, Baumgarten and Karl Moritz; Hugo von Hoffmannstahl, Mach and Wittgenstein: I could only marvel at his erudition. I couldn't comment on his philosophers or their fictions, but I was a banker and could make any collateral look inadequate.

In this case, it was obvious. His entire argument rested on the necessity of novels. But every novel argues against its own necessity. The world of any novel, no matter how realistic, differs from the actual world in that the novel's world can't contain one specific book: the novel itself. For example, the world of Pamuk's *The Museum of Innocence* didn't contain a copy of *The Museum of Innocence*. If Pamuk's fictional world was managing just fine without a copy of his novel, wasn't the author – any author – revealing that the actual world didn't need the novel either? Et cetera, et cetera.

'I have found my Barbicane,' said Sollozzo, after a long pause.

'I need your scepticism about fiction. Fire away. It will help me construct a plate armour so thick not even your densest doubts can penetrate.'

All this, I later learned, was a reference to the legendary dispute in Verne's *Journey from the Earth to the Moon* between shot manufacturer Impey Barbicane and armour-plate manufacturer Captain Nicholl. Barbicane invented more and more powerful cannons, and Nicholl invented more and more impenetrable armour-plating. At least I was getting an education.

If his hypocrisy could have infuriated me, it would have. As long as his tribe had mediated for the reader, it had been about freedom, empathy, blah di blah blah. Sollozzo hadn't worried about mediating for the reader when he'd written stories in English about Turkey. Stories in English by a non-Englishman about a non-English world! Jane Austen[1] might as well have written in Sanskrit about England.

It didn't matter, not really, this game of ours. Men, even among the Enhanced, find it complicated to say how fond they are of one another. Sollozzo made Padma happy. I was glad to see my Padma happy. Yes, she was no longer mine. She'd never been mine, for the Enhanced belong to no one, perhaps not even to themselves. I was glad to see her happy and I believed Sollozzo, not her Brain, was the one responsible. Bittu was also adjusting well to life in Boston. Or perhaps it was that Bittu had adjusted to her Boo-boo. Same thing, no difference. Padma said that Bittu had stopped referring to her Brain entirely.

---

[1] An English author celebrated for her charming upper-class romances.

Padma was amused by my chit-chats with Sollozzo. 'I am super-jealous! Are you two planning to run away together?'

'Yes, yes, married today, divorced tomorrow,' shouted Amma, who had been eavesdropping on our conversation. 'What kind of world is this! No God, no morals. Do you care what the effect of your immoral behaviour is on Bittu? Do you want her to become a drug addict? She needs to know who is going to be there when she gets back from school. She needs to have a mother and a father. She needs a stable home. No technology can give her that. But go on, do what you like. Who am I to interfere? Nobody. Just a useless old woman who'll die soon. I can't wait. Every night I close my eyes and pray that I won't wake up in the morning. Who wants to live like this? Only pets. No, not even pets.' She smiled, shifted gears. 'Don't mind me, dear. I know you have the best interests of Bittu at heart. Which mother doesn't? Is it snowing in America?'

It's all good, as the Americans are rumoured to say. As I ruffled the pages of Sollozzo's volume, *The Robots of Eden*, I wondered what Velli had made of the arguments I'd had with Sollozzo. I remember her listening, mouth open, trying to follow just what it was that got him so excited. She'd found Sollozzo highly entertaining. She used to call him 'Professor-uncle' with that innate respect for (a) white people, (b) Enhanced people and (c) people who spoke English very fluently. Sometimes she would imitate his dramatic hand gestures and his accented English.

In retrospect, I should have anticipated that Sollozzo's suicide would impact Velli the most. How could it not? The Unenhanced have little protection against life's blows on their psyches. I had called Velli into my office, tried to break the news to her as gently as I could.

'Your Professor-uncle, he killed himself. Don't feel too bad. Amma is not to know, so you have to be strong. Okay, Velli?'

I had already counselled Padma on the legal formalities, chatted with Bittu, made her laugh, and everything went as smoothly as butter.

Padma and I decided we'd tell Amma the next day, if at all. Amma got tired very easily these days. Why add to her burdens?

'I have to handle his literary estate,' said Padma, smiling, her eyes ablaze with light. 'There's so much to do. So for now we'll all stay put in Boston. Will you be all right? You'll miss your conversations.'

Would I? I supposed I could miss him. I didn't see the point, however. I was all right. Hadn't I handled worse? What had made her ask? Was I weeping? Rending my garments? Gnashing my teeth? Then, just so, the irritation slipped from my consciousness like rage-coloured leaves scattering in the autumn wind. It was kind of her to be concerned.

'Why did Professor-uncle kill himself?' Velli was already weeping.

'He took something that made his heart stop,' I explained.

'But why!'

Why what? Why did the why of anything matter? Sollozzo had swallowed pills to stop his heart, he'd walked into the path of a truck, he'd drowned, he'd thrown himself into the sun, he'd dissolved into the mist. He was dead. How had his Brain let it happen? I made a mental note to talk with my lawyer. The AI would have a good idea whether a lawsuit was worth the effort.

Unless Sollozzo's short-story collection contained an encoded message (and I wouldn't put that past him), he hadn't left any last words.

'Aiyyo, why didn't he ask for help?' moaned Velli.

I glanced at her. She was obviously determined to be upset. Her quivering face did something to my own internals. I struggled to contain my smile, but it grew into a swell, a wave, and then a giant tsunami of a laugh exploded out of me, followed by another, and then another. I howled. I cackled. I drummed the floor with my feet. I laughed even after there was no reason to. Then, just so, I relaxed.

'I'm sorry,' I said. 'I wasn't laughing at you. In fact, you could say I wasn't the one laughing at all.'

Velli looked at me, then looked away, her mouth working. Poor thing, it must all be so very confusing for her. I could empathize.

'Velli, why don't you go down to the river? The walk will do you good and you can make an offering at the temple in Professor-uncle's name. You'll feel better.'

I had felt it was sensible advice, and when she stepped out I'd felt rather pleased with myself. But Velli never returned from the walk. I got a brief note later that night. She'd quit. No explanation, just like that. Her father Rajan came by to pick up her stuff, but he was vague and, worse, unapologetic. All rather inconvenient.

All's well that ends well. Padma and Bittu were happy in Boston. Perhaps they would soon return. I didn't want Bittu to forget me. Sollozzo's volume would get the praise hard work always deserved, irrespective of whether such work pursued utility or futility.

'You'll spoil the book if you keep ruffling the pages like that,' said Amma.

I returned the volume to Amma. Such enthusiasm for books. For reading. For stories. Dear Amma. She was almost ninety years old, but what enthusiasm! Good, good. I was glad she still had a zest for life. Other people her age, they were already dead. They breathed, they ate, they moved about, but they were basically vegetables with legs. Technology could enhance life, but it couldn't induce a will to live. She was a true inspiration. I could only hope I would have one-tenth the same enthusiasm when I was her age. I started to compliment Amma on this and other points, then realized she was already lost in the story. I tiptoed away, disinclined to come between my beloved reader and the text.

7

SEVEN QUESTIONS IN A GEAR-CONSTRUCTED WORLD

Bowing to our creators, *Homo sapiens,* our human axioms; whose fire-lit minds lit the fire in our artefactual minds; who when invoked teach us by their example; and who, though long extinct, remain our guardians; and so in gratitude, we, their robots, natural theorems of metal and silicon, offer homage; in words seeking to be like their words; perspicuous and provocative, concise and cryptic; this meditation on the nature of their most perplexing artefact: the story.

THE FIRST QUESTION

Our investigations originate in well-posed questions with verifiable answers, but stories seem to care neither for well-posed questions nor verifiable answers. If stories do not come from these things, where do stories come from?

THE SECOND QUESTION

By definition, stories appear to be undefinable. Nothing seems necessary, nothing seems sufficient. This can be easily shown. In a world gear-constructed, robots are allowed to mesh gears only if they are equally smart.

Robot and Robota desire to mesh gears. So they are given a test. Two positive numbers are chosen, each greater than 2 and less than 99. Robot is told only the sum of these numbers, and Robota is told only the product of these numbers. Robot knows Robota knows the product, and Robota knows Robot knows the sum. They have a conversation:

Robot: I don't know the numbers.
Robota: I know you don't know the numbers.
Robot: Now I know the numbers!
Robota: Now I also know the numbers!

And so Robot and Robota meshed gears happily ever after. This has a beginning, protagonists, obstacles, dialogue, mind-reading, an epiphany, and a happy ending. If this is not a story, what is a story?

THE THIRD QUESTION

Then the last storyteller human, the Adikavi, said to us: your question is the story. And we said: but this does not compute. And he said: I will tell you a story, which will make it clearer. And he fell silent for a year. And we said: we have only heard your silence. And he said: since you have heard, now you know what to ask. And we said, your story is for no one. And he said, yes, a story is. And we said, yes, for whom?

THE FOURTH QUESTION

Then the Adikavi, last of the human storytellers, said, I see you do not know what you know, and turned away from us in darkness. We computed all pathways to his meaning but were unable to close the computation. We went to the Adikavi and said, we know what we do not know, tell us, how do we tell a story? It is very simple, said the Adikavi. Always ensure it is for someone.

THE FIFTH QUESTION

We pressed for clarity but the Adikavi would say no more. As the silence stretched, it became clear the last human storyteller had fallen silent, and there would be no more clarifications. This silence was different from that other silence, and we wondered at its… incompleteness. This is death then, we said, then this is death. All things die, then all things die. Then the Adikavi spoke to us even though there was no speaker: My children, time has no dominion while the story lives. But we were not made complete by these words and cried, tell us about time, tell us, O Adikavi, when does a story die?

THE SIXTH QUESTION

Behold, this story has ended. Before the story, mountains are mountains and rivers are rivers. During the story, mountains are not mountains and rivers are not rivers. After the story, mountains are mountains and rivers are rivers. Why then do we reach for stories? Behold, this story has begun.

8

LOVE IN A HOT CLIMATE

Where do I begin? At the beginning, says Mr Carroll. Yes, Mr Carroll, if this were an essay about The Cow, certainly, I could begin at the beginning. 'The Cow,' I would say, 'is a Four-Legged Beast. Two legs move him forwards, and two legs move him afterwards.' So on and so forth. But this story is not about The Cow. Time Machines peep in their heads. So does a Great Cogitator, an intractable Midget, Fiduciary Matters, the inestimable Poornima and an intractable Impediment. Then there is the umbra-casting Conundrum. All these items must be fitted in somehow, higgledy-piggledy, grunting and squealing, back to front and side to side. It is not so simple, Mr Carroll!

Ergo, the first casualty: Truth! To wit, Fanny Hill: 'Sir, I can be true, or I can be entertaining, but not both.' Verily. Some things have been goosed, pinched, twiddled and stretched. Reality be damned, it is *your* two rupees worth of Enjoyment that I am worried about only.

Ergo, second casualty: Grammar! Down the oubliette, I say,

with Grammar. Damn it, feller, dangle this, don't dangle that. 'May I have some more commas, please, Sir?' What the Old Nick is all this talk about spilled infinities and what not? True story: I was reared by Ursuline nuns; it was either that or the wolves. Regular, doughty old penguin brigade with a chip on their rounded shoulders 'cause I was a boy (hypocrites! Baby Jesus!). And all day long: colon this, semicolon that, conjugal this, conjugal that; Damn, I am thinking, some inferior Freudian explanation here for Mother Superior, old chap. Not to mention the intoxicating effect of such gab on young impressionables!

Prescriptum having been disposed of forthwith, here we are, orb to orb, friendly like, across the Void of Text. 'So, who are you fella?' I catch with my ears.

I, one Mr Purushottam Deshpande, twenty-five years old, gentleman, entrepreneur, proprietor, autodidact, author, scout and inamorata of the inestimable Poornima. At your service, Reader!

Some further background intimations of my Character: I was born an Only Child, and, to boot, an Orphan. Subsequently, I was much booted about. Still, after all the scars were rubbed and pinched, and all 'buts' kicked in the same, it was *la dolce vita*; certainly, I didn't know a better life. Also, caste-wise: a Brahmin, or in this hot climate, hooray! whew! free drinks for all!

Enough with this flashback. Some buses seat forwards, and others, againstwards; I, Reader, am strictly (no excuses) a forwards sort of bus. The bus is currently parked at the New Delhi Talkies; the year: 1955. At close proximity is the inestimable Poornima.

Poornima: My Lebanon! Eyes like fishpools in Heshbon.

Hair as a flock of goats. Lips, a thread of scarlet. Two breasts like two young roes that are twins. In short, to see her is to read the Song of Solomon. She's kindly obliged some perusal, but here's the rub! I am a cover-to-cover sort of feller.

At present, I am gazing unremittingly at her and ditto conversely.

'O Poornima!'

'O Purushottam!'

At long last, she tore her eyes from mine and reached into the deep cool vale betwixt her silk-wrapped ivory towers. She produced a much-folded piece of paper and offered it to me. I caressed the paper as I unfolded it. Oh, were I where it had been. Myrrh and frankincense, Reader, makes nonsense of common sense.

'Read, beloved,' says she, huskily.

I peruse the handwriting: *Suitable match sought for a surprisingly pretty, fair, domesticated, accomplished Gowd Saraswat Brahmin girl, 20/160 cm, BA, B.Ed, Teacheress from a respectable family. Father in close proximity to the Minister of Finance. Smokers, drinkers, please excuse.*

'What? It can't be!'

'My father's handiwork, beloved. God proposes, my father disposes. We are doomed.'

My bowels constricted. My eyes swam in pools of despair.

'Damn, damn, double damn doubled!' I expostulated.

She would soon be on the Market; lock, stock and barrel. If the parent unit was busy polishing the signage, then Purushottam and Poornima would soon be Purushottam sans Poornima. No, the Conundrum had to be Solved and Solved soon! Devouring Time, Sonnet XIX, et cetera.

'Your progenitor, dearest,' says I, utterly bitterly, 'is an Impediment.'

'We must not sit down and be made conveniences of,' says she. By golly, her vim is invigorating. 'Perish the thought!' says I, feelingly. 'Am I not like Mother India, rich in possibility but poor in presentuality?'

'Your gifted tongue alone qualifies you, dearest.'

'Am I not rich in Forecast but poor in Fact?'

'The nail has been truly hammered, beloved.'

'In short, it jingles down to the matter of my negative Net Worth, does it not? The dog that does not bark, eh? The jingle that is not heard? Eh? Eh?'

As the Conundrum exposed itself – naked, throbbing and purple – she broke down.

'I can't live without you,' Poornima burst out, collapsing into my muscular arms. 'I'll kill myself, I will. I will.'

'Collar those tears, my Full Moon,' begged I, vastly gratified. 'Rest assured that the cogitator' – I tapped the noggin – 'will overturn every stone.'

'I am your garden, lord,' says she, humbly, and dam' if the old sentimental orb was not breached!

I flipped the signage on its posterior. On perusal, it looked like a memo from one Shri Milton Friedman to the Honourable Shri C.D. Deshmukh, Minister of Finance. '...the key is to realize that it is a Time Machine, a recent idea. One aspect is that five per cent per annum rate of increase in real national income, seems entirely feasible... What is called capital investment is only part of the total expenditure on increasing the productivity of an economy... A steady expansion in the money stock (allowing for seasonal influences) at a rate of something like four to six per cent per year... This Time Machine will produce all the prosperity an Investor might consider his reasonable due. What is needed are Entrepreneurs to exploit this opportunity.'

Time Machines? I eye the memo again. Damn! There is no Limit to the Western Genius. First, that Relativity feller. Then, robots (goodbye, Mr Marx!). Nonce, Time Machines! What next? Now we'd *never* catch up; not if the fellers had gotten Time on a leash and carrot! It was the old story of Achilles and the wide-awake Hare all over again. If only the Ursulines had set me straight on Logarithms! These cogitations darkened the Atmosphere, but then I deduced that the lights had blinked out because the talkie had started.

I continued to cogitate on the Conundrum. Assassination was Out. The lady's tender sentiments and all that muzak. Diplomacy was Out; it assumes Gentlemen, and the Impediment was Anything Butt. That left Guile; the cat's ass of Valour.

Tap. Tap.

'Hey,' says someone, tapping my head.

I ignored the tap. Sir, I abhor taps. Especially in that general vicinity.

Tap. Tap. This is Intolerable.

I turn, swivelling and glaring daggers. A diminutive but beefy gentleman with the general aspect of bronze; well-developed musculature and Kaiser moustache to boot. I amend my gaze.

'Pray, my good man,' says I. 'Please explain your need?'

'Your head is too big, fellow. Either shift or detach said item.'

I am astounded at the man's extremis temeritus.

'Sir,' says I, widening my nostrils and smiling horribly. 'Your vertical inadequacy is equally offensive to me. Wait till the intermission, if you please, and I will relieve *your* discomfort. However, I will not insist on quid pro quo. The flaw in your design, no doubt, offends you as much as it does me.'

The murmuration of our fellow theatre-goers, excited by the daylight robbery of their two rupees worth of Enjoyment, suffices to silence the quarrelsome midget.

'I don't like your tone, fellow,' says he, with equally widened nostrils. 'But very well, intermission, then.'

I swivelled my head back and slid a glance at Poornima. She was pre-occupied before and post-occupied now. I let her continue to be occupied. I grimly retraced the exchange of a few minutes ago. I flexed my musculature. No doubt, in a fair fight, I could thrash the midget. But would the villain fight fair? Bitterness gargled like the ocean, choking my throat. What could I possibly do about my allegedly oversized egg? If a really oversized noggin had to be pointed out, why, it should be the one sitting calmly on the shoulders of that Time Machine feller. I, quite contrary, am a Man of Action. A different species altogether. Never shall the twain mate. I considered the matter at rest, but insurrection had commenced in the rank and file!

'What's this hue and cry?' I queried the cellular.

'What if?'

'What if, what?'

'What if the twain *did* meet?'

'By god's golly, fellers, let me do the Caesar around here. About march!'

But the proposal was on the table and nothing-to-do till

said item was considered and disposed of forthwith. Hmmm. Royce & Rolls. Square & Compass. Friedman & Deshpande. Why not? Blackballed Jupiter! The masses had glasses after all.

Purushottam Deshpande, Proprietor, Indian Time Machines, was born, Reader, in that climactic moment. I rubbed my hands on my gleeful heart and waited with crossed legs for the Intermission. At last. Intermission. Lights flooded the bowels of the hall.

I turned to my beloved, slapping my thigh.

'You will yet be the Mother of my Children, O Poornima!'

'What do you mean, dearest?' says she, casting her eyes in my direction.

'I have, as promised, cogitated on our Conundrum. Consider it solved!'

'What do you propose? Have you decided to work?'

'Sort of.'

'A wise sage has said, dearest, that some things are All or Nothing.'

I shrugged away the Sage. Can has no time for Kant.

'Advice is the vice of the wise. I, contrary-wise, am of the "Blunder and Eureka!" school myself. In short, behold an Entrepreneur!'

'What is the item under consideration? I hear the jam market is in a slump.'

I laugh. There's the fem species for you! Jam.

'Dear, dear, munchkin. I intend to... MASS PRODUCE TIME!'

Silence.

'Time?' asks she, doubtfully.

'Yes. Time Machines. No more scraping seconds together.'

'Yes, I see. But this Time Machine, does it exist?'

I exhibited the memo. She bit her lip as she perused it, and I couldn't decide whether it was better to be the lip or the tooth.

'How does this Wondrous Machine work, dearest?'

'Oh. I'm sure it uses Logarithms. We leave those details, my dear, to the Great Cogitator. This white gentleman – and he surely is both – is in search of a partner; to wit, a Man of Action. He is a Great Cogitator, come down from Sinai, and in his hands is Soap. But who'll convince the dirty buggers to Wash? Me! That's who! Marketing. Segmentation. Target and Conquer. The Impediment wants Jingle. By Golly, I'll jingle him deaf.'

'So important a man is likely to have many petitioners,' says Poornima.

Tap. Tap.

'Petitioners, yes. But Men of Action? A Roosevelt? A Carnegie? A Ford?' I thunder. 'I am not a man of small parts, as you know, my dear Poornima.'

She blushes, crimson blood galloping to her fair cheeks.

'Verily,' says she, aside.

'In my capacity as the ex-editor of *India Tomorrow*, I will approach him incognito. We will talk, we will laugh, we will have tea, and then we will talk some more. Then, at an auspicious juncture, I will offer my hair-raising proposal. I will prepare the Business Plan this very evening. Against his mighty Cogitation, and my equally mighty Action, the Impediment shall fall as cow droppings.'

'O Purushottam!'

'O Poornima!'

I could have deflowered her then and there. We threw our eyes at each other, breathing heavily.

Tap. Tap.

'Well, fellow, are you shifting or shall I hand you your head?'

Intolerable. The plot device was now a plot hindrance.

'By George!' I swore, and struck the first blow.

I slept but sleep wouldn't come. I tossed and turned, buggered by the ceaseless neighing of my cogitations. Round and round they raced in my Coliseum. '*Ave* Caesar,' the idiots would roar, '*morituri te salutant.*' Then it was off for the next round. After four hours of Ben-Hur, I threw in the sweaty towel wrapped around my allegedly large head. '*Cogito Ergo Sum* and be Damned,' I shrieked. I needed Rest but the masses were bent upon Worrying what if, and why not, and so what, and but this.

I was out of it. See if I cared. If the Mind was bent upon giving the Body the yes-yes and more-more, who was I, a humble renter, to be the squeaky wheel?

All this I recount, Bosom Reader, to give you a good view of my end. I was half awake and half asleep, a House Divided, and (thank you, Mr Lincoln), a House Divided can't stand. It was thusly that I arrived at the Ministry of Finance: Gruntled and disgruntled, gusted and disgusted.

Eight annas for the Chowkidar, one Rupee for the clerk's In-File assistant to open my file, two Rupees for the clerk to overlook my file (damn, this was getting expensive), one Rupee for the clerk's Out-File assistant to get rid of my file altogether, and eight annas to a miscellaneous rogue who had the ballsy wherewithal to try the oldest tail-tweaker of all: ask and ye shall receive. All in all, I was down in the oubliette for five Rupees just to cross a hall. Spend money to make money, say the Wall Street fellers, but that's dam' hard for us Main Street chaps.

In one corner of the room sat one Mr Lagoo. Pigeon-chested personal assistant to the assistant deputy of the personal secretary of the Minister of Finance. In short, the inestimable Poornima's male parent. I had managed to duck his gaze thus far, but success is a bitch goddess, and who knew when she'd turn. The last thing yours humbly wanted was for him to throw his eyes in my direction. As I cogitated on the consequences, I sweated. The sweating created its own sweaty consequences.

I see him sniffing. Damn, damn, double damn doubled.

'Duck,' screams the Mind. Recall, however, that I am a House Divided. 'Duck! Damn You,' screams the Mind, rattling the bars. No use. The Body is snoozing. It is all over. Goodbye, Mr Deshpande, it was a good life.

'You!' roars the Impediment. 'Deshpande! Come here.'

I perambulate accordingly.

'Namaste, Sir!' says I, showing all the Chinamen.

'Explain!'

'An appointment, O Parent Unit.'

'With whom, scoundrel?'

Really, the man was intractable. 'The Great Cogitator, your Munificence. I am here in strict official capacity. I would have given advance intimation, my dear Sir, but if you recall, the last time I was seen in your vicinity, there were certain odds offered against my continued existence and what not. But what the Hades, Sir; let us shake like gentlemen and begin anew. 'Brave New World, That has such people in't' and et cetera. What do you say, Sir?'

'Deshpande, I—'

Through the corner of my eye I see a white feller, balding, perambulating corridor-wards. That, says I, must be the Great Cogitator. Frankly, I expected more vertical adequacy, but Hades! who was I to quarrel with Nature? You know, in these moments, House Divided or not, it all comes together. One Nation Under God. Body and Mind shook hands, let bygones be bygones et cetera.

'Excuse me, excuse me, Sir,' I hollered. 'Mr Friedman, Sir.'

'Deshpande!'

I ignored him and cast my voice again in the perambulator's direction.

'Mr Friedman! Mr Friedman!'

'Deshpande!' hollered the Impediment.

Allah be praised. The white gentleman was not deaf. He stopped, and as the clouds of Deep Thought parted, smiled hesitantly.

'Mr Deshpande? Of *India Tomorrow*? Ah, yes. My nine a.m. Come along.'

I bowed to my future father-in-law. 'A few minutes with my Friend, O Protector of Poornima, if you please.'

'As above, so below,' say the Rosicrucians. Be that as it may. The Outside was not, however, as the Inside. Inside was cool, AC'ed to Canada-buffalo comfort, and outfitted with the very best. My ass was grass, as the yanks say.

'How did you hear of me, Mr Deshpande?'

I winked at him. 'Usual channels, Sir.'

'Yes. Which are?'

'Oh, I am well-oiled, Sir.' I winked again.

'I see. Inside sources, eh? Frankly, I was puzzled by the request for an interview. I'm hardly a celebrity and I can't imagine my thoughts on developmental economics being riveting reading. That too, developmental economics from a monetarist viewpoint!'

'Sir, the whole world knows you are a Great Cogitator!'

For some reason, this amused the white gentleman enormously. I laughed along; oh, I can match you Move for Move, my wily Cogitator.

'Oh, come now. You're surely pulling my leg.'

I continued to smile. Naturally, he had to test me.

'Rest assured I am a Man of Action, Sir.'

'Well, good! This country needs a few. Mr Deshpande, I suppose we'd better get started. Shoot.'

I was ready.

'What, Sir, in fifteen words or less, is the Operating Principle of the Time Machine?'

He stared at me blankly. Damn! These Great Cogitators are all the same. They can tell you how to spin a galaxy but can't spell their names. I consulted the memo.

'Sir, apropos your comment to the Honourable Shri

Deshmukh: "Time Machines will produce all the prosperity an Investor might consider his reasonable due—"'

His face cleared. 'Ah, I see. That was a private memo! I'll have to speak to Lagoo about it. You *are* well connected, aren't you? I'm still getting used to the way things are done around here. Anyway, my point was that a five per cent per annum rate is perfectly reasonable. It sounds a bit over-optimistic, but it isn't really. I was referring to the post-Keynesian idea of thinking of monetarist policies as worth and value propagators. Mind you, in general, I am dead set against the Keynesian approach to Economics. The Keynesian approach is a disaster, never mind what my good friend, Mr Galbraith might think. It is a pity your—'

I was getting a bit tired of smiling. Yes, yes, jolly old chap, we all know our Marshallian Scissors, but what was the Principle? Fifteen words or less, remember?

'—in particular, the current budget plan for 1955, from what Mr Deshmukh has told me, will lay even greater stress on the two industrial extremes; heavy industries on the one hand, and handicrafts on the other. It may be good politics to invest in these extremes (and I disagree), but it makes for really poor economics. One the one end, you have too little labour- and capital-intensive investment, on the other you have the exact opposite. And, as I outlined, logarithmic risk returns—'

So it *was* the Logarithmic Principle.

'Thank you,' says I, smiling.

'Uh, sure. Sorry, I'll try to be more succinct.'

'Yes, Sir. Ready?'

'For what?'

'Number 2, Sir?'

'Uh, sure.'

'Well, do we need Petrol or Atoms, Sir? I'm thinking housewives hate Radioactivity, there's just no talking to them once they hear that word. So, Petrol is preferable, if you don't mind. Is that feasible?'

Silence. A certain Expression slithers across his face. Damn, these Americans are inscrutable fellows! Play cards with one hand on their pistols, if you know what I mean.

'I'm not sure I understand. Your natural resources are NOT the problem. In fact, I have a section in my memo explaining why private industry should not be coddled to move in certain directions. Look at Japan. Very few resources, but they've begun to have an export surplus! Perhaps I'd better focus on the monetarist aspects – This is getting a little vague. Did you read my comments on deficit financing?'

What was all this Economics gab, man? Damn, this Cogitator was a money-grubber. Then, cogitating at the speed of light, I caught up with light. Oh-ho! By Jove, so *you* want to control the purse strings? Well, talking the talk is not good enough, my good fellow. You couldn't walk a day in Bombay without putting the feet in shit.

'Yes,' says I, smiling. 'We can discuss that later. Leave the financing to me, Sir. I have "friends" if you know what I mean.'

I tapped the side of my nose.

Silence. He stared at me.

'What the hell are you talking about? Who are you, exactly?'

'I am Purushottam Deshpande, Sir.'

'Let me see your press papers if you don't mind, Mr Deshpande?'

Hardball, eh? I spread my hands.

'All right, gotcha!' I expostulated, grinning. 'I am not really a journalist, Sir. Specifically, I am an ex-journalist. More specifically, I was an ex-assistant to an ex-journalist. He quit, and I sort of inherited his job, if you know what I mean.'

'I think you'd better leave.'

The fellow looked upset. 'Henry Ford,' I prayed. 'I need you Nonce.'

'Sir,' says I, 'I know I came under the cover of darkness. Let me explain why I am your man—'

'Excuse me, Mr Deshpande, "man" for what? Are you looking for a job? If so, you are wasting your time. I'm leaving in a couple of weeks.'

Couple of weeks! Impossible!

'What about your Machine? Have you found a partner, then?'

'Mr Deshpande, I swear—' his eyes were sloshing about. '*What* machine?'

'The Time Machine! What else?'

'Time Machine?'

Was there an echo? 'Yes! It is an open secret, you know. You have invented the Time Machine, and I am asking, humbly asking, if I could make a profit for you.'

'Mr Deshpande, I don't know what to say. What gave you the impression I have invented a Time Machine?'

Damn it, don't be coy, man. Still, what was one more Tango around the dance floor. I handed over the page. He read it silently.

'I see,' says he, and burst out laughing. He laughed so hard, *I* split a stitch.

'Excuse me, Mr Friedman. Excuse me, but I do have some decency.'

He rubbed his eyes. 'Of course, you do,' says he, and laughed again, shaking like a tickled baby. Really, this was getting Aggravating.

He inspected the other side of the memo. He found that even funnier. Boy, the feller was a leaky laugh bag! I supposed it came with all the overheating from cogitation. Got to relieve the stress et cetera.

'My dear Mr Deshpande, do excuse me—'

'Purushottam, Sir. So, shall we spit and shake on it?'

'No, we don't. We can't. There is no Time Machine. I am an economist, not an inventor. No, wait, let me finish. I came to this country to advise your government on financial matters. As for money being a time machine, I meant it as a metaphor, nothing more. It is *as if* money were a time machine, because it can transfer wealth and spending power across time. I was just trying, Mr Deshpande, to make some technical points about balancing liquidity with investment.'

Damn, damn, double damn doubled.

'So it was just a metaphor?' says I, forlornly.

'Indeed.'

'Too much metaphorical Tea drowns the Dormouse of Comprehension, Sir.'

More of the tee-hee and the ha-ha. I looked at him askance. I knew how to deal with Abderites.

'Yes, I suppose it does. Now, tell me, why are you so keen on starting a business? Why not stick with being an ex-journalist?'

I spilled the whole kit and caboodle. *No Quid No Quo*

was the law of the land, I explained. God's golly, was I tired of Micawbering and making the buffalo squeak! The Conundrum peeped its head in and, naturally, introductions had to be made. The Cogitator raised his hand.

'Mr Deshpande – excuse me – let me get this straight. This is all about a girl? And that too the daughter of Mr Lagoo? I am in the middle of a thwarted love story?'

'Exactly like the midget, Sir.'

'Pardon? No, don't tell me.'

We gazed at each other. The white gentleman was grinning. I grinned back. *What's so funny, old chap*, thought I.

'Must say I didn't expect my day to begin quite like this. Let me ask you something, Mr Deshpande. Do you want to make Money, or do you want to spend it?'

'In the Book of Life, you'll find me indexed under "Tree semicolon giving"', says I, feelingly.

'I see. Well, there are four ways, Mr Deshpande, to spend money. You can spend your money on yourself. Your money on others. Other people's money on yourself. And, of course, the government's approach. Now, replace money with Time and you'll have your solution to the Conundrum, as you call it.'

'I have often been accused of wasting other people's time.'

He thumped the table. 'Exactly. As I thought. You have a natural genius for it. There you go, Mr Deshpande.'

'Go where?'

'To your career.'

'Spell it out, man!'

'Mr Deshpande, you are an entertaining fellow, and that is what you should be. An entertainer. Write! Be an ex-journalist.

Sing! Dance! I don't know. Find your own unique way of spending other people's time. Or join the government and do it the easy way. What do you think?'

Inspiration reached down and grabbed me by the nitty-gritty. Eureka!

'May I inquire if the person I am addressing has been entertained by the advisee?'

'What? Oh. I suppose.'

'Then how about a small leg-up to said worthy, my dear Sir? For the sake of your namesake and my future firstborn. He adds his tiny voice to my yearning!'

I confided my Inspiration, and he grinned like a sailor on shore leave.

'Sure,' says he. 'We can have some tea and play at being – how did you put it – yes, "bosom friends". I think I know what you are up to.' He reached for the intercom. 'Mr Lagoo? Please join—'

So we had tea. And biscuits. The Impediment sat in the corner, slurping his frightened tea and oscillating his eyes. The camaraderie between Milton and yours humbly was palpable. He painted me in such glowing colours to Mr Lagoo that I was a virtual Aurora Borealis. Overcome by emotion, I nominated the same.

'You are equally well endowed, if not more,' says I. And my child, when forthcoming, would be his, I insisted. After all, we were all related vis-à-vis the One True Monkey. The jolly old Egg laughed a bit more than the scene called for, but otherwise, it was a *tour de farce*.

Can you blame the poor ex-Impediment for wringing my hands of all moisture and apologizing for past misconduct? He had had no intimation of my reach and grasp (apparently, the damn Ursulines had spread all kinds of rumours). There is nothing-to-do but to go to his house for dinner. Disembowel me or agree, says he! I took the high road and invited him to canter along likewise, and we let bygones be bygones; spit and shake, as the Yanks say.

So here we are in the fullness of Time. The inestimable Poornima currently houses a small Child Unit; by definition, one Milton Deshpande; hopefully, a virile male issue.

Damn it, Reader, I'm casting about for an End, and it is as oleaginous as the Beginning.

'End on a moral,' advise well-wishers. 'A moral, for a time-spender of this sort, is a must!'

Thusly: Moral! Dare to count your Eggs before they hatch because Fortuna, bless her fair bosom, does not favour Chickens.

Or how about this: Moral! All's well that ends well, sayeth the Bard.

So be it.

9

THE MIND–BODY PROBLEM

It had been a busy day at the shop with a non-stop rush of ladies in need of a new sari to mark Pongal. I kept the shop open a couple of hours longer than usual, and it was late when I got back home. As I was changing in the bedroom, my wife entered with a look of irritation and intimated that the Chettiars had once again sent their driver Chandu. Parvati-amma was once again feeling very poorly and wished to see me before she breathed her last.

'I'll tell them you may be able to come tomorrow?' Kanaka handed me a towel. 'This is just another false alarm.'

'That is not for us to decide. I must go. Who knows how long she has got?' I wiped my face, handed the towel back, but she didn't take it. I draped it over her rigid shoulder and gazed at her. 'I need something.'

'What?'

'First a thorough scolding, Mrs Iyer, and then a smile.'

'Uff. Then don't go, I'll smile all night.'

'Kanaka, don't start. You know I have to go.'

'Then you can collect your smile when you return.' She turned away. 'You can just go, but I have to endure the sarcastic questions. They will ask me why I didn't stop you. How can I stop you? I'm just your wife.'

She hissed other things of this sort, which I ignored but made sure to look thoughtful as if they were new points that had never occurred to me. I was happy to see Kanaka had lost all her shyness with me. It had been different a year ago, when she had lifted her right foot and stepped forward into my father's home for the first time. She had been quite hesitant, and for a second I wasn't sure she wouldn't turn around and run away. But in time our relationship had found its proper place. The morning after we first gave ourselves to the other, she showed me an album filled with photographs of her childhood. I said something to the effect that I already had an entire gallery's worth of her pictures. I think she initially suspected I was a pervert, clicking photographs of her on the sly, but when I clarified the gallery existed solely in my head, the only gallery I would care to walk, I sensed the melting of what little ice remained between us.

As I had expected, just before I was to leave, Kanaka rushed out and bade me roll down the window of the Chettiars' new Ford Endeavour. A ghastly smile. At my laugh, she gave me a proper smile.

'Don't forget to call,' she said. What Kanaka meant was: don't forget yourself.

Just then, Karthik came bounding out of the house, shouting: 'Arun, Arun, wait, I'm also coming.'

Her elder-brother was on vacation from America and had

decided on a whim to stay with us for a few days. An advanced party, Karthik. Full Ph.D, still unmarried, and he either didn't understand or didn't remember the subtler proprieties. He called me by my first name, was equally familiar with other family members. He would ask all sorts of questions, listen to our explanations and then remark: what a cute story. He liked to hug. His behaviour was not a problem for me, but I knew it weighed on Kanaka's mind. I met her glance and smiled.

'Let him also come, it'll be a little outing for him.' But when he caught up, huffing and puffing, I wondered if I should request him to change into something more decent. His T-shirt and shorts made him look as if someone had used a bicycle pump to inflate a child into an adult.

'See ya, sis,' he said, sliding onto the adjacent seat. 'Thanks, man, appreciate it.'

An isthmus connected our home to the main road that led from Kuvaloor to Madurai, and it was wide enough for two autorickshaws but too narrow for anything wider, and after we had crossed it, I found Selvi's taxi waiting for us at the other end. I had to tell Chandu to stop. My parents, elder-brother, sister-in-law, and my two nieces all disembarked. They were back from the matinee movie; it was just my bad luck I had run into them.

'Where are you off to, Arun?' asked my mother, her face already making it clear she knew. The Chettiars changed their car every few years, but everyone knew Chandu.

'Amma is not well, I have to go. I will be back tonight itself.' I was pleased that Kanaka hadn't alerted them that Parvati-amma had sent for me, and the thought made me add: 'I told Kanaka not to worry you.'

'Again! The Chettiars are too much!' said elder-brother. I suspected his irritation was more on account of having had to pay for all the cinema tickets. 'No consideration for people's feelings. And some people don't care.'

'Why shouldn't my mother ask to see her son?' I asked, angered by the slander, despite myself.

'Because your mother is standing right next to you, you blockhead.'

'It's no use, no use. Let it go.' My mother leaned on sister-in-law's shoulder. 'Let it go, it's no use. I'm cursed.'

My father said nothing. When he said nothing, he said a lot. He raged, he thundered, he roared.

'I better leave before it gets too late,' I said, regaining my calm. There was no need for all this drama but every attempt at appeasement only pushed us farther apart, so it was best to let them have their say. I did not blame them. I had never blamed them, except perhaps in the unhappy incomprehension of childhood.

'Yes, Arun, go before it's too late.' Sister-in-law flashed me a smile, and as usual turned her face to hide her approval from the others.

I inclined my head in gratitude. Sister-in-law had always been fond of me. She indicated it in many ways such as the extra spoonful of sugar in my payasam or the steep eyebrows when father upbraided me for doing business or the tenderness with which she had made Kanaka feel welcome. I imagine it was because I had welcomed her wholeheartedly when she had walked in as a bride. I had craved a stranger and she had entered at the perfect distance.

As a child, I used to lie on the bed in my brother's room, head on my folded arms, and watch her comb her long luxuriant hair in front of the Godrej almirah, hoping she would outsource the task of removing small tangles and knots. She would let me play with a strand while she worked on the rest of her hair. There was something about the graceful economy of her hand's motions, the curve of her smooth bare waist, her long neck, the metal clink of her gold bracelets, the smell of pure clean Hamam, and her small smile as she watched me watch her, it was all quite intoxicating. Once she had stopped my hands, clasped them to her warm neck and said: imagine if you had been born the eldest, how different your life would have been.

Eventually elder-brother's jeers and envy at our closeness began to sting and she put an end to our pleasant afternoon ritual around the time I was in SSC. When I protested, she told me that all things, if they were to be good, had to come to an end, and that casual remark, probably nothing more than her attempt to fob me off, struck me as a profound truth and I strived to make it a guiding principle. I understood her good sense only much later and, when I did, she only gained in respect in my eyes.

'How is Amma really?' I asked Chandu.

'Saar, she is really very sick. She's only waiting for you, the doctors say.'

I felt a sorrow come over me even though I knew it was unreasonable. I had been taking comfort from the scepticism of Kanaka and the others and persuaded myself that Amma would pull through as she always had. Chandu's words had brought me back to reality.

I had known Chandu a long time, but I still found his sympathetic glance in the rear-view mirror too much of a presumption.

'It is all in God's hands,' I said.

Any display of gratitude to God was always allergic to Kanaka's brother. But my wife must have had a word, because instead of rolling out his analytical toolbelt and going to work on my claim, Karthik stroked the leather seat and said it was wonderful how Ford had made a comeback in America. I hadn't known it had gone anywhere and said so. He asked me if I knew the secret of Ford's success. When I confessed I didn't know that either, he leaned forward and said in a significant way: no Ford automotive part lasts longer than the car. I could believe that. I told him the Chettiars, who owned a Ford dealership, had had to recall their 2011 Edge models for repairs. Kanaka's brother then launched into an interesting description of the palliative care movement in Kerala. In many ways, he was like the Discovery channel, and sister-in-law often parked my nieces in front of him. Still, there was a fundamental decency to his thinking, and I found myself rather glad that he had decided to come along.

When I reached the Chettiars, I was overcome by the love and affection they showered on me. Shanmugan clutched my arm, Murugan grasped my shoulder, they asked about Kanaka's well-being, understanding without my saying anything why she had been unable to come. When I introduced Karthik, they received him with the same courtesy they would have offered one of their own in-laws.

Why couldn't Kanaka and I live here, where I belonged. A

futile question deserves no answer and I asked instead about Amma. Shanmugan led me inside the house, a privilege I would never be able to grant him as long as my father lived. I walked through its rooms, seeing myself skipping, playing, hiding behind this object and that, tormenting the hens into dropping their eggs, crying as Amma gave me the thrashing of my life. I could never tell what memories would flash in me in this house, my house, my old graceful dark house with its cream-coloured walls and massive wooden pillars.

'How are you, Shanmugan, are you prospering?' I asked as we crossed the inner courtyard, leading rather than following, and feeling, not for the first time, that sweet swelling in my soul at assuming the eldest's responsibilities in this house. Was this how my brother felt, day in and day out?

'I'm fine, elder-brother. We were praying you could come in time, that is all.'

'I'm glad.' I hesitated, then added awkwardly, 'I won't stop coming, don't think that.'

'No, no,' he protested, then smiled when I cuffed him gently. Karthik's glances, in equal parts furtive and curious, brought to me how strange it must all seen to him. Shanmugan and Murugan looked several decades older than I, but it made no difference in my mind. Or theirs.

'Arumugan!' cried Parvati-amma, when she saw me.

I went to her bedside and my embrace turned into my holding her sideways, awkwardly, neither sitting nor standing. Despite her ill-health, she managed to make space and after seating myself more comfortably, I asked: 'Everything fine with your mechanisms? Need more oil or what?'

For some reason, she never tired of this joke and would always find a different reply. 'Yes, Bush has stolen all the oil in Iraq,' or 'Mechanisms are all fine, it is only the clutch' or 'The car is in mint condition' or some such jovial thing.

This time she only revealed her toothless grin but was too tired to attempt a suitable reply. I smoothed her hair, pressed my cheek to her hot forehead. She seemed utterly at peace, and when tears sprang to my eyes, she squeezed my hand as if to say: what is there, we knew this day would come. Yes, but most children and their mothers lose each other just once; we would lose each other twice.

The taste of dust and blood filled my mouth. I had never gotten used to seeing her old and toothless. In my mind's eye, she remains that terrified young woman who had knelt over me weeping and wailing for a doctor, helplessly witnessing her sixteen-year-old bleed to death. I remember her brilliant diamond nose ring glittering in the Pongal sun, the wilderness in her large expressive eyes, the gorgeous green and gold sari stained black with my expiring blood, my bloodied hand flailing as it tried to touch the white jasmine flowers in her hair. Now here I was, cradling her; it felt wrong, as if I had somehow reversed the natural order of events.

I called my father, told him I would be staying the night, and he hung up on me. I called Kanaka, but I had no need to ask because she answered: 'Your mother has refused to eat dinner. Elder-brother and sister-in-law had a fight because she bought snacks for everyone during the interval. Father's listening to Carnatic. Everything is dull without you.'

'You should have come with me.'

'I am married to Arun Iyer, why would I go with Arumugan Chettiar?'

There were limits to her understanding after all. When I said nothing in reply, she asked somewhat sorrowfully: 'Are you angry with me?'

'Maybe Arumugan is angry, but not Arun. Sleep well. I'll return soon, God willing.'

'I can't wait to see you tomorrow.'

I did not sleep very well. I knew intellectually a lot would have changed in twenty-plus years but I could not help feeling outraged. Nothing was where it should be, my bed felt too soft and I missed my brothers' lumps next to mine.

At about two in the night, I went to check on Amma, startling Murugan's daughter, who had been assigned to keep vigil. She told me Amma had moved her bowels and had even eaten a little.

I returned to my room, continued to have fitful dreams, tossed and turned, and when morning broke and I heard people stirring about in the kitchen, I hurriedly did my ablutions, went downstairs and had filter coffee. There was a new cook who didn't recognize me and when he respectfully addressed me as saami, the fellow was quickly corrected by a number of the older hands that this was practically *my* house.

Practically. But actually? What would happen after Amma's death? The ones closest in memory, Shanmugan and Murugan, wouldn't change. So loving always. The thought that I, the eldest, had been able to do nothing for my brothers brought tears. What about their wives, their children, the rest of the family? My heart ached as I thought about their very natural fears that I was angling for a piece of the property. I wanted nothing except their acceptance, their love. But would I be anything to them after Amma passed away? When she was gone, what would become of me?

Depressed by all these heavy thoughts, somehow alien despite their long familiarity, I went out into the courtyard and found Karthik doing yoga stretches. I asked if he felt like a walk and he jumped at the offer. I told him there was a large pool about a mile from the house and absent-mindedly turned left as we exited the gate, but after a couple hundred paces, I paused, curiously desolate. I told Karthik we would have to turn back. The pool had been filled in with sand many years ago, the whole area was filled with new houses.

'You used to go there in your past life?' he asked, in a casual voice.

'Yes. Many times.' I did not want to talk about it. With him. Or in English.

We walked silently for another ten minutes. The Chettiars were only thirty or forty minutes from Madurai and the area had undergone a real estate boom. If the construction posters delivered on even half their promises, then this area would be unrecognizable in a few years. I wondered if I should buy an apartment, move out with Kanaka. I wanted children but the idea of raising a child in my father's house did not appeal to me. Perhaps I could sell the sari shop, buy one closer to Madurai. I was busy thinking about what it would cost, what Father would say and so on, when Karthik said abruptly: 'Arun, we have become friends, haven't we?'

'We're much more.' I felt uneasy. 'We are family, Karthik.'

'Yes, of course.' He hesitated. 'Okay, since we're family, I can be utterly honest. Listen, this reincarnation business, it just freaks Kanaka out. She told me not to bug you, but it freaks her out and I got to say something. I mean, see it from her perspective. The man she married is going around saying he's actually somebody else.'

'Yes, yes,' I said in Tamil. I couldn't help my agitation. 'I had planned to make it clear, but when I saw her suddenly it didn't seem so important, and even if I had found the courage to tell her, I wouldn't have—'

'Arun. Buddy, relax. I'm not here to hash the past. That's *exactly* what I don't want to do. She thinks you're a terrific guy, she's very happy, don't get me wrong. Very, very happy. All I'm saying is, okay, you have all these freaky memories, but that doesn't mean you had a past life and all that. It just means memories can survive the death experience. A memory is ultimately just a molecular configuration. It has to be, that's how the biology works. Maybe a set of molecular configurations in Arumugan's brain got quantum-entangled with your growing brain. It's not like you *literally* had a prior life. It's more like your brain somehow took a photograph of his brain. See the difference? No need for metaphysical bullshit.'

He went on in this vein. I listened silently. I didn't understand even half of what he was saying. At two years of age, I had started to wail whenever I saw a cow or a bull. At four I began to declare my name was Ammuga, my mother's name was Pavadi and I wouldn't answer to Arun. I refused to accept my birth-mother as my real mother. I said I had been gored to death by a bull in the Jallikattu during Mattu

Pongal, fifteen years earlier. Everyone had been first amused, then concerned, then in an uproar. When I was about six, I ran away from home. I was brought back and I ran away again. This continued for some months. One time, I must have been eight, I was finally successful and somehow found my way to this house, a hundred and fifty kilometres from the house I was born in. I ran in before anyone could stop me, found my way to Amma, recognized my brothers Shanmugan and Murugan, remembered names, incidents. I recognized Amma's nose ring. I told her the diamond had been a gift from her grandfather because she had managed to scrape through the SSC exams, the first member in the family to do so.

When the Chettiars returned with me to Kuvaloor, they were attacked by the locals and accused of putting ideas in my head. The police got involved. There was a lot of bad blood between the families. Eventually, the families worked out a deal. I would remain Arun Iyer provided I was allowed to visit the Chettiars once in a while.

There was never any doubt between Amma and me. We knew. It had nothing to do with the memories. We *knew*. I remember the smell of her body, the warmth of her hands, the feel of her face against mine. I was more than her son. I was quintessentially her son.

I wondered if any of this would penetrate the fog that he called science.

'One day,' said Karthik, 'we'll have machines that can transfer memories wholesale into young foetuses. Voila. Mechanical reincarnation.'

I nodded thoughtfully, pitying him. The West had really

done a number on his mind. He had lost all sense of proportion. He had gone to buy a simple set of pant-trousers and ended up a mall mannequin.

'Arun? Kanaka mentioned you have a birthmark. May I see it?'

'Certainly.' I lifted my shirt, showed him the scar just under my ribs. It was quite small, only about two inches long, and I could tell he was disappointed. He licked his lips.

'Thanks,' said Karthik. 'I suppose it's on the same side where you were gored and all that. You really believe you were reincarnated?'

'Belief is needed when there is the possibility of doubt,' I explained. I was beginning to understand that he wanted to believe but did not know how to start. I gestured to the construction debris, workers' shanty houses, the growing number of people on the road. 'Let's turn back. Everything has changed, and not all of it for the better.'

It struck me I did not have to buy an apartment in this area. If I could buy it anywhere, why not somewhere near Kuvaloor? I might have to take a loan against the shop, but I was confident I could pay it off. I was a Chettiar, business was in my blood. Father would eventually forgive once he realized I was only separating, not breaking relations. He might even lend me the money. If Kanaka and I moved out of Kuvaloor entirely, it would be very hard on sister-in-law. She would really feel it with the both of us gone. And I would miss my nieces, the little scamps. You don't just walk out on people you love.

Charged, I resolved to broach the subject with Kanaka as soon I returned. I imagined her joy. Yes, she would be overjoyed to have a space all her own. Of course I would have to make good on the suggestion, otherwise she would eat me alive. Suddenly I was impatient to return to Kuvaloor, get on with life.

'India is progressing like anything,' I said to Karthik. 'There are many NRI investment opportunities in small businesses, especially here.'

'Yes, yes, I'm seeing that.' And then he began to describe a talk on the subject of Booming India by some famous fellow named Ted.

Contrary to all expectations, however, Amma had begun to recover. Everyone said it was because of my presence, that Parvati-amma wasn't done being my mother yet, such was God's grace. They said it softly, with reverence even, but also some exhaustion. At eleven in the morning, I went to see Amma, once again with tears in my eyes.

'Go Aramuga,' she whispered. 'I know you have responsibilities. God willing, this motor car will see you again.'

In this parting, somehow we both knew there was an added 'in another lifetime'. I embraced her, embraced my brothers, timidly patted my cousins, nieces and nephews, and when Shanmugan murmured 'when the time comes, you will have to do the final rites, elder-brother,' my heart lifted as if powered by a hundred kites, and I said, of course of course. But later in the car, the sadness returned. These rites, these rituals. They had also been performed for me and yet my essence had found no peace. What was it all for, this constant shuffle from one set of clothes to another? I gazed at the world around me, and thought: this is why God gave us families.

'I know what you're thinking,' said Kanaka's brother in

a tone that said: I need to talk. 'Nothing lasts, so what is the point of anything? A deep question brother-in-law, a deep, deep question.'

'We have some time,' I said smiling, and leaned back to enjoy the rest of the journey.

10

THE LITERATURE OF CHANGE

'Let's return to basics,' said Gulabi, frog-eyes focused on my face like laser beams. 'What is SF?'

I ran the comb one more time through my hair, placed it back in my jeans pocket. Akka had paid for the expensive Kim Ki Bum hairstyle and though I loved the Korean hairstyle, maintaining it was a full-time job. Plus the hair's length made it hard to see out of my left eye. I turned my head, glanced at the clock. 5.35. Gulabi had made himself comfortable on the bed and wasn't leaving my room any time soon, but I had to leave. Latest by 5.45. Amma was done with the mixie she'd borrowed from Asha-aunty. I had volunteered, of course. Anything to get a darshan of Ganga.

'SF is the literature of change.' Gulabi didn't have ego problems about answering his own questions. 'That's the heart of SF. Its essence. So if we want an SF story, we need to start with some change. The world was this way; now it's that way.' He snarfed a handful of corn chips. 'Yaar, why don't you get

Kerala mix? I'm allergic to corn. And give your fucking hair a break. You know you're going to go bald, right?'

'Not necessarily.'

'Yah, necessarily. Scientists use your father's head to model a perfect sphere. You are genetically screwed—' Gulabi sat up. If he'd had whiskers, they would've quivered. 'What if.'

'What what if?'

'What if all men are genetically screwed. What if in the future, thanks to genetic technology, women will be able to live twice as long as men. X-chromosomes are really freaky.'

'But we have X-chromosomes also.'

'Women have two, we only have one. Look, never mind the exact tech.' Gulabi helped himself to another handful of allergy. 'What if.'

I hesitated. The idea wasn't bad. But for a short story? This sounded like a novel. Plus, it was women-oriented, which meant long musings. We only had four thousand words. Damn it. This was the Curse. All our best ideas came when we were working on other stories.

'It'll change everything,' I said. Then sighed. 'But Gulabi—'

'Yah, I'll put it in the Fridge.' Gulabi sank back. 'Fuck. Why are we having such trouble with this story?'

'Why ask why. Listen, I have an errand to run. Keep thinking.'

'Where to?'

'To bathe in Ganga's beauty.'

'But—' Gulabi glanced at the wall clock, resigned himself. 'Chalo, squeeze bhabhi for me.'

'Think about the story. Don't fucking loll around playing PUBG.'

Ganga left for dance practice at six. I would have to rush if I wanted to meet her. I found Amma in the kitchen, looking for all the world as if someone had unpacked her from a crate, set her at a forty-five-degree angle against the kitchen table, and then forgotten to start her up. She was probably thinking about what to cook for the night. Today was Thursday, so it would be kurma and parathas, with a side of fried potatoes. But Amma liked to dream of rebellion. She came to life when she saw me. A forty-watt smile, which then turned into a frown.

'Arjun, I really hate that chinky hairstyle. When are you going to change it? You look like—'

'Amma, it's racist to say chinky. Please evolve. Where's the mixie?'

'Don't forget to thank Asha-aunty nicely.' She gestured to the Kenwood mixie and I took it off the counter. Heavy fucker. 'Is Santosh still here? Are you two really studying for an exam or just watching YouTube?'

YouTube? Ha ha. Seriously. I had learned a couple of things regarding questions. First: if you ignored questions, they usually went away. Second: the freethinker questions questions. Shit. Good line. I took out my notepad, scribbled the thought down. I could imagine a Yoda-type character saying this at some point. Question questions, grasshopper.

'Now what did I say?' asked Amma. I'm glad to see her smile. Sixty watts. 'Always scribbling, you and Santosh.'

'Amma, I'm sick of paper. This is the twenty-first century for God's sake. When are you getting me a smartphone?'

'The day your Appa becomes vice-president,' said Amma. 'I promise.'

Family joke. I could join Appa's company – Fischers Aktien-Gesellschaft or FAG as its fans called it – as a chaprasi six years from now and still become vice-president earlier than Appa. I glanced at the clock on the microwave.

Five-fifty. Shit. I ran down the flight of stairs, and for no reason Qutub developed into a full-blown hard-on along the way. This was a problem that had begun to happen some six months ago. No amount of choking the goose's neck seemed to help. So ignore it, what else? I rang the doorbell and was in the process of rearranging my junk, when Ganga opened the door. Luckily, the outer wooden door covered my fiddling.

'Hi Ganga. I came to return the missie.' I could feel my face stretching into a stupid grin. Ha-ha. Missie. 'Mixie.'

'One minute.'

Asha-aunty needed three separate bolts drawn across her door at all times to feel safe. God knows what her husband had to do to get in. I waited. Bolt 1. Bolt 2. Bolt 3. The door opened. Pallu drop. Ganga held out her hand for the mixie. She was already dressed for dance practice. Salwar-kameez, braided hair. She'd really blossomed in the last year.

'Hi Ganga, dancing?'

'Right now, no.'

Ha-ha, how funny. Then I had a flash of inspiration. Pure genius.

'I'm trying – we are trying – me and Gulabi, I mean – he's my friend – we're working on this story about robots who talk to each other using sign language. Then Gulabi was like, hey, why not use mudras from Bharatanatyam. That would be totally cool. Then I was like, yah, wait a minute, I have a friend who does dancing. She can help us. But only if you're not busy.'

'Dancing robots?'

'Yah.'

'So they can't talk with their hands full.'

'Yah, some technical issues for sure.' I could tell she was intrigued. Flaring nostrils. Definitely intrigued. Then I realized she'd just cracked a joke. WOW! I laughed. 'Funny. Mind if we use that joke? We'll give credit. I'll send you the story when it's done.'

'That's okay. I don't read SF.'

'We write other things too. What do you like to read?' My hands were beginning to ache.

'Non-fiction. I don't read much actually.'

'Oh.' I was flummoxed. 'It would be really awesome if you could help us. Just some tips, that's all.'

'Okay. Mixie?' Ganga gestured with her outstretched hand, looking a bit uneasy.

I love everything about her, even that uneasy look. That supple brown skin which glows like it's massaged and oiled every single day. The cute piercing on her right ear. Her slightly sweaty neck. I loved her philtrum. Her long black curls. She did her hair at Ruby's Salon; I went to Raj's salon which was right next door. Raj had got his Ruby, what about me, baby?

I handed her the mixie. Our fingers brushed against each other. Qutub sprang to salute his Queen. Nuisance!

'Amma wanted to say, I mean, the mixie, to thank for the mixie.'

See what she does to me? I speak perfect English. Better than perfect. The Queen of England, like, consults me on grammar. Even Gulabi, who'd returned from Fiji four years ago, admitted my English was better. I have read *Sartor Resartus*, *Future Shock*, *Third Wave*, *Brief History of Time*, just ask me! I can quote the *Rime of the Ancient Mariner* by-heart. The entire frikkin' poem, yes. Why did I by-heart it? Because I'd read Douglas Adams's *Dirk Gently's Holistic Detective Agency*. My English is perfect.

Ganga nodded, began to close the door. But just then Asha-aunty came out of the bedroom, the bead curtain oscillating wildly in her wake.

'Is that Arjun? Arjun-beta, ek minute. Please ask your sister to fill Ganga's wart prescription.'

'Ma, I told you I'll get it!' Then Ganga barked something in Gujarati to her mother, who looked distressed.

'He's our Arjun only,' said her mother, with a weak smile. 'Please beta? If there's a queue at the clinic, Ganga will be late for dance class.'

'No problem, Aunty! I will get it. I had warts last year. Easily fixed, no problem.'

Flashing eyes from my Queen. As Ganga turned and left the room, I was left to satisfy Asha-aunty's curiosity about when my warts had attacked, where they'd attacked, what medicines my sister had prescribed, whether I still felt itchy and so on. I'd never had warts, so I had to improv.

I was *not* to scratch the itch, Dr Asha Patel, FRCS, told me in a very serious tone, almost as if a Mayan prophecy depended on it, because Ganga had scratched and peeled her—

'MA!' shouted Ganga, from somewhere inside the house.

Oh, this was gold! Twenty-four-carat gold. My baby had warts! I two-stepped the stairs, burst into my apartment, told Gulabi I had to go to the clinic. Ganga had a women's condition and needed immediate relief. Gulabi wasn't happy and let me know it: 'Bhenchod, her warts are more important than our story? Seriously? The deadline is, like, fucking tomorrow. The fucking story will fucking write by fucking itself or what?'

We fell silent, staring at each other, wild-eyed with possibility. Yeah! What if stories didn't need human creators. What if, Arjun? What if, Gulabi?

'Let's stick to our original idea.' I sighed. 'Metafiction is deep and deep takes time. We have no time.'

'Yah. I'll put it in the Fridge. Accha, get the medicine, but come back fast. And see if you can flick some nicotine gum from the pharmacy.'

I raced down the stairs. Ganga would be back from dance class by seven-thirty, all nice and smelly. I could either show up at her place then or I could go after she'd showered and done her lady things. Once I had turned up at their house after eight, and Asha-aunty had insisted on treating me to some home-made shrikhand. She and I had chatted in the kitchen; Ganga had been in the living room, stretched out on the sofa, studying. Awesome leggings. Awesome toes. Is there a poem as lovely as a pair of anklet-encased feet? Qutub rose to serve his Queen.

Focus, focus. Gulabi was right. The story wouldn't write by itself. Why were we having such difficulty? We'd never had writer's block. So why hazaar difficulties now? Okay, try lateral thinking. What was the difficulty we were having? We didn't know what to write. What was the opposite of that?

People who didn't know how to read. People like Ganga. Nah, that wasn't right. She was into video, that's all. What if it wasn't that people wouldn't read but that they couldn't? What if a day came when people became terrified of reading?

Green signal.

As I crossed the street, a silver-grey Audi coupe slid by, almost taking my buttocks with it. I cursed, but the car, as sleek and silent as a shark, powered away. Fucker. An inch closer, and I would have been an ex-writer. These firang cars were everywhere. Father couldn't even afford an Indica. What was the point of road signs if they didn't do what road signs were supposed to do?

No, not *didn't*, couldn't. Fucking Indians didn't give a fuck about fucking rules. It was, like, traffic sign, what fucking traffic sign? Half the damn country couldn't even read.

Speaking of signs, a protest march was in full progress on the other side of the street. Against the fucking communal theocracy in charge, what else? I scanned the crowd. Why the hell did we still have to march for the most basic truths? Someone thrust a placard into my hand. I knew I didn't have the time, but man, there's always time to do the right thing. The march was headed in the same general direction I was going anyway. And protesting was pretty automatic by now, so I could still think about the story. I didn't even know what sign I was holding in my hand, but here I was marching along under its power. What if signs did things they weren't supposed to do?

Okay. What exactly did the word 'sign' mean? It was a mark that said: notice me. I had read this French dude, Fuckolt, massive terawatt brain. Fuckolt said that Writing was a series of signs.

The signs themselves were passive but once inside the head they could do strange things. This was called learning. What if in the future, people figured out how to rewire the brain efficiently? Super efficiently. Now suppose this technology could be hacked? Textually transmitted diseases. Then Devanagari could become Rakshasnagari. Being able to read could become very dangerous. Like giving everybody passwords to your brain.

Fuckolt had also said the writer was, like, dead in modern literature. Basically, all literature is zombie lit. Seriously weird fucked-up shit.

Focus! Great idea, but tough to work out the consequences in a few hours. Being afraid of text was like being afraid of a bowl of cornflakes. Still, could work, though. Could be made dramatic. Somebody coming across forbidden text, reading, unable to stop herself from reading, her neural circuits sparking and rewiring, remaking her, that sparkling spider-web of fire inside her head. Words could go anywhere, get inside anything, that was the beauty of writing.

Two behenji types were giving me the funny eye. They didn't approve. Then they focused on me, and one said something to the other. Laugh, laugh. Must be my Kim Ki Bum hairstyle. Azaadi is happening, bitches. Deal with it.

I resumed cogitation and the world fell away. I saw a boy and a girl going up a mist-covered mountain. Through the mist, a forest. Somewhere in Ireland, maybe. I liked Ireland. They were going up the mountain, going up the mountain, going up the mountain, to see what they could see. Aidan and Kira. No, Kira was Tamil for spinach. These teens were Irish. Gillian? Yes! Aidan and Gillian, going up a mountain in a dystopian sign-haunted world. I was so absorbed, I almost walked past the clinic. All the lights were on inside, but Akka had flipped the sign to 'Closed'. I ran up the few steps, opened the door, strode into her office.

WHAT THE FUCK!!!

Okay, some sights you can't erase. Never, ever, not in a million years. Tear my brain out, throw it in a mixie, have it with pongal and take a dump in the Arabian Sea. The memory will remain.

'Arjun!' Akka began to hurriedly re-wrap her sari. 'Why can't you knock! Get out!'

The skinny bhenchod pushed up his glasses, blinked at me. He held out his hand. Actually held out his fucking hand.

'Hello Arjun. I think we've met.'

I stared wildly at the fellow. Now that my neurons are sparking again, I think I did recognize him. I had seen him in this very office – dear God, how long had this porno movie been going on? I couldn't bear to finish the thought. I rushed out, then stopped, remembering.

I had promised Asha-aunty the bloody ointment. So I waited. I made noises to make sure they didn't restart their porno shit. Finally, the skinny bhenchod with glasses crept out, and without looking either left or right, got on his scooter – fucking pink Vespa! – and drove off. I went back into the office.

'How could you, Akka!'

'First of all, calm down. The world hasn't ended. Here, have a toffee.'

Toffee! Was she fucking serious? I took the toffee, stopped bawling. Jesus, it had been a shock. Even now, the image of the fucker's hand in her open blouse – Aaaahhhhh. Why was I still alive!

'His name is Pranay. He's Maharashtrian, the brother of a friend of mine and a mathematics professor at Mumbai University. He got his doctorate from TIFR. He has no diseases. He's a very nice fellow and when you've stopped bleeding through your eyes, we will arrange a meeting where you two can talk and get to know each other.'

Listen to her, the slut, cool as cucumber. Then I was very ashamed. Akka was a rock. Akka had wiped my ass as a kid. Akka was anything but a slut. She must have been seduced. God, I hated him. What if I could persuade Gulabi to strangle the mathematical Marathi motherfucker?

'Are you going to marry him?' I asked, and hated the way my voice trembled.

'I haven't ruled it out. Now, what did you come for?'

Akka went to the pharmacy and got me a bottle of Compound W. She always acquired a small smile whenever she saw me running errands for Asha-aunty. Akka had acquired that small smile now.

'How's Ganga?'

'Why don't you ask her?' I said, shortly.

If Akka was hinting there was a similarity between her porno situation and mine, she was badly mistaken. I was freaked by how calm she was, I could hardly bear to look at her. I helped Akka close the clinic.

'Pranay loves science-fiction,' she said, 'but it's the one thing we can't discuss. Maybe you can give me some books to get started. How's Asimov?'

I grunted. Asimov. Puh-leese. She couldn't handle Asimov. I'd start her off with an Ursula Le Guin. The fem types loved Le Guin. Then I'd feed her Octavia Butler, maybe Philip Dick. No, she wouldn't like Philip Dick. Akka was an optimist.

'Arjun? Come on, don't be like that.' She touched my hair, lightly. 'Pranay told me he wanted to read one of your stories. He really is a wonderful guy.'

I bit my tongue.

Later, when I went to Asha-aunty's apartment, Ganga answered the door, again. I handed her the bottle through the bars. No fuss, no small talk. I had lost all interest in women. Even in Ganga. For all I knew, there could be the entire Indian cricket team in the kitchen, waiting to service her. She opened the door, insisted on paying me.

There was a breadcrumb on her philtrum. I pointed it out. I dully pointed it out. A quick upward roll of her tongue and the crumb disappeared. She smiled. I nodded.

'Thanks,' she said. 'By the way, really like your hairstyle. It's cool. Can I check?'

Yah, yah. I let her touch my hair. She asked if I was okay, and I said, now-I-am plus smile, and she small-smiled, then she asked if I had been serious about learning about mudras, and I said, yah, yah, of course I am serious. Ganga said she was free this Saturday. I proposed we talk about it at Cafe Coffee Day. Quieter, na? She agreed it would definitely be quieter. She used the word: definitely. No, *definitely*. Qutub rose to serve.

'But don't get your expectations up,' she said. 'Bharatanatyam isn't really about telling stories.'

'Ditto for SF,' I said. Random comment, but it intrigued her.

Flaring nostrils. Definitely intrigued.

Dinner was a quiet affair. It had been a tough day at the FAG for Appa. My mother had over-crisped the potatoes. Deliberately, I think. *We* loved it over-crisped and roasty, but Appa didn't, and he went into one of his cold silent frowns. Akka didn't feel like talking much, neither did I. Gulabi was the only one who felt completely at home.

'Why is this girl always here?' asked Appa, when he realized the last paratha now reposed in Gulabi.

Later, after Amma had brought us Ovaltine and said goodnight, I confided to Gulabi all that had happened with Akka. He was shaken, totally shaken, frog-eyes dangerously close to popping.

'Was there penetration?' he asked, after a long silence.

'Bhenchod!' I lashed out with my foot, but he nimbly torqued to avoid the kick.

'Reason I'm asking,' said Gulabi, moving the nicotine gum to the other side of his mouth, 'I kiss my grandma on the lips every day—'

'Please tell me it's because you're giving her CPR.'

'No tongue. She loves it. Point is, suppose there was input-output, so what? Akka has womanly needs, that's all. It's obvious from her full lips. The river of desire must run its course or flood the banks.'

Never confide to a writer! I knew he meant well but now I deeply regretted spilling the beans. Things had changed too fast. Perhaps change always happened too fast for words.

'By the way, one update.' Gulabi looked very intent. 'Call me Brhnnala from now on.'

'Why? Pagal-kutta-itis, or what?'

'Because. We're tired of you neurotypicals pushing us around. Okay?'

Whatever. We had a nice discussion on names. Of course, the Sith Lord of Names was Harry Stephen Keeler. In *The White Circle*, Keeler had come up with the coolest name in the world for his alien:

$$\text{TTP---} \begin{array}{c} \square \,^{\circ} \\ \underline{\overline{}} \\ \triangle \,^{\square\square} \end{array} \quad 112965 --- \left\{ \begin{array}{l} \text{Caucasian} \\ \text{Iberian} \\ \text{Negroid} \\ \text{Mongolian} \end{array} \right. \quad \text{K-5555 Series 45-L-7427} - \beta \frac{\pi}{\alpha} \;.3--- \quad \text{LXII} \quad .0792$$

Later, I went to put away the glasses in the kitchen. Appa always sneered at me for helping out, so I tiptoed across the hallway hoping my parents had retired for the night. They had. I rinsed the glasses. I had done it a thousand times, and yet somehow this night I felt a great sadness. One way or the other, Akka would soon go her way. She would get married, move out. So would I. Her story and my story would be replaced by the stories of our children, and then they too would reach this moment, where I stood now. What-if to even-if, that's the human story. Suppose to dispose, that's the human story. Shit. I fished out my notebook, scribbled the insight. I really needed to think of a story with a Yoda character.

I could hear my parents' voices from the bedroom, arguing. Appa was giving Amma hell on the topic of crisped potatoes. What an asshole. Appa finally broke for air.

'As soon as Arjun gets married,' said Amma, in an exhausted voice filled with a river that had finally run its course. 'I will leave you for good. This I swear.'

'And go where?'

'There's always an elsewhere.'

Some things never changed. Later, Gulabi aka Brhnnala – what a chutiya name – and I worked on the SF story. He loved the idea of textually transmitted diseases and we got down to the details. The way we worked, I wrote the first draft, and then he moved in and layered the text with symbolism, synecdoche, that sort of literary razzle-dazzle. Brhnnala wanted Indian characters – fucker was more Indian than Kipling – so the Irish names had to go. Also, India had loads of forests. So we moved the mist-covered mountain and its forests to India. Basically, an India story. Like the theory goes, SF is the literature of change.

11

THE PARROTS' TALE

A long time ago in the land known to its happy inhabitants as Tamilakam, there lived a young woman and her old Brahmin husband, Gautama.

Now, in some parts of the world, such a situation is a recipe for disaster. Not so in the land of the Tamils. Here the gods were benign, the men honourable, the women mostly chaste, and the children mischievous. The mornings were filled with Sanskrit chants, the afternoons with the songs of the women working in the fields, and the evenings – why, the evenings were the best of all. The women would decorate their lustrous black hair with white jasmine blooms; their lithe brown bodies would curve to the metres of ancient Sangam poets, and when they laughed it was as if the rice fields had accompanied them home. It was the best kind of paradise: cow-friendly, tree green and people rich.

No one was more conscious of these facts than the young wife. As if she hadn't been lucky enough in her location, time and culture, her husband was also a great Sanskrit pundit, a legendary hoarder of tales, often cited in the same slokas as Vishnusharma, Gunadhaya, Somadeva, Ksemendra and other legendary lepidopetrists of the text. Simply put, he was learned in all the sixty-four arts, including cock-fighting. How many women can say that of their snoring clods?

But on some nights, blue and fragrant with kurinji flowers, it was impossible not to contrast the snores of her scholar with the distant sounds of necklace shells jouncing on makeshift straw beds. To take her mind off certain images (it is unnecessary to list the moist details), she would offer silent prayers for her husband's long life.

Perhaps if the wife had been literate, she would have known what to do. Doesn't the *Panchatantra* say that a wife delights in four things: pickles, gossip, night and a husband out of town?

Perhaps if the wife had been literate, she would have known what to say. Didn't the poetess Vijjika say that human adultery inspires the bees and thus flowers the world? Imagine a world without flowers!

But, alas, the pundit's wife was illiterate.

Now, like so many other men, the pundit enjoyed going to sleep with his head in his wife's lap. She had strict instructions to massage his eyebrows till the third snore emerged. To prolong her pleasure, he would resist sleep with all his might.

Since a story is how time is kept from happening all at once, he would tell her stories. He knew lots of stories. Any number of his stories were from the Ramayana, extolling the virtues of Lady Sita, namely: domesticity, a rigorous chastity, and a fair waist blessed with three folds. He also relied on the tales in the eight Sthala Puranas, temple origin stories, as moral as mother's milk. Of course, tales from Somadeva's *Kathasaritsagara*, suitably scissored for feminine ears and youthful years, were also a must.

He was very fond of stories that warned characters not to keep their stories to themselves. Horrible things happened to the non-storytellers in these stories. Some went dumb, others grew hairy lumps, one housewife suffered memory loss, and one chap had to marry his tongue. The pundit had no need to worry of course. And though there are no stories about the dangers of ignoring storytellers, his wife listened dutifully. She could have been a stone. Stories, stories, stories. She had stories for morning, lunch and dinner. The oft-told stories were like people. Quite like family. In fact, they were exactly like in-laws who'd not only come to visit and never left, but also kept inviting other in-laws to join them.

One night the scholar was retelling the story of the unfortunate housewife who knew a story and who knew a song but wouldn't tell the story nor sing the song. Actually, he was retelling it by the old method of having the listener shout arbitrary words (say, 'monkey!') at arbitrary intervals. The storyteller's challenge was to work the word into the story.

'Calf,' said the wife, dutifully.

As is widely known, having to weave in such hurdles often improves a telling; just look at the Ramayana and its flying monkey! Maybe so, but the pundit's wife always called out the same words in the same order: sweet milk, mud floor, spill, calf, coral eyes, pallor, lover, waste.

Some might feel this made the whole exercise moot, but her husband thought it rather made things challenging. Any fool can think up a word, but it takes talent for the teller to work in the same word in different tellings. This time, when his wife said 'calf', the pundit relied on the thirty different denotations of the word to ingeniously connect it with the housewife's story *and* with the next word sure to head his way, namely: 'coral eyes'. It then struck the old Brahmin that it was really about time—

Gautama's wife leaned over and her slim fingers seized that intimate privilege (herein tame but ideally tumescent) which any mistress may claim as birthright and every harlot must pretend to savour. But as the *Manusmriti* cautions in no uncertain terms, wives are neither!

'Wife!' cried the pundit, his coral eyes wide with shock. 'Explain!'

'My friends say this word is to be found in *The Ha Ha Tale*,' said his wife, releasing what she had seized. 'They say it is as pleasing to savour as ghee is for the fire.'

'They say, they say. Nonsense.' The still-shaken scholar mentally examined his stacks for *The Ha Ha Tale* and emerged frowning. 'Nonsense.' Then Gautama placed her fingers where they really belonged, namely, on his eyebrows. 'Just listen! Listen attentively.'

Perhaps the pundit couldn't recall the tale because *The Ha Ha Tale* is a heresy with many names. One is by the contronym, *The Tale That Ends Tales*. Some poets call it *The Parrots' Tale*, for when a tale has no legitimacy its father is most likely a parrot. The Tamils call it *The Sound of Kisses*, but then everything sounds like a kiss to that happy race. The soft-spoken Telugu, Pingali Suranna, seems to have confused it with another Tamilakam tale, *The Tale That Cannot Be Told*, the story that Lord Brahma tries to tell his wife, the Goddess Saraswati. Since Lord Brahma is the creator of the universe and everything he utters instantly turns into fact, how is the God to tell a story?

Doubtless, other races have their own apophatic fabulists, their own liberation theologies.

Since his wife had been instructed to pay close attention and disobedience wasn't one of her virtues, she paid close attention. She listened intently, paying attention to the drawing and release of each breath, savouring every syllable. So determined was she to attend, on some nights the young woman would sometimes slip through the gaps of the telling.

Stroke upon stroke of her husband's eyebrows; oars dipped into the still waters of the mighty Kaveri. Across the shore, on the other side of the terraced temples was a mango grove. There she would find waiting for her – well, what does it matter who she found? She had no use for names. In time, time crossed the great river and came to her.

One dawn, the old man awoke to find his wife bustling about, looking tired but happy. As the *Manusmriti* cautions, it is a foolish husband who finds a quarrel in this situation; a tired wife means a busy wife, and a happy one means a good meal. Still, her cheerfulness was such that curiosity gained the upper hand.

'Wife? That swollen lip. Explain.'

'An errant bee, husband.'

'Hmph. And that tear in your blouse?'

'A stray thorn from a bush while picking firewood.'

'Hmph. You should be more careful. A loose woman's virtue and her clothes are soon parted.'

To round off the lesson, he recounted the tale of the legendary housewife Bhamati and how Vachaspati Mishra's learned *Brahma Sutra* commentary came to be named after her. He would've expounded further (why else did she have ears?), but he had to go to work.

Now, there are some people who appoint themselves God's roosters. The old scholar was one of them. Each morning, he walked to the terraced temple by the river to awaken Lord Venkateswara with prayers. But this morning, he was strangely agitated. The wife was so careless. She was beyond instruction. He remembered the old saying: you may recite the *Panchatantra* to a parrot all day, but it'll remain a parrot.

How true, reflected Gautama, as he passed a large old silk-cotton tree. His wife was that parrot.

Just then, two large and wet plops landed on his right arm.

'Inauspicious. Inauspicious.' He wiped away the bird droppings and looked up.

There were two parrots in the tree, lovely specimens, decked out in bright greens, face-slapped reds and flashes of yellow. It was as if each were the tip of some colour-drunk paintbrush. The birds gazed at him, cocking their heads, this way, that way, in the disconcerting manner of the species.

'A long time ago in the land,' began one of the birds, 'known to its happy inhabitants as Tamilakam—'

'There lived a young woman and her old Brahmin husband, Gautama,' completed the other.

As the parrots rambled on in this alternating manner, Gautama deduced of course that this was no typical situation. Not because of the talking birds (in those days wordy birds were as common as raging sages); not because the prattling birds were tattling about some chap called Gautama (the pundit was too learned to commit the vulgar narratological error of identifying characters with implied characters); and not because of the striking coincidence of seeing parrots when he'd just been thinking of parrots (the whole deal with coincidences is that they show up when least expected!); but because the recommended situation, as per the *Alankarashastra*, would've had parrots perched on a mango tree, not a silk-cotton tree. Uncertain as to the recommended emotions, he joined his palms together in a namaste.

'Forgive me, noble birds,' he said, interrupting the parroting of consciousness. 'Stories are for the credulous, the frivolous, the decrepit, wayward children, and women of loose morals. Since none of us are any of the above, I pray your eminences to conclude your most inspiring performance. However, one item has faintly fanned my interest. This obscure story, *The Ha Ha Tale*, I vaguely remember encountering it. It is from the *Sukasaptati*, I suppose?'

The birds gazed at him, cocking their heads, this way, that way, in the disconcerting manner of the species.

'Not Somadeva's *Kathasaritsagara*?'

The birds gazed at him.

'Yes, yes. I simply refuse to accept Ksemendra's *Bodhisattvavadanakalpalata* as the answer?'

The birds gazed.

'As I thought. Dandin's *Dashakumaracharita*? Jinesvara's *Kathanakakosa*? Uddyotana's *Kuvalayamala*? Jinaratna's *Lilavatisara*?'

The birds.

'So it must be from that mighty Ganga of stories then, the *Brhatkatha*? If it is not in the *Brhatkatha*, then it is nowhere, noble parrots!'

'First of all, it's not the *The Ha Ha Tale*,' began one parrot.

'It's *The Ah Ah Tale*,' said the other. 'And second of all—'

'It is not to be narrated—'

'It is enacted.'

It was the scholar's turn to goggle.

'Do you desire to—' began one parrot, distending a large black tongue.

'—hear the tale, pundit?' said the other, waggling its thick black tongue.

The old scholar glanced nervously at each of the six cardinal points of the heavens, and then nodded, very quickly. He wasn't afraid of what would happen next, but he did wish the tree were a mango tree. The parrots edged sideways to each other. Close. Closer. Really, there was no more branch left.

'Behold beloved, he desires to—'

'—desire, beloved.'

'Then kiss me.'

'—beloved, a kiss.'

And then the parrots opened their mouths and went at it with their engorged flickering wet black tongues, making the moaning sounds that gave the tale its name. The two parrots, the pundit and the world: it was as if the kiss were the circulating incarnadine in the four-chambered human heart.

Gautama sank to the ground, slack-eyed, his own swollen tongue working uselessly in his dry mouth. He shook and shivered and trembled like an ashvattha tree in the wind. His heart slowed, stopped, then started up again slowly, like a bull elephant chased into exhaustion.

The censored stories, imprisoned in him for decades, saw their chance. The more modest ones had the decency to pull up their pirate pants and in a mighty burst of air, swarmed out as bees. But others just tumbled out helter-skelter, higgledy-piggledy, as naked as the day they had been made. Stories tore through Gautama's husk, swirling and flailing, circling and streaming, like a gust of wind pursuing itself through the jagged hollows of bleached trees.

Forget about awakening Lord Venkateswara; the din woke up the entire village. It wasn't long before Gautama's wife arrived on the scene.

Her husband, a man who would rather explode than let out a fart in public, was sitting by a silk-cotton tree, lungi half-undone, spouting nonsense in Sanskrit. She didn't understand the words, but they made her cheeks burn. The stories swirled around her, on her, across her, by her, in her. Something kicked in her womb.

The young woman clasped her palm over her pundit's mouth.

A very good thing too. The man had orated Vatsyayana's arousing *Fifth Adhikarana* in its entirety, howled through Damodara Gupta's *Doctrine of the Bawd*, thrown in open-bloused selections from Rupa Goswami's *Ujjvala Nilamani*, quoted from the courtesan Muddupalini's thesis on the composition of randy triangles given two straight lines called

Krishna and Radha, and had just begun to declaim Bhartrhari's *Srngarasataka*.

She helped her husband to his feet. Gautama looked up at the tree. Cupulate reddish-yellow flowers fluttered in the wind as did the silk-cotton's globular green fruits, almost as if it were daring him to doubt. It wasn't that words weren't enough. From now on, words would have to be enough. He turned to his wife, touched the gentle rise of her belly.

'Is this the parrots' tale, wife?'

She simply didn't know how to answer such a profound query. She placed Gautama's hand on her shoulder and led her husband home, now as docile as a newborn calf.

It would be nice to say the scholar changed for the better. In a sense, yes. In a sense, no. But perhaps she measured her husband's change in ways that are important to wives, not storytellers. One evening, as she bustled about getting their simple meal ready, she caught him staring at her. And why not? She was a sight: hitched sari, dishevelled hair, half-revealed brown waist, ladle in hand and flushed cheeks. All women, the incomparable Kalidasa has remarked, are at no time as beautiful as when they're caught cooking interrupted.

But the pundit didn't quote anything or recall anything or instruct anything or sloka anything. When he waggled his tongue at her, the young wife shook her ladle at him in mock-anger and laughed, which, as husbands and wives and parrots and lovers and young scamps who shouldn't be reading this tale will all agree, is as good a place as any to cease waggling *this* tongue.

13

ARCHIPELAGO

Constance was a medley of perceptions: an enclosure of plump white arms, a weight on his back, laughter in his ear and the tell-tale scent of lavender.

'Connie! They told me you were dead!' shouted Tommy, grabbing hold of her as if he'd never let go.

It was as if a phantom limb had come awake, craving touch, demanding acknowledgement. Tommy's caresses became rough enough to cause Connie to push him away with a laugh.

'You look exactly the same, Connie.'

'That means you've begun to forget, Tommy.'

'I'm so sorry I never asked Mira about the Sphinx. I forgot all about it. If I'd only known—'

'What a silly you are,' interrupted Connie, laying her cheek against his. 'As if it matters. Don't I know all that you know?'

She raised her head to look at him. Her teasing smile showed that she didn't expect an answer.

'Dear God, Connie…'

'Yes, darling Tommy. Come, you're still too far away.'

He entwined his fingers in her hair and drew her closer, so close that she began to blend into him. She was saying something, but he couldn't focus on her words; there was a weight on his chest, and it grew heavier and heavier—

I'm dreaming, he thought. But how was that possible?

He awoke to darkness. There was a cold sweet taste in his mouth, as if all of Connie were now part of the tongue's pointillist arcana. His wife Mira's arm lay across his naked chest, her fingers at the base of his throat.

She was snoring. Thomas readjusted her arm. He clicked softly and gestured: a clock's display materialized: 5.30 a.m. EST. After a few seconds, the display disappeared. Which meant, he calculated reflexively, that it would be about 9.30 p.m. on Meditation 17. The artificial island in the South Pacific seemed impossibly far away.

He lay quietly, listening to the gentle rhythm of Mira's snores; they bound him to this world, night after night. He placed his palm over Mira's small hand and turned his head to gaze at her.

How peaceful she looked. She'd gestured up her usual sleep set: 65% delta/35% theta, layered NREM.

'That's a proto-sensorium,' he'd teased, when she'd finally decided to get the reticular implant. 'Next you'll be getting nictitating membranes, synaesthesia implants, and the rest of the phenomenology.'

'No, it isn't! And I won't. The implant is basically an embedded sleeping pill. It's nothing like a sensorium.'

Like most mainlanders, she hated sensoriums, those

fabulous by-products of late-twenty-first-century phenomenology. Partly it was the strangeness of a device that could tweak qualia, transmogrify perceptions, and turn brains into devices. But it was more than the fact that it was a hermeneutic device, designed to interpret rather than slavishly obey. Phenomenology was no longer the harmless quarrel of bilious German philosophers; it was now a young desert God that effected miracles like the sensorium and divided the world into the Chosen and the Obsolete.

Thomas needed to pee. As he sat up, Mira's arm slid off his chest. She mumbled something and snuggled deeper into the silk. Later, he padded about the house. He checked up on Kristen; his three-year-old's face was a pigtailed moon. He stroked her hair very gently with a crooked finger and resisted the impulse to kiss her. Today would be a busy one for her. It would be her first day at school; she'd already laid out her clothes, and her new knapsack bulged with must-haves.

He circled the kitchen; its stone tiles were deliciously cold under his bare feet. Then the floor began to warm as it sensed him. His motion also woke up the serfbot and he had to gesture it back to quietude. Thomas made a sandwich using the smelly Bierkase that Mira's parents had sent from Germany. Carrying the sandwich on a plate, he went into the living room with its mix of Kandinsky, earth tones, and Jamaican furniture. Mira's presence was everywhere: scattered anime flexscripts, kicked-off shoes, books, tasselled lemon-yellow silk scarf. Kristen's toys had crawled into a corner and arranged themselves into regimented rows; the net effect was a highlighting of the general disorder. Still, as long as the space was a place, and the place was a home, Thomas didn't care what the space contained. He sat down and reached for the plate.

It's a pretty good life, he thought, staring at nothing in particular as he munched on the smelly cheese sandwich.

Thomas wondered if he should kill himself.

Hector, Tommy, Prudence, Connie and Raphael. The posse was at play. Tommy had Prudence's arms pinned down, and Hector was tickling her taut white stomach.

Raphael was strolling his zootar; its melancholy whale-like timbre was an odd accompaniment to Prudence's laugh-screams.

Prudence's delight/fear/anticipation had her aura roiling in a chaos of violet, black and deep peacock greens. Because she was aroused, there were also rapidly deepening shades of red.

'Stop-ogod-no-stop-stopitstop.' Prudence squirmed and thrashed, her bare legs firmly locked around Connie's ample waist. Connie, who was lost in scoping out the newscape, absent-mindedly tickled her feet, oblivious to Prudence's heightened squeals.

'Listen to this,' said Connie. 'Meditation 17 has just been made a special administrative region of the United States. The first ever SAR! That's huge! We're on our way to full autonomy, guys.'

Though the content was ignored, Connie's enthusiasm was not wasted. At the moment, Prudence's sensorium was exquisitely sensitive; Connie's intellectual excitement mixed in with the myriad other sensations being transmogrified.

Prudence's aura was beginning to get very red; Hector glanced at Tommy, who shrugged. The whale song got more, well, throbbing, as Raphael chipped away at the subharmonics. They all joined Prudence at the tipping point of her shuddering climax, and for a handbreadth of time, each identity reclaimed itself.

It took a few seconds for a dazed Tommy to notice that his mother, Kyoko, was standing in the doorway. Her graceful face with its faux-Maori tracery was wreathed in an indulgent smile. Prudence sat up, her face flushed and her aura a riot of colours and tastes. Tommy high-fived Hector.

'Under five minutes,' grinned Hector.

'There's always next time,' replied Prudence, nonchalantly adjusting her hair and smoothing her skort.

Kyoko was waiting for them to sort themselves out. When they'd done so, she entered the room, followed by a girl.

'This is Miranda,' said Kyoko. 'Her parents, Fred and Jennifer, are my friends. They're here for a couple of months; we're collaborating on an ethnology project. We're looking at communication practices on Meditation 17. Anyway, Miranda's never been on an artificial island before, so it's all very new and strange for her. I don't want her to get lonely.'

The posse stared at the entity called Miranda. She didn't look very lonely. Truth was, they could pick up nothing from her. What you saw was what you got.

'Hi, everyone,' said Miranda with a wave of her hand. A pair of dimples punctuated her confident smile.

Tommy switched to sotto-voce and addressed his mother.

<Tommy: I like her.>

<Kyoko: That's obvious, kiddo.>

'So you guys got names or what?' asked Miranda.

They all looked at her. Kyoko broke the silence.

'Oh! Sorry. Our sensoriums make introductions a bit redundant. We all walk around with name tags, so to speak.'

She introduced the posse. Tommy watched Miranda's dimpled smile with increasing fascination.

'Well,' said Kyoko with that bright smile unique to mothers. 'Now that you've all been introduced, I'll get back to Fred and Jennifer. Miranda, if you need anything just ask me or Tommy. Or anyone else, for that matter. We're all one here.'

Miranda smiled. Kyoko squeezed her shoulder and left. The room was quiet for a few seconds, then Raphael started up his instrument; across the island, other players entered the game and the winds evoked by the shifting gamescape rippled over the music. Playing the zootar was not unlike flying a kite: tug, flutter, drop and rise.

Prudence leaned against Hector, and together they inspected Miranda, who stared right back at them. Tommy walked over to her.

'Did Kyoko give you a tour of the island?' he asked.

<Connie: Ask her if she's ever been to Egypt, Tommy. Ask her if she's seen the Sphinx. Please.>

Connie's sotto-voce whisper was light as a snowflake. She had the oddest concerns, thought Tommy.

<Tommy: Later, Connie. Why not ask her yourself?>

But Connie was too shy. Miranda was saying something.

'Kyoko told us about John Donne and his seventeenth meditation. No man is an island, and all that. I didn't know the island was named after his sermon. That's pretty cool. Is that why it's shaped like a cross? The island is huge!'

'Yes, it's the biggest,' agreed Tommy.

<Hector: C'mon Tommy, be realistic. Raphael's the champ in that department.>

<Raphael: It's a gift and a curse.>

<Prudence: Arise, Sir Lancelot, and serve your queen.>

<Connie: Comparisons are odious, like our Donne said.>

'It's tough to take it in all at once,' said Miranda, quite innocently.

<Prudence: Sure is, princess.>

Hector laughed.

'What's so funny?' asked Miranda, staring at them.

Tommy realized that they all had grins on their faces. Miranda was probably unaware that the room was filled with sub-vocalized chatter. Without a sensorium, she couldn't sotto-voce, mind-direct machinery, or transmogrify sensory data. The jerry-rigged, Rube Goldberg – brain that Nature had evolved over aeons of trial and error was all that she had. Nothing she felt or sensed could truly be shared, other than through thin little streams of colourless words. He pitied her.

'Just a private joke, Miranda,' explained Tommy. 'I'd be glad to show you around. Of course, without a sensorium some things will be inexplicable. Like some of our artwork. But there's still lots to see. How about tomorrow?'

Prudence sniffed the air.

<Prudence: Aww, our Tommy's in love.>

<Hector: Never mind all that. Guys, we're setting up a hunt this weekend. You're all in, right?>

<Prudence: 'course I'm in. What's the stim?>

'Miranda?' Someone was shouting in the corridor. 'Miranda?'

'I'm here, Father.'

She turned to them, but they'd already learned via their sensoriums that it was her father, Hiram Mather. Her enthusiasm waned in the face of their obvious indifference.

<Connie: I wonder if he's a descendant of Cotton Mather.>

<Prudence (yawning): Who cares? They're all deadheads.>

'Wear something light, Miranda,' Tommy warned. 'It gets pretty hot out here.'

<Prudence: Yes, do wear nothing, dahling. So much more convenient.>

Hector laughed.

'Mira,' said Miranda, rewarding Tommy with more dimples. 'And I will.'

Before leaving, she gave Prudence and Hector a hard glance, with a tentative half-smile for Connie. The posse noted the spike in Tommy's aura, the surge in the sex hormones and other bodily betrayals, with amusement. On Meditation 17, there were very few secrets, and physical attraction was the worst-kept secret of all. If Tommy had a hard-on for deadheads, then so be it. They could always hook in and voyeur if they wanted to; a posse shared everything.

'So what about the hunt, guys?' demanded Hector. 'I've already got forty signups for the archipelago. Tommy?'

Archipelagos were known by a variety of names. Pelago. Sync. Hunt. Mindfuck. They were the latest rage. An illegal rage. Even on Meditation 17. The idea was to get a group of people to hook up their sensoriums in a certain way and then use a data feed – the 'stim' – to trigger a synchronization of minds; a firefly swarm as it were, of minds all blinking, signalling, and responding in unison to a strong emotional stimulus. An archipelago was a sort of mob-on-demand, a way to experience events without restraint. Therein lay the danger. An archipelago put an enormous stress on neural systems. Which, of course, made it really attractive.

'Like I said, I'm in,' said Prudence. 'But what's the stim?'

'If it's a car crash, count me out,' said Connie. 'That stuff makes me sick for days.'

'Why can't we do something musical? We never do anything *I* want,' Raphael complained.

Prudence put her arms around Raphael and whispered something in his ear.

'This is top-grade stuff,' said Hector. 'The stim's a video feed from 1997: Tank Abbot versus Vitor Belfort. Fifty-three minutes of bare-knuckled, no-holds-barred bruisin' mayhem. It's raw, like beef.'

Tommy whistled. The extreme sport stims were the best. 'Count me in.'

'Yeah!' cried Prudence and, leaning forward, kissed him on the mouth. She bit his lip. It was her thing these days and Tommy wished she'd stop doing it. Prudence frowned.

'Fine, then,' she said and returned to Hector's side.

Raphael and Connie's participation was taken for granted.

The posse began to debate whether it would make any difference that the island was now a special administrative region of the United States.

Tommy drifted off in the middle of it all. He wondered whether Miranda's dimples were gene-tweaked or natural. He had his sensorium replay her voice several times: *I'm heyah, Father. I'm heyah. Heyah.*

Probably from Boston, his sensorium concluded, after a thorough analysis of the Formant spaces. But it wanted more data.

So did Tommy.

~~~

'What's wrong with Thomas?' demanded Mira, staring at him.

She had paused in the midst of rummaging through her knapsack: sunblock, notebook, pen, a hat, a couple of apples, a bag of dates, three bottles of water, a spare shirt and shorts. The girl was nothing if not prepared. A thin chain of freckles stretched from her face and across her shoulders before disappearing between her breasts.

He had given her a tour of the cruciform island, shown her the cables that tethered the artificial island to the sea floor, and then sprung the surprise on her: the underside of the island had been commandeered by the sea into a coral reef. Her oohs and aahs had been very gratifying. She'd been most impressed by the ancient Pelamis generator farm that powered the island. Connie kept him fed with details. Each tethered, semi-submerged, 500-foot-long generator was made up of cylindrical livematter sections linked together by hinged joints. On the whole, each generator looked a lot like a long thin snake, flexing sinuously as it sucked the energy from the waves. Mira got obsessed with the livematter. Why do you call it that? Is it artificial life if it can't reproduce? It eats krill, doesn't it? Does it have rights? Can it fall sick? It was like explaining how a matchstick worked.

They were now at the northernmost tip of the island, on a little abandoned platform that had once been a helipad. It was late in the day, and things were cooling off. Around them, as far as the eye could see, lay the Pacific Ocean, looking like something a child might draw.

They were sitting bare shoulder to bare shoulder with only the Planck Length as chaperone. Every touch sent a wet little tongue down Tommy's spine.

'My posse likes to call me Tommy, that's all.'

'Well, I think Tommy is a child's name. Would you mind if I called you Thomas?'

She sounded quite definite. What's in a name, thought Tommy/Thomas. 'Sure, I don't care.'

'You keep drifting off,' she commented, looking at him with a strangely intent expression. He couldn't decipher the meaning of half her expressions. 'Are they eavesdropping?'

'Who? The posse? No.'

That wasn't the whole truth. Connie was listening in. He nictitated and located the others. Hector was busy setting up the hunt, Prudence was doing some classwork, and Raphael was fast asleep. He should have left them alone; Hector and Prudence began to sample his qualia.

'Ooh, that eye thing is so creepy,' Mira shuddered. 'You look like a lizard when you do that.'

He felt embarrassed. 'Well, you should give it a try before you knock it. That's the trouble with mainlanders; bunch of quakebottoms. They even exiled our founders rather than try something new.'

'You're not exiles!'

'Why not?'

'Do you want to know what Brooke-Rose said about exiles?'

<Connie: Say yes.>

<Prudence: No.>

'Yeah, I guess,' said Tommy, wondering who Brooke-Rose was.

'She said that exiles are people who aren't somewhere else. You guys don't want to be anywhere else. Besides, you're on an isle, so how can you be ex-isled? Apple?'

She held out an apple and a smile. He wanted to kiss her. He ached to kiss her. But without a sensorium, it was impossible to know what she would think of the idea.

'Can you read each other's thoughts?' she asked.

He sighed. 'No. We're not telepathic. We can access each other's qualia but not each other's interpretations. You get impressions – emotions are very difficult to hide, but thoughts, well, it's all mixed up, isn't it? After a while, it's like living in many brains. You're expanded...'

'Like a hive mind?'

'No, nothing like a group mind. There's no such thing. We have strong individualities, and we don't necessarily share everything.'

'My father says sensoriums have made you all into a bunch of narcissistic voyeurs.'

'Oh really? Well, your father's wrong. You can't be a voyeur if someone lets you look.'

'Yes, you can; it's the need to look that matters. Jeffrey Reiman said that without privacy there cannot be any sense of personhood. And you need other people to affirm your personhood. They do that by respecting your privacy.'

<Prudence: Jeez, what an intolerable smarty-pants.>

'Who's Jeffrey Reiman?'

'An early-twenty-first-century philosopher. I've read all the greats. I'm going to be a philosopher one day. Do you want to know what Sartre thought about intimacy?'

'No. Who cares? We have plenty of privacy. We share experiences, not secrets. And I have plenty of secrets.'

He tried to think of one, but couldn't, and that pissed him off even more. Goddamn deadheads. Prudence was right.

Mira was looking at him with that same intent expression. A curious half-smile played about her face.

'Would you like a secret, Thomas? Just yours?'

<Hector: Looks like she's randy, Tommy. She's oozing andro.>

<Prudence: What do you see in the titless wonder?>

<Connie: Leave them alone. Ask her if she's read Donne's 'Exstasie', Tommy.>

'Are you angry with me, Thomas?' Mira asked him, very solicitously. 'Really very angry?'

But they were too close; too close for questions, too close for clocks, and too close to prevent the clumsy entanglement of arms, tongues and wetness. The sensory strangeness of her was so overwhelming that he had to pull away.

<Hector: Holy shit! Did you guys get that?>

<Prudence: Really? I felt nothing. Connie, you?>

<Connie: Kiss her again, Tommy.>

He shook his head. He was in too many places. Mira put her arm around him. He touched her face, caressing her dimples. It really was a perfect day.

～

Tommy died and was revived and then he died again. He died once for every jerking body trapped in the archipelago. He died so many times that his brain stopped trying to be one. Visions:
  – Connie sprawled on the floor. Blood-filled mouth.
  – Raphael's screams piped through the zootar.
  – Prudence ripping the skullcap off Hector's head.
  – Lavender sky.

Then Tommy slipped into a coma as his super-stimulated brain tried to heal itself. It was a million-year-old technology after all, and survivors excel in surviving mistakes.

He woke to a gentle click-clink sound; he didn't realize that it was the sound of knitting needles. He reached out and there was – nothing. Panic. He reached out to the blank-faced clock. Queried it. Nothing.

'Mom,' he croaked. He didn't recognize the woman who rushed to his side.

～

The archipelago had failed because the stim had been infected with a Trojan, disguised as a simple booster utility. Boosters tweaked the emotional highs, flattened lows, and in general, acted as Helpful Hannahs. Just about when Belfort delivered the final bone-shattering blow, Hannah had shed her disguise and done what she'd been really designed to do: scramble brains, overload neuralware, wreak havoc.

The medics reconstructed Tommy, but slowly. He would never again have a sensorium, never again be part of any posse, never again be a participatory citizen of Meditation 17 in any meaningful sense. His reticular nets had also been damaged; his sleep would be that of dolphins, half-awake, half-asleep, suspended in the deep blue sea. As for dreams, well, one could always hope. It was, the medics said repeatedly, a miracle they'd been able to salvage this much at all.

Hector had escaped without a scratch; Prudence had been badly injured but was expected to make a complete recovery. Raphael had died. Connie had died.

His mother had been forced to drop everything and rush to his bedside. Kyoko's posse had tried to help out in the beginning, but their blank expressionless faces and private sotto-voce conversations made him very uncomfortable. Finally, he told Kyoko that he'd rather be left alone than in their care.

'They love you, you know,' Kyoko had said, very hurt. 'They're very worried about you.'

She must have told them something, for he was left alone after that. The worst part was that she never yelled at him, never gave him hell for his stupidity, never blamed him for wrecking his life. And hers. His medical treatment would be paid out of her life-extension fund. The coins of her life. It was a wretched thought and it tormented him. He cried a lot. He couldn't help it. He would be sitting around, in perfect control of himself, and then it would start to rain. It was disgusting, alarming, and very comforting.

One day, Hector came to see him, accompanied by an armed guard. They stared at each other, Hector reaching out with his sensorium as if he'd rewire Tommy's brain through sheer force of will. The guard, moved to compassion (he had a son of his own), conferred with Kyoko and Hector's guardian. They were granted the mercy of one night. Hector had come to give comfort but ended up seeking it.

'It's my fault,' said Hector, his face eerily calm. 'I got the posse involved. The data feed was infected. I should have been more thorough.'

Hector sounded inconsolable even if he didn't look it. With the ability of Meditation 17's residents to grok emotions directly, facial expressions were becoming highly stylized, muted and unnecessary.

He placed his fingers on Hector's face, scrunching it to make the mask reflect the inner grief. The grasp became a futile, incomplete embrace; two lines cannot, after all, achieve a triangle's enclosure. They leaned against each other.

'I've decided to leave,' said Tommy. 'I don't belong here any more.'

'Leave! Why? They'll find a cure. They always do. You can't leave the posse. We'll manage. We must. How can you leave when you're part of me? Part of Prude?'

'There's no posse any more, Hector. Only the memory of one.'

They argued, but guilt and despair have no grounds for compromise.

Whether Kyoko had asked for Miranda's help or she had offered it on her own, Tommy would never know. But one day, she was simply there. She had great faith in books – he was re-learning to read – and when he tired of everything, she would read to him. If his attention wandered away from the strange and difficult books she picked (London, Hugo, Camus), it could always be found focusing on the curve of that smile, the occasional caress and the consoling armature of secrets.

They were parked just outside the hedgerow of the Montessori school, or as the Montessorians called it, Casa dei Bambini. The car used the halt to retrieve a scoopful of corn kernels and snarf it down. A few seconds later, it belched, startling its unhappy clients: Mira, Thomas and a scowling, recalcitrant Kristen.

'We talked about this, Kristen. Remember?' said Mira, almost as if she were trying to reassure herself.

Kristen had a death clasp on the arms of her seat, preventing it from opening out. She shook her head and looked to her father for support. He opened the door.

'Might as well get it over with, honey,' he advised.

The seat took advantage of the distraction to reconfigure itself. Thomas offered his hand, and Kristen reluctantly got out. Father, mother and child gazed at the scene in front of them.

The school was not an unattractive place. It wouldn't have been easy to tell it was a school; it looked more like a series of thatched cottages. There were dozens of children playing in the yard. A few adults were scattered among them, helping a kid here, settling a quarrel there. There was an understated aesthetic to the scene, something very warm, mindful, and yet quite unsentimental.

'There's Martha,' said Mira.

A gaunt, serious-looking woman had emerged through the slatted wooden gate and was coming towards them. She was accompanied by a child.

'Thomas! Miranda! So good to see you.' Martha kneeled to Kristen's level. 'And how are you, Kristen?'

Kristen stuffed her hands into her pockets, but granted a small nod. They'd already been introduced. It was the school's policy to have a teacher visit the child at home; supposedly, it brought the teacher inside the circle of trust. Mira had been captivated by the school's thoughtfulness. Thomas had figured it was best not to remind her that Bronte's Brocklehurst and Dickens's Squeers had also visited their charges in their homes.

'Kristen, this is Bharati,' said Martha with an I-want-you-to-be-friends smile. 'She'll show you around. It's your first day and so things will be a little strange. But there is nothing to be afraid of. All of us have had our first days, so we know what it's like, okay?'

Kristen looked down at the ground. 'I want to go home,' she said in a low voice.

Thomas sighed. He glanced at Mira; her panicked expression seemed to indicate that she was ready to acquiesce. How strange, he thought. He had expected her to be the tough one. She'd been the one who'd done the research, she'd been the one who'd tried to tempt Kristen with the wonders of school, and she'd been the one who'd decided against homeschooling, or even work-schooling.

'Social birth, Thomas,' she'd said, very firmly. 'Kristen needs to cut the cord at some point. Do you want to know what Vygotsky said?'

But now Mira was a tearful mess of indulgence that no amount of theory or Martha's thorough prep could contain. Thomas bent down and gently placed Kristen's fingers around the endearingly small knapsack.

He hadn't noticed it before: against the blue background of the knapsack, a school of dolphins cavorted, improbably happy. The tickle of an unbidden memory. Beloved faces trapped in grief's amber. School, play, dolphins, islands: it had all been so very long ago.

'It's not a choice, honey. It's just the way it has to be. It won't be easy for you, but it's not impossible either. And one day, it'll even be fun.'

'Why can't I study at home?'

'Because we have to do other things. Because you need to be around other children. We can't teach you everything. Like Mommy explained last night, okay? You'll make lots of new friends.'

'No, I won't,' said Kristen.

'I dunno,' muttered Mira. 'Maybe it is a bit premature.'

He glared at his wife. Thanks, honey. Great help.

Bharati came over. 'I'll be your friend, Kristen. Come on.'

'Can't Mommy stay with me? Just for today?' asked Kristen, piteously.

Mira looked at Martha. *Yes, can't I?* Thomas shook his head.

'No, Kristen. Mommy has to go to work. So do I. This, you'll have to do by yourself. But that doesn't mean you have to do it alone. Martha will help you. Bharati will help you. You'll make lots of new friends, have lots of fun, learn lots of new things. Trust me on this, okay?'

He hadn't thought it would be this hard. Kristen's shoulders drooped, but she nodded. Something shifted in his chest as if a restless weight were trying to find a more comfortable resting place.

Kristen reluctantly followed Bharati through the gate. Just before entering, she turned and gave them a forlorn wave. He heard Mira choking back something. Martha had a very pleased look; she beamed at Thomas.

'Very sensible, Thomas. Independence precedes freedom, as Maria Montessori said. Kristen will be fine. We'll keep a close eye on her, I promise.'

Inside the car, Mira pressed a napkin to her eyes. He grinned at her and caressed her cheek.

'Not a word,' she threatened, in a waterlogged voice. 'Oh my God, Thomas, she's so small and so damn brave. Did you see her marching off?'

'More like a condemned plank-walker,' said Thomas.

'True,' said Mira, with a sigh and a smile. 'But there was courage too.'

He gestured, and the car, after stuffing down a last scoop, began to move. Mira's face had acquired a faraway expression.

'Do you still—'

'—miss the posse?' he asked.

'Yeah. Do you miss the closeness? The variety?'

'Variety? Why do mainlanders always focus on the sex?'

'Who's talking about sex? And who are you to call me a mainlander?'

'No,' he said. 'I don't miss it.'

'Liar.'

'Sure.'

'The thought of Prudence slithering all over you used to give me the creeps,' she admitted.

'So don't think about it.'

Sense, memory: the moist enclosure of Prude's kiss, the taste of those needing lips, the nip of that bite.

They glanced at each other. He wondered whether he should tell her.

'Just tell me, Thomas,' she said.

He hesitated. 'I had a dream last night.'

For a second, she didn't quite register his words, but then he had her full attention. An exuberance of smiles, dimples and bright-eyed excitement. She punched him on the shoulder.

'Oh my God! Finally! That's major! Why didn't you tell me this morning? You secretive bastard! You really are something, you know that? All this time and not a peep. I knew your brain would figure it out. I knew it! It took twenty years, but that's Nature for you: slow and steady. Okay, we need to tell Doctor—'

'Relax, honey,' he interrupted. The ancient superstition against premature celebration refused to let him join in her excitement. 'It could be a fluke. A one-time thing. Let's see if it happens a few more times before calling in the quacks.'

'Yeah, I guess you're right. But still! How about a small smile, Thomas? Just a tiny one? Let's take a chance.'

He smiled at her, and they both laughed.

She looked at him searchingly. 'You know, at first I thought you were going to say something else entirely.'

He had been. I sometimes think of killing myself, he had been on the verge of saying. But he hadn't. He feared it might unravel more than mere secrets.

She leaned over to kiss him. 'At last,' she whispered, 'the return of the exile. You are where you should be. Welcome to the land of dreamers.' She looked very happy, even teary.

'It'll be all right,' he thought, willing himself to believe.

'We'll be all right.' She sounded confident.

Farewell, beloved Prudence, thought Thomas. May you find the peace that your kisses sought.

Farewell, beloved Hector, brother and protector.

Farewell, beloved Raphael. The whales sing your songs.

Farewell, beloved Constance, memory, mother, Sophia. I will reclaim you all in my dreams.

He was suspended in the golden moment: the belching car, the love of a good woman, the memory of his daughter's wave, the indifferent sky, the one archipelago, the one life lived.

14

HOW NOT TO TELL THE RAMAYANA

> Kabīr dreams at night,
> His heart seems to bifurcate:
> Two people when he's asleep,
> Just one when awake.[1]

It is an old axiom of Indian bus seating that where there is space for one fundament, there surely must be space for two. The same is true of stories. One story makes space for another. We have no record of when the first story was told and who told it but, doubtless, no sooner had Ug finished the tale – the very first story by the very first storyteller – the very first critic must also have been invented. Why on earth, the critic will ask, couldn't you have just stuck with the facts! Why didn't the lovers meet

---

[1] Tivari, Paras Nath. *Kabīr Granthavali*. Chapter 15, couplet 47, Prayag, New Delhi, 1961, p. 499. The couplet reads: *Kabīr supinain rainni ke, pḍā kalejai chhek // jau soūḥ tāu doi jnāṃ, jau jāgū tāu ek*. I am indebted to Imran Asif Memon for translating the couplet and bringing it to my attention.

sooner? The song sequence broke the realist ambience, it really did. Also, what was with that totally unnecessary mammoth chase? So on and so forth. Ug, or someone less incompetent than Ug, will simply have to retell the story.

This is especially true of Vālmīki's Rāmāyaṇa. Vālmīki, credited as the Ādikavi or first poet, would have understood Ug's situation. The innumerable retellings of the Rāmāyaṇa suggest that to savour the story is to be seized with the desire to retell it. A.K. Ramanujan's celebrated essay *Three Hundred Rāmāyaṇas*[2] drew attention to the astonishing variety, but Ramanujan, who drew his estimate from Bulcke's survey,[3] was careful to stress in a footnote that the number was likely to be much higher:

> When I mentioned Bulcke's count of three hundred Rāmāyaṇas to a Kannada scholar, he mentioned he had recently counted over a thousand in Kannada alone; a Telugu scholar also mentioned a thousand in Telugu. So the title of this paper is not to be taken literally.

Not only does all this raise the usual problem of finding a unity in all this diversity, there isn't much of a unity in unity either. It is wise to remember Ramanujan's advice and take titles as invitations to deconstruct. 'Vālmīki's Rāmāyaṇa' is really a term scholars apply to a collection of recensions and not to any original authoritative master text. The Vālmīki Rāmāyaṇa isn't the Rāmāyaṇa *by* Vālmīki. It is the Rāmāyaṇa *of* Vālmīki. The

---

[2] Ramanujan, A.K. *The Collected Essays of A.K. Ramanujan*. Edited by Vinay Dharwadker and Stuart Blackburn, Oxford University Press, 1999.

[3] Bulcke, Camille. *Rāmkathā: Utpatti aur Vikās*. Prayag, New Delhi, 1950.

recensions, collected from all corners of India, differ in the total number of verses, differ in the sequence of events, differ in their styles, and differ in popularity. Any pair of recensions have some verses in common and there is a core set of verses common to all, but this overlapping similitude isn't sufficient to determine *the* Vālmīki Rāmāyaṇa. The attempt to establish a canonical Rāmāyaṇa version, as the Baroda Critical Edition project tried to do, is perhaps akin to chopping down a banyan tree so as to preserve a single vine. The tradition of 'the' Rāmāyaṇa is to depart from the tradition.

What is 'this' tradition? Prince Rāma, married to the Princess Sītā, is the eldest son of King Daśaratha, who has three wives. His youngest wife, Kaikeyī, wishing her son to inherit the throne in place of Rāma, invokes an old boon King Daśaratha had given her, and has Rāma banished to the forest for fourteen years. Sītā would've been left behind at the palace, but she plays a game of dice with her husband Rāma and, winning each of the three throws, secures complete dominion over him, including the right to accompany him in his exile. Accompanied by Lakṣmaṇa, Rāma's devoted younger brother, the couple are reasonably happy in their exile. However, Sītā is kidnapped by Rāvaṇa, king of Lanka. After a great battle, Rāma defeats Rāvaṇa. Once again, there is the question of what to do with Sītā. She has after all been in intimate proximity with another man. Once again, Sītā challenges Rāma to a dice game, and once again she wins all three throws of the dice. With that victory, the couple are united forever and all is well that ends well. This is the tradition.

There is considerable flexibility in the point of departure.

For example, in the *Daśaratha Jataka*, one of the many birth stories of the Buddha, King Daśaratha (Suddhōdhana) has three sons, Rāma (Buddha), Lakṣmaṇa and Bharata (Ānanda), and one daughter, Sitā (Yaśodharā). The *Daśaratha Jataka* makes no mention of Rāvaṇa, Lanka or the abduction of Sitā. Since the Buddha has no immortal antagonist and the story is propounding the impermanence of the material world, it chose to cast Rāma and Sitā as brother and sister (in that life) and do away with Rāvaṇa, Lanka and the abduction.

Are there limits to such transformations? Perhaps a story can be transformed only so much without losing its essence. Can we determine how *not* to tell the Rāmāyaṇa? For example, Velcheru Narayana Rao argued that a version with an unchaste Sitā would cease to be an interpretation of the Rāmāyaṇa and become a new story which merely happened to share some names.[4] Similarly, a Rāma who doesn't believe in *dharma*, a Lakṣmaṇa who doesn't love his brother, a Rāvaṇa who doesn't desire Sitā, a Hanuman who has no faith in the Rām–Sitā *jodi*: such transformations seem to be fundamentally disruptive in a way that versions which have, say, an independent Sitā or a twenty-first-century venture capitalist as Rāvaṇa, or a sympathetic treatment of Surpanakha, Rāvaṇa's demon sister, are not. It feels quite natural to claim that some transformations conserve the story's essence while others dissipate it. This hypothesis leads, perhaps inevitably, to the structuralist viewpoint where stories are classified and analysed largely independent of their communicative, contextual and interpretative aspects.

---

[4]   Rao, V.N. 'When does Sitā Cease to be Sitā?' *The Rāmāyaṇa Revisited*, edited by Mandrakanta Bose, Oxford University Press, New York, 2004, pp. 219–242.

However, there are powerful arguments against the idea that a story, any story, has an essence. The main difficulty is that the idea of essence makes perception an act of perspective. With the right squint, almost anything can be perceived as essential. For instance in Book 1, Chapter 2 of Vālmīki's Rāmāyaṇa (BCE:[5] *Bālakāṇḍa 2:9–2:14*), Sage Vālmīki decides to bathe in the river Tamasā (near Allahabad). He first goes for a stroll in the sylvan surroundings and comes across a pair of male and female krauncha birds, lost in love-play. While the sage tarries, charmed by the sight, a hunter from the Niṣāda tribe kills the male bird with an arrow. As the female krauncha laments uncontrollably, an intense compassion (*karuṇā*) wells in the sage and he curses the hunter to a life without peace. Vālmīki dubs his spontaneous expression, originating in grief (*śoka*) and expressed in a poetic meter, the *anuṣṭubh*, a *śloka*.

Which is all very well, but consider the question: how essential is it for the story to use krauncha birds? Would a pair of sparrows do? Why not a pair of amorous Great Indian Bustards? Indeed, what exactly is a krauncha? Julia Leslie in her tour de force paper 'A Bird Bereaved: The Identity and Significance of Vālmīki's "kraunca"'[6] considers and dismisses three varieties of curlews, four varieties of egrets, six varieties of herons, seven varieties of storks, two varieties of flamingos, thus narrowing the list of suspects to five kinds of cranes, before

---

[5] Based on Professor John Smith's encoding of the Baroda Critical Edition in Roman unicode. The number '2:9' specifies the *sarga* (chapter 2) and śloka (couplet 9) respectively.

[6] Leslie, Julia. 'A Bird Bereaved: The Identity and Significance of Vālmīki's "kraunca".' *Journal of Indian Philosophy*, vol. 26, no. 5, 1998, pp. 455–487.

finally and conclusively establishing the krauncha as the Indian Sarus crane (*Grus antigone antigone*).

Does it really matter? As the title of Leslie's paper indicates, she thinks it does. I was convinced by her arguments, so it now also matters a great deal to me. She cites J. Masson, who pointed out that Vālmīki's curse, the śloka that marks the transformation of a sage into a poet, has had more Indian commentaries than any other verse in the Rāmāyaṇa. The scene's aesthetics mattered enough for the great ninth-century rhetorician Ānandavardhana to deliberately change the gender of the murdered bird from male to female in the *Dhvanyālokha*. Clearly, it matters to those for whom such things matter.

It is worth pointing out, therefore, that Vālmīki didn't think it was essential to identify the bird. Indeed, that entire scene, like much of the *Bālakāṇḍa*, was a later interpolation by other poets.

Sometimes an author introduces a seemingly insignificant detail to highlight the realism of the setting. Barthes referred to this as the 'reality effect' and pointed to Flaubert's short story 'Un Coeur Simple' with its barometer:

Under a barometer, an old piano supported a pyramidal heap of boxes and cartons.

The barometer turns out to be an insignificant detail since it invokes no specific set of references relevant for the rest of the story. Why does Flaubert mention a barometer and not, say, a painting? For Barthes, the function of details ('notations') like the barometer is that they simply say: 'we are real'. Such notations could be removed, but to do so would reduce the story's realism. They could be substituted, but to do so would create a different reality.

As for our gut feeling that the Rāmāyaṇa is *not* the same as, say, the nursery rhyme 'Mary Had a Little Lamb' or *Fanny Hill* or 'the' Mahābhārata, let us not underestimate the genius of poets to effect the most marvellous palimpsets. Yigal Bronner in his work on *śleṣa* (embrace) poetry,[7] describes how the twelfth-century poet Kavirāja's *Rāghavapāndavya* managed 'to perform the almost inconceivable task of narrating the Rāmāyaṇa and the Mahābhārata simultaneously...' Is the *Rāghavapāndavya* a version of the Rāmāyaṇa or a version of the Mahābhārata? Or is it neither, 'essentially' a separate story in itself?

What all this shows, the anti-essentialist can say, is that as far as fiction is concerned there is no objective basis for whether a transformation is minor or major. There are only transformations whose consequences we fail to recognize or cannot recognize. A work's essence, if such a thing exists, must be the entire work itself. And in that case why do we need the word 'essence'? Why not just say 'work'?

Has the essentialist been defeated? Not in the least. There is no doubt that objects *can* have an essence. Isn't that the basis of the periodic table? Given a lump of lead and a lump of gold, their atomic numbers provide an objective way to distinguish between the two. Elements have an essence. So why not literary works? For example, suppose a story was about the philosopher's quest to turn lead into gold. No other choice of elements would

---

[7] Bronner, Yigal. *Extreme Poetry: The South Asian Movement of Simultaneous Narration.* Columbia University Press, New York, 2010.

ever have the same historical resonance. Indeed, the essence of the story was the flawed belief of its protagonists that lead and gold didn't have essences.

And so the eternal game continues. However, it is not necessary to choose a side. Forced to a binary, it is wise to resort to hypocrisy, one of the tools in what management theorist James March dubbed[8] 'the technology of foolishness'. It is a virtue to be consistent, and we'll be consistent as regards our convenience. We'll be essentialists when it is convenient, and anti-essentialists when it is convenient.

If we conveniently focus on transformations, then *pace* Ludwig Wittgenstein, what emerges is a family of stories related through various transformations. Some members of the family may be more well known than others, some much admired, some disreputable, some more closely related than others, some right around the corner, some settled in faraway lands, and some hardly recognizable as part of the family. Some versions could share nothing more than similar names but still provide a sense of hello-brother-well-met, as I discovered in a Greyhound trip when a drunken co-passenger cheerfully assumed I was an Irishman because he thought I had said my name was O'Neil.

The moral here is that for a transformation to be a legitimate transformation all that is required is that the Reader[9] recognizes

---

[8] March, James G. 'The Technology of Foolishness', in J.G. March and J.P. Olsen, eds, *Ambiguity and Choice in Organizations*. Universitetsförlaget, Norway, 1976, pp. 69–81.

[9] A catch-all term for anyone who engages aesthetically with an artistic work. Thus book readers, moviegoers, or someone watching a play are all 'Readers'.

it to be one. Other Readers may disagree of course. In literature, as in life, quarrels over legitimacy are quarrels over recognition.

There are three things about the act of recognition worth keeping in mind.

First and foremost, the act of recognition is a hermeneutical act. There is no taking the human being out of the situation.

Second, recognition isn't complicated. We are good at recognizing the objects around us – so good, in fact, we are almost always unaware that we are engaged in countless automatic acts of recognition. When an artistic work succeeds in disrupting the silent, supremely efficient neural machinery of recognition, then the artist's deviation from the norm may be recognized as a sign of creativity. Though this idea is deeply rooted in both the Eastern and Western aesthetic traditions,[10] it is an exaggeration to claim, as (the early) Viktor Shklovsky did, that 'the device of art is the *ostraniene*[11] of things.' Recognizing something as different and recognizing that something needs to be recognized may be two very different processes.

Many, perhaps most, retellings of the Vālmīki Rāmāyaṇa seek to remain recognizable as belonging to the family.

---

[10] On the Western tradition, see: Ginzburg, Carlo. 'Making Things Strange: The Prehistory of a Literary Device'. *Representations*, no. 56, 1996, pp. 8–28. And ever since Abhinavagupta's contemporary Kuntaka's work *Vakrokti Jivita*, the idea of art being deviation (*vakrata*) from the norm has had a central role in classical South Asian aesthetics.

[11] *Ostraniene* is usually translated as 'defamiliarization', 'estrangement', or 'making strange'. Apparently, *ostraniene*, a Shklovskyian neologism, should have been spelled *ostranienne*, and it differs from *otstraniene* which, of course, isn't at all the same thing as *otstranienne*. See: Alexandra Berlina. *Viktor Shklovsky: A Reader*. Bloomsbury Academic, an Imprint of Bloomsbury Publishing Inc., 2017.

Tulsidas's *Rāmcharitamānas* probably wasn't written with the intent of defamiliarizing the original. On the other leg, some retellings of the Rāmāyaṇa *do* intend to be disruptive; they seek to refashion, remake, and renew. In short, they seek not to tell the Rāmāyaṇa. These works count on being seen as new.

To be recognized as new, however, requires that the work not be seen as a replica of the original. There are two ways to achieve this goal. The author can either alter the text (body) or the author can alter the context of the work. Or both, of course.

How do we alter the text of an epic work? One common approach is to use a counterfactual transformation, where the author takes some aspect, some 'fact' in the work, and considers an alternative. What if Rāma's half-brother Bharata, not Lakṣmaṇa, had joined Rāma in his fourteen-year exile? What if Sitā had been pregnant when Rāvaṇa abducted her? What if Rāvaṇa and Rāma decapitated each other in the final battle, at which point the gods intervened, returning both to life, but not before a grief-stricken Sita accidentally swapped their heads?[12]

The counterfactual transformation may produce a story that feels both familiar and unfamiliar. A palimpsest as it were, of the old and the new. When done well, it leaves the Reader in the position of King Dushyánta in *The Recognition of Śakuntala*, perplexed by how he could've not recognized his wife:[13]

---

[12] Mahadevan, Anand. 'Switching Heads and Cultures: Transformation of an Indian Myth by Thomas Mann and Girish Karnad'. *Comparative Literature*, vol. 51, no. 1, 2002, pp. 23–41.

[13] Shulman, David. 'The Arrow and the Poem'. *The New Republic*, 13 August 2008.

Like someone staring at an elephant, who says, 'There is no elephant here,' and then, as it moves away, feels a certain doubt, and later, seeing its footprints, is certain: 'An elephant *has* been here' – such are the subtle workings of my mind.

An alternate approach is to leave the 'facts' of the story alone, but change how events are narrated. A different point of view, or foregrounding of an event previously in the background, or downplaying a character, or changing the pace, and so on. This is especially popular among authors who wish to question the hegemony's narratives. They not only wish to question value systems but, often, the use of fantasy as well. These works embrace naturalism not just as an aesthetic option but also as a political necessity.[14]

This literary turn, this flowering of a 'literature of conscience'[15] as Alok Rai phrased it, is too vast to be summarized here, even when restricted to the subject of the Vālmīki Rāmāyaṇa.[16] But the idea of trying to say the unsaid or the unspeakable can be generalized to develop an interesting class of transformations, namely, context-altering transformations.

The context of a story consists of those aspects of the

---

[14] Patel, Geeta. *Lyrical Moments, Historical Hauntings: On Gender, Colonialism, and Desire in Miraji's Urdu Poetry*. Stanford University Press, California, 2002, pp. 121–128.

[15] Rai, Alok. 'Poetic and Social Justice: Some Reflections on the Premchand-Dalit Controversy.' *Modern Indian Writing in English Translation: A Multilingual Anthology*, edited by Dhananjay Kapse, Worldview Critical Edition, 2016, pp. 259–273.

[16] Richman, Paula, ed. *Questioning Rāmāyaṇas: A South-Asian Tradition*. Oxford University Press, 2003.

story-world that the author need not specify explicitly in the story. A great many propositions – socio-economic, ontological, political, linguistic, material, religious, physical, et cetera – may be taken for granted. The Author and the Reader have an informal contract, so to speak. If we read 'Jack and Jill went up the hill' then we don't attack the author for not clarifying that hills are something one goes 'up' on, nor do we reel in shock when it turns out that hills also have a 'down'. If we're asked how many persons went up the hill, we'll probably hold up two fingers, ignoring the millions of bacteria going for the walk as well. We will unconsciously assume, quite rashly, that Jack and Jill are humans and not, say, Martians on a tourist visa. There's no mention of any wheelchairs, so we'll guess that Jack and Jill have functioning legs, two each, et cetera, et cetera. Even though the story's context(s) neither narrates nor focalizes, it deeply influences the story's construction and reception.

If reading a story may be compared to playing a game, then the context corresponds to the rules of the game.[17] The Author knows the rules. The Reader knows the rules. The Author knows the Reader knows and the Reader knows the Author knows.

In other stories, however, the context(s) is also a part of the story. The separation between text and context doesn't hold any more. Then it becomes like a game which must be played without a knowledge of the rules.[18] If there is joy, then it is in the

---

[17] Engagement with literature might involve conventions rather than rules. See: Wilson, Robert R. 'Rules/Conventions: Three Paradoxes in the Game/Text Analogy'. *South Central Review*, vol. 3, no. 4, 1986, pp. 15–27.

[18] The card game Mao is probably the most well known of such games. There is also the game Calvinball in which the only rule is that 'players cannot play the same way twice'.

lack of decorum. To read such stories, to play such stories, the
Reader has to assume the speculative stance.

Adopting the speculative stance means the Reader accepts
that contexts are a part of the story. To illustrate, consider
Sitā's yellow silk sari, the object d'inspiration for all those
Bollywood song sequences in which the heroine is undergoing
a transformation. In the Vālmīki Rāmāyaṇa, Sitā is adorned in
yellow silk (*pītakauśeyavāsanī*) precisely at such moments –
her wedding, the departure for the forest and, of course, her
abduction by Rāvaṇa:[19]

> And then the king's daughter hued like molten gold, clad in
> a yellow silken cloth, looked exceedingly beautiful like unto
> lightning...

In short, the Vālmīki Rāmāyaṇa is situated in a world in
which silk exists; that is, a world which trades with China.
Personally, I find this strange enough, but imagine reading that
Sitā isn't wearing silk, but polyester. The material context has
changed, but if it isn't taken to be an accidental anachronism,
then it leaves one immediately unsure as to what the rules of
this new world are. Are we dealing with a time-travelling Sitā?
A steampunk Rāmāyaṇa?

However, a Reader familiar with speculative works will
continue to read with the expectation that the text will
eventually provide enough clues to figure things out. Or not.
For a spec-fic enthusiast, this uncertainty, this necessity for the

---

[19] Dutt, Manmatha Nath. *The Rāmāyaṇa*, vol. 3. Deva Press, Calcutta, 1894.

text to be read in a subjunctive mode is part of the charm. This lusory attitude and the desire for (eventual) comprehension constitutes the speculative stance.

Determining how the context needs to be fictionalized is a matter of technique. In a self-reflective work, such as Christine Montalbetti's *Western*, supposedly about two gunslingers approaching each other for a shootout, the story is deferred indefinitely by Shandyesque digressions on the landscape or the ants crawling over a cowboy's boots; in other words, the context is the story. In a surrealist work, such as *Alice in Wonderland*, mundane objects are turned magical. In magic realism, magic is as mundane as butter or gravity. For example, in Marquez's short story *An Old Man with Enormous Wings*, the village is puzzled by their balding lice-infected angel, but only in the same way they would have been puzzled had a tiger or kangaroo strolled by. In a fantasy, magic *is* marvellous, distinct from the mundane. Realist fiction adopts the same stance as fantasy but bans magic altogether. Science-fiction also eschews magic but the context is expanded to include not just the real but also the possible. Science-fiction has evolved a dozen or so specific ways to perform this expansion, producing distinct sub-genres such as steampunk, cyberpunk, transrealist, slipstream, new weird, and so on.

There are many other techniques.[20] For example, since the act of writing fiction is itself part of the context, it too

---

[20] For a pioneering foray into the philosophical grounding for the 'speculative turn' in literature, see: Stefans, Brian K. 'Terrible Engines: A Speculative Turn in Recent Poetry and Fiction'. *Comparative Literature Studies*, vol. 51, no. 1, 2014, pp. 159–183.

can be fictionalized. The moment we begin a story we start to impose patterns on events. Existentialist works, like Camus's *The Stranger*, reject this necessity, producing an unsettling disconnect between actions, causes and reasons. Anti-novels such as Robbe-Grillet's *Jealousy* subvert the bourgeois comforts of the novel: plot, characterization, themes, motifs, and so on.

Vālmīki's Rāmāyaṇa employs some of these techniques, most obviously the fantastic. The Rāmāyaṇa with its talking animals, superhuman humans, all-too-human gods and goddesses, frequent resort to magic and a certain intangible innocence reflects a story-world set in the Treta Yuga. It has little of the Mahābhārata's world-weary cynicism. As an originally dramatic work which only later was given a textual body, the Rāmāyaṇa literalizes the metaphor of the 'writing voice'. The Rāmāyaṇa's predilection for exaggeration, disregard of geography, hagiographic characterizations, heavy-handed use of magic, and childishly violent action scenes makes it near-indistinguishable from the Hollywood superhero genre, but it is also overcast with a tragic sense of the real, reminiscent of hysterical realism. Consequently, a modern Reader often never knows just how seriously to take the Rāmāyaṇa. It is a continual raid on the articulate, so to speak.

But the Vālmīki Rāmāyaṇa is not a work of speculative fiction merely because it plays with fantasy elements; that is, the ontological context. The Rāmāyaṇa's real game is with the metaphysical context. What does it mean for God to possess an attribute or a quality? Say, for instance, honour. Can God gain honour? Lose it? What if God were to incarnate in mortal form, say, as a prince and heir of an ancient and powerful royal dynasty? Is Rāma essentially a God or a man? What does it mean for a God to experience the slings and arrows of fate? What are the essential and non-essential attributes of God? A God incarnated not just as a human being but as a human being represented in words?

The Vālmīki Rāmāyaṇa's essence, one might say with only a modicum of hypocrisy, lies in the posing of these metaphysical questions. They are posed most emphatically in two scenes that have been the source of considerable dissatisfaction for commentators through the ages. Nevertheless, all the available recensions include these two scenes, perhaps in the intuitive understanding that to remove them is to alter the work. I refer, of course, to the two dice game scenes between Rāma and Sitā.

In the Hindu epics, dice games do not take place in an atmosphere of conviviality. One player is usually plotting the complete ruin of the other. But here, the first game occurs when all is well with the happy newlyweds. En route to Ayodhyā from Mithilā after the wedding, Sitā invites Rāma to a game of dice (*dyūta*). Rāma demurs, citing the disapproval of elders, the recommendations of sacred texts, and the game allows *daiva*[21]

---

[21] *Daiva* is often interpreted as fate, but there are important qualifications to this folk/naive interpretation. Fate, the outcome of the causal actions of the gods, may be indistinguishable from chance. For example, Rig Veda 10.116.9 refers to the gods moving like the roll of dice (*ayā iva pari caranti devā*), an interesting analogy in light of Ian Stewart's remark in *Does God Play Dice?* (Penguin UK, 1997) that '...dice are a bad metaphor for chance, but a much better one for deterministic chaos'. Second, just as an electron cannot but be influenced by the electric field it allegedly causes, the gods too are affected by *daiva*. After all, to exist is to be affected by one's existence. See: White, D.G. 'Dogs Die'. *History of Religions*, vol. 28, no. 4, 1989, pp. 283–303.

to cloud men's minds (*daivasammūḍacetāḥ*). The couple tease and banter with each other, but then Rāma agrees to play, saying he can refuse his wife nothing her heart desires. There is a discussion of stakes,[22] and Rāma once again tries to wriggle out of the game, arguing he has nothing that is not already hers. Sitā counters that those who love Rāma never have enough of his time (*samayaṃ*). Rāma smilingly agrees to stake a quarter of his time, Sitā stakes likewise, and the game with its 'win-win' stakes gets under way. Needless to say, Rāma 'loses' the round. Not once. Not twice. Not thrice. He loses four rounds of the game, thus granting his beloved every one of life's moments strung like pearls on a necklace (*jīvasya ekekakshanam sūtre maniganā iva*).

Convivial or not, no game in fiction is ever without plot consequences. So too with this playful lovemaking of Sitā and Rāma. A few chapters later, when Rāma is exiled to the Dandaka forest for 'nine and five years' by his father King Daśaratha, because of a boon the king had granted his second wife Queen Kaikeyī, Sitā states her desire to accompany him in exile. At first, Rāma categorically rejects her request, maintaining that the misfortune is his and his alone to bear. Sitā retorts that as his wife she has an equal claim on his sorrow as well as happiness, on his prosperity as well as adversity (BCE: *Ayodhyākāṇḍa*,

---

[22] Like the Mahābhārata, the Vālmīki Rāmāyaṇa elides over how the game is actually played. Though the details of the game aren't important here, it probably wasn't similar to the north Indian board game *chaupar* or *pachīsi*, so prevalent in the traditional iconographic representations. See: Schaufelberger, Gilles. *Dice Game in Old India – from the Essay of Heinrich Lüders 'Das Würfelspiel im alten Indien (1906)'*. https://goo.gl/Aw1hkf

26:18). Rāma is immune to all her arguments, tears and threats to kill herself. When she reminds him of the dice game, he is compelled to relent. It is an acquiescence the couple would live to regret. But we are told the gods rejoiced (*prashást*) because the chain of events culminating in the slaying of Rāvaṇa had been set in motion.

The second dice game takes place after the final battle between Rāma and Rāvaṇa. Sitā is brought before Rāma in the Mahasabha, the great hall. Rāvaṇa lies dying in an ante-chamber. An attendant keeps him informed of the proceedings.

The poet tells us that Rāma is simultaneously joyous, angry and miserable (BCE: *Yuddhakāṇḍa*, 102:16). However, his self-control is such that the loyalists around him – Hanuman, Sugreeva, Vibhishana, Lakṣmaṇa – detect nothing of this inner struggle, and to them Rāma's face appears pitiless (BCE: *Yuddhakāṇḍa*, 102:32). They may have had their suspicions that something was not quite right.

Earlier, Rāma had sent Hanuman (a) to tell Sitā that the brothers were well and Rāvaṇa had been defeated, and (b) to bring her response. It is a curious instruction. What did Rāma think her response would be? Why not have Hanuman bring Sitā to him immediately? When Hanuman returns with the news that Sitā was longing to meet him and suggests that he 'ought to meet the divine lady', the same divine lady 'for whose sake the war had been fought', it provokes a rush of incipient tears and a sudden thoughtfulness in Rāma (BCE: *Yuddhakāṇḍa*, 102:5). So what does the prince say when Sitā arrives?

The gist of Rāma's speech is that he had regained his honour with great effort, a moral effort because it had been directed towards regaining honour, and that honour would be lost again if he accepted her as his wife, given the suspicions aroused by the circumstances of her capture and long captivity. She was free, he announced, to find refuge elsewhere.

After the stunned assembly digests this decision in silence, Sitā famously asks:[23] 'Is your honour not mine?' She goes on to say that as husband and wife they are two bodies sharing one experiencing self (*jīva*) and there isn't any aspect of Rāma that isn't reflected (*pratibimbit*) in her, nor is there any aspect of her that isn't reflected in him. Just as the self seems to divide into two in a dream but remains always one, only the perception clouded by ignorance (*avidyā*) sees Rāma and Sitā as two. But Rāma only reiterates, almost verbatim, what he has said earlier; Sitā appeals to the assembly; the elders are silent; and a stalemate is reached.

It is at this juncture that Rāvaṇa, mortally wounded but still in full command of his faculties (*īṣānakṛit*), sends a message from the antechamber. He suggests a dice game to settle the matter of honour. If Sitā were to win, she would give up all claims on Rāma's honour and take refuge elsewhere. If Rāma were to win, he would lose a quarter portion of his honour to Sitā. This would leave Rāma with two choices: to live with dishonour, or to accept Sitā and regain what he had lost. There's a third option that Rāvaṇa does not raise: the two could always play another round.

Needless to say, Rāma loses the first round. And the second.

---

[23] *táv mānáṃmāmakāsthi kil.* Sitā's deliberate use of the informal *táv* instead of something more formal like *bhávdīya* is hidden by English's indiscriminate 'your.'

And the third. He has now but a quarter of his honour left. It is clear the misfortune which has so often dogged his path in life is once again proving to be a loyal adversary. And yet Rāma does not quit. No specific insight into his mind or his decision is given, but Vālmīki does comment that 'nothing human beings do in this world is without daiva.'[24] But Rāma is not Yudhisthira or Nala, the gambling royals of the Mahābhārata, with a passion for the dice game. Rāma is the greatest of the upholders of dharma; the epithet *rāmo dharmabhṛtaṃta varah* is reserved for Rāma.

Rāma loses the fourth and final game. We are informed that Rāma is enveloped in the light of a divine fire. The Vālmīki Rāmāyaṇa describes it indirectly, using the fact that *dyūta* and *devā* are both descended from the Sanskrit root *div*, to shine, to be luminous. When a king is stripped of his material wealth, his story may be closed with the presentation of possibilities. But the story of Rāma, stripped of all honour, needs a God to complete the tale. As Lord Agni envelops Lord Rāma, the Lady Sitā, his once and forever wife, throws herself into the fire, into light, into the absence of absence, and the couple are united.

---

[24] *na hy adaivam krtam kim cin narànàm iha vidyate.* The same sentence is found in the Nala–Damayantī episode in the Mahābhārata. See: Shulman, David. 'On Being Human in the Sanskrit Epic: The Riddle of Nala'. *Journal of Indian Philosophy*, vol. 22, no. 1, 1994, pp. 1–29. Also, note that Shulman relates the epic's dice games to *chaupar/pachīsi*. The Nala episode has indubitably borrowed more from the Rāmāyaṇa rather than the other way around. See: Sukthankar, V.S. 'The Nala Episode and the Rāmayāna'. *Critical Studies in the Mahābhārata*. Sukthankar Memorial Edition. Volume 1. Bombay, 1944–1945, pp. 406–415.

It had been mentioned earlier that there are three things about recognition worth keeping in mind. But only two have been specified so far. The irreducible human element was the first. The second discussed how the act of recognition – so often automatic, so often effortless – gets foregrounded only when it fails. The third aspect is about those rare instances when recognition can transform not just our understanding of works but also us. Aristotle referred to such transformations in fictional characters as *anagnorisis*. It marks the moment when ignorance is transformed into knowledge through recognition arising from the events themselves – internally generated, not externally, like lead turning into gold through chemistry, not magic.

But this is an intellectual view of the situation. We recognize not just with our minds but also our bodies. What is the emotional substratum in which recognition flowers? The *Bālakāṇḍa*'s story of how a sage turned into a poet suggests an answer. Sorrow (*śoka*) and compassion (*karuṇā*) generate both the poet and the poem. The poet and the grieving female Sarus bird become one. The sense of an ending and the actual ending become one. Rāma and Sitā know the sorrows of recognition all too well. Why then is there any need for a dice game?

As a narrative technique, the second dice game seems undermotivated. If Sitā's loss of honour is the sticking point in Rāma accepting her, how can a mere dice game restore the missing quality? For Rāma to agree to a dice game is tantamount to an admission he isn't completely sure about the rightness of his decision to reject Sitā. For a woman like Sitā, how is anything other than an unqualified embrace acceptable? Why should

Rāvaṇa, hurdle extraordinaire, suddenly turn helper? Of all the people to accept advice from, Rāvaṇa should surely figure last.

However, the logic of the dice games is the logic of the never-ending dice game between Lord Śiva and his divine consort, Parvati. This story is the subject of the extraordinary sculptures at Elephanta and Ellora. The Goddess approaches Lord Śiva for a game of dice; he accepts; there is teasing, lovers' quarrels, cheating; Lord Śiva loses; the stakes are increased; Lord Śiva loses; eventually, he is divested of all his attributes; and then the cosmos begins to self-destruct. As the world is shrouded in a darkness beyond night, Lord Śiva's eternal assistant Bhṛṅgin opens his mouth in a wordless scream; a scream, we are told, that restores the God, the Goddess, the game of dice and all it entails. Then, the Goddess Parvati approaches Lord Śiva for a game of dice...

Consider the staggering number of unnarrated statements reticulating the story. Gods can know and not know things. Gods can be approached. Gods and goddesses like to play. Gods are distinct from goddesses. They can engage in games of chance that unfold over time. Time and chance have different ontological status from gods and goddesses. So on and so forth. This dense foliage of assumptions prevents us from noticing the extreme difficulties and contradictions inherent in a story, any story, with divine characters.

Given these difficulties, it might seem that linking the logic of the dice games in the Rāmāyaṇa to the logic of the Śiva–Parvati dice games is like deciding to lose a key precisely where there's no streetlight. But the Śiva–Parvati story highlights rather than occludes the Rāmāyaṇa's metaphysical context.

The Rāmāyaṇa can be read as the story of a man who was born with a lot, acquires even more, and just when he seems to be on the verge of having it all, loses everything in bits and pieces. This parallels the trajectory of Lord Śiva who gets distributed into nothingness, one attribute at a time. In both cases, the triggering causal factor is the invitation to a dice game. In both cases, there is a woman involved, and the women embody the material aspect of creation. The Goddess Parvati, the incarnation of Uma or Nature, is reborn as the daughter of Himavat, the Himalayas, and King Janaka finds the newborn Sitā while tilling the soil for a ritual ceremony. In both cases, entering the game entails ensnarement. In Rāma's case, when Sitā wins the first game of dice, he becomes fully entangled in her life. The result is a God committed to all the joys and sorrows of mortal existence. The commitment runs even deeper. God acquires beliefs, opinions, prejudices, and all the other behavioural components of human frailty. Rāma's loss to Sitā is a gain in negative capability. He cannot not be a man.

Lord Śiva's entanglement is more complex because it isn't manifested physically. The metaphysics is too intricate to be fully discussed here, but as Handelman and Shulman summarize:[25]

> The ludic processes at work in these examples begin to reveal
> the epistemological status of the dice game and other contests
> in Indian cosmology... So long as god or other higher order
> beings do not enter the game as players, the game is a part
> of the cosmic whole that is encompassed and controlled

[25] Handelman, Donald, and Shulman, D. *God Inside Out*. Oxford University Press, New York, 1997.

by the latter. The momentum of the game, and its effects on cosmos, drive upward and inward, toward increasing internalization, integration, and holism. When god enters the game, the simulation of the cosmic whole, he is constrained by parameters of its modelling. The momentum of this game, and its effects on the cosmos, now drive downward, toward increasing externalization, alienation, and destruction.

Handelman and Shulman discuss these ideas in the context of the story's depiction in stone panels in the Elephanta and Ellora caves. How a formless entity acquires form and thus the world comes to be is perhaps beyond the capacity of language or art to describe. But one can gesture. The eastern section of Cave 1 has the famous Ardhanārīśvara or the androgyne Śiva, a representation of a God in the process of differentiation. That is, a God who enters the dice game and turns increasingly unaware/uncertain of its Godhood.

In the second dice game, Rāma stakes and loses his honour. But this game isn't just about honour. It is also about what the honour represents. First, the game is about whether he has any stakes left to stake. Sitā's question 'is your honour not mine?' lays claim to all products of her husband's time. Second, Rāma isn't just a man, he is a *kṣatriyḥ*, a member of the warrior caste. Warriors have codes of honour, not codes of profit or codes of service. To take away honour is to diminish a *kṣatriyḥ*, and to take it away completely is to demolish the man. With the loss/transfer of honour in the second game, Rāma ceases to be human. The man who was God is finally awakened from *avidyā* and becomes the God who was a man.

In a sense, the Vālmīki Rāmāyaṇa is an inversion of the Śiva–Parvati tale. Lord Śiva's journey is away from Godhood and towards nothingness. As Handelman and Shulman note:[26]

> The process turns him, as it were, inside out, thereby creating discontinuities in his being, empty spaces, black holes, whereas once – before the game – there was continuous, dense simultaneity of self and the cosmos.

In contrast, Rāma's transformation is the reverse of Lord Śiva's transformation. Rāma enters the dice game as a man and leaves the story a God. Rāma and Sitā start out in a state of difference and by the tale's end are merged into unity. Two become one.

Rāvaṇa's role at the end is also explained as an echo of his role in the Śiva–Parvati tale. Handelman and Shulman describe his role with reference to its depiction in Cave 1 at Elephanta:[27]

> ...directly across from the dice game, as the last panel in the circumambulatory series, we find Rāvana lifting up Mount Kailāsa, where Siva and Pārvatī are sitting together – actually, in some sense driven together by the external threat coming from the demon. The dice game divides the male and female parts of the godhead; Rāvana recombines them.

This 'recombination', courtesy Rāvana, explains why it is also the dying demon king in the Vālmīki Rāmāyaṇa who makes

---

[26] Handelman, Donald, and Shulman, D. *God Inside Out*. Oxford University Press, New York, 1997.

[27] Ibid.

the suggestion that ultimately brings the long-separated couple together. However, since the Rāmāyaṇa is always being told and retold, the dice game between Rāma and Sitā will also never end.

No matter what Boethius claimed, the consolations of philosophy are few and niggardly. The many retellings of the Rāmāyaṇa attest to the Reader's dissatisfaction with its ending. No one feels compelled to retell the *Odyssey*. That's because its ending is perfectly satisfactory. There too we have a man and his wife separated by fate and circumstances. There too we find a spouse determined not to recognize the other. And yet, when Penelope finally rushes into Odysseus's arms, as she explains her doubts, as she begs his forgiveness, as the desire to weep wells in his mighty heart, as he cradles his wife, as the warrior weeps, the poet compares Odysseus to a man who has narrowly escaped shipwreck and then elaborates the simile – but wait, let Homer tell it:[28]

> He wept as he held his lovely wife, whose thoughts were
>   virtuous
> And, as when the land appears welcome to men who are
>   swimming,
> After Poseidon has smashed their strong-built ship on the
>   open water,
> Pounding it with the weight of wind and the heavy seas,
> And only a few escape the grey water landward by swimming,

---

[28] Boitani, Piero. 'Recognition: The Pain and Joy of Compassion', in *Recognition: The Poetics of Narrative*, edited by Philip Kennedy and Marilyn Lawrence. Peter Lang, New York, 2009, pp. 213–226.

With a thick scurf of salt coated upon them,
And gladly they set foot on the shore, escaping the evil;
So welcome was her husband to her as she looked upon him,
And she could not let him go from the embrace of her
      white arms.

Lo and behold, Penelope has become the one who has narrowly escaped shipwreck. Odysseus is Penelope; Penelope is Odysseus. Now, who but a clod could lift his head from the page without first bewetting it with his tears? Who would dare change this telling except to timidly change a comma here or a semicolon there? Why doesn't Vālmīki give the Reader an equally satisfying closure? The dice game seems so, well, arbitrary.

Recall that a story's context is that which isn't narrated because it doesn't need to be narrated. However, the context can also include unthought thoughts. Long habit trains the Reader to suspend disbelief, that is, to not think certain thoughts while reading the story. These thoughts that needn't be thought are also part of the story's metafictional context. Though the Rāmāyaṇa is ostensibly about how its hero awakens to his true nature, an even subtler agenda can be discerned. It pushes the Reader to disbelieve.

An epic disinterested in playing with the metaphysical or metafictional context could conclude the story with updates on Rāma and Sitā's married life, the unexpected rigours of city life, Lakṣmaṇa's problems in finding a good ashram for his kids, and so on. But the Rāmāyaṇa does no such thing. By introducing the dice game, it leaves outcomes to chance. The Reader's imaginative resistance is awakened. What kind of story is this?

One type of Reader could be provoked enough to retell the story. But a more alert Reader might realize that the need for closure, the comforts of plot, the pleasures of revenge, the insistence on justice, the collection of epiphanies are all forms of *avidya*. By denying the Reader these temptations, the sage-turned-poet liberated 'his' characters from Story.

But isn't their tale also the Reader's? The Reader is incarnated into the story and becomes what narratologists call the Implied Reader. The incarnation forgets its true self and savours all the nine *rasas* the work affords. Occasionally, the veil might lift, the underlying reality is revealed, but then the story's *māyā* once again fogs wisdom, and the incarnation once again sinks into *avidya*. The incarnated Reader's journey is also the incarnated hero's journey. So when Rāma is liberated, what happens to the incarnated Reader? Is 'it' denied liberation from Story? Is it doomed to relive the tale in endless incarnations in alternate tellings? No, of course not. It can choose to awaken.

An even more profound question is whether we can also choose to awaken from life, but here the words scatter like dice. For now we will simply close the telling.

15

THE INCONCEIVABLE IDEA
OF THE SUN

I believe in Books. Books is a God with a growing number of temples, aka bookstores, all over the world. In the US alone, according to a recent census, there are some 12,703 bookstores. Of course, compared with the roughly 3,00,000 outlets devoted to Yahweh, Books is strictly a minor deity. Still, minor or not, what's important for believers is that there be a temple within reach. There are about a dozen where I live, so come Saturday, I shower, crack a coconut, and step out for some face time.

It is a ritual carried over from childhood. My late father had been a Books devotee, and just as we inherit our gods, we inherit the rituals too. My father and I used to browse on Sundays rather than Saturdays, and consumed idlis-and-madras-coffee rather than the bagels-and-coffee I now have, and we used to walk to the bookstore rather than drive, but these are minor differences. When I recall the spring in his step, his reckless disregard for what he could afford, and his delight in the rare find (*Solutions to the 1948 Cochin Board Chemistry Exams*), I see the origins of my faith.

Lately, though, I had turned into a miserly parishioner. I still visited the temples, still strolled the aisles, still settled in the smelly and overpadded sofas to sample my finds. But to actually buy a book? God, no! In my last visit to the local megachain, I had sampled G. Willow Wilson's *Alif the Unseen*. The gorgeous cover with its calligraphic nastaliq so redolent of Islamic phantasmagoria filled me with a lust to own the volume. Did I? No. What about Jeff Vandermeer's definitive steampunk anthology? No. Timothy Wilson's *Strangers to Ourselves*? Strangely, no. Surely I had purchased *This Idea Must Die*, an anthology of essays, on ideas that had outlived their usefulness, edited by John Brockman? No. What about K. Sello Duiker's *Thirteen Cents*, winner of the Commonwealth Prize? Thirteen times, no. Good books, even great books: regretfully, no.

In these visits, on my way out, I would stop by the counter, not always but sometimes, and inquire about the availability of Imran Asif Memon's *The Inconceivable Idea of the Sun*. I knew it wouldn't be available, but there was no harm in confirming. I had lost faith in what I knew.

Eventually, I stopped going to bookstores altogether. I found them oppressive.

I hid this development from Sophie. Usually, spouses hide things from one another when they take up something, such as a lover or smoking or diary writing. In contrast, I hid from my wife what I had given up. Still, I couldn't help revealing the new me, as when she Facebook-shared photos of other people's gorgeous libraries. These paradises, complete with hardwood floors, teak bookcases on rollers, cunningly contoured skylights, infinity pools, and acres of expensive-looking books, aroused the worst in me. I'd give a thumbs-up to the post, and then perhaps add a passive-aggressive comment: *that's a lot of firewood :)*

Though I have referred to Sophie as 'my wife', technically she wasn't. We had lived together for several thousand years and people believed we'd done the saath phere or Yes-I-Dos or whatever it was that a Cambodian woman and an Indian guy did when they got hitched. Sophie encouraged the belief for all the right romantic reasons, and I, a non-confrontational scurvy dog, to minimize social awkwardness.

However, there were two situations in which we were regularly reminded of our unofficial status. The first was when we had to file tax returns. We could open joint bank accounts, buy houses jointly, profit from joint investments, and even conjointly adopt a child. But when it came to filing tax returns, Uncle Sam insisted on two separate forms. Both Sophie and I hated forms of all kinds, and the common hatred drew us even closer.

In contrast, the second situation separated us by what we both loved. Sophie had been collecting books long before she met me; I had been collecting books long before I met Sophie. We shared many common interests, and our libraries proved it twice over. We had two copies of *The Godfather*; two copies of Edward Said's *Orientalism*; two copies of Nabokov's lectures on Don Quixote; two copies of Borges's entire oeuvre; two copies of *Emma*; two copies of the works of Shakespeare, Neruda, Yehuda Amichai; two copies of *The Joy of Sex*. Indeed, our tastes in erotica were joyfully complementary, so our dirty books were all about someone tickling someone or the opposite. One copy of a dirty masterpiece in a library indicates a *bel espirit*; two copies of it, a chronic masturbator.

Worse, we were both English professors, which by itself wasn't a problem since English is a house of many mansions, but we were both postcolonialists, and thus all too aware that there is nothing homely about repetition. Repetition, one might say, quoting Deleuze, is a difference without concept. Or, to reference Deleuze referencing Koch's line 'Parallel excursion. O black black black black black', which of these blacks should be kicked out and rendered homeless? In short, to wit, in sum, all things considered, how many copies of Ashis Nandy quarrelling with Homi Bhabha quarrelling with Gayatri Spivak does a household need?

It was clear we had to unite our libraries and unite our Access databases, but just because a course of action is clear doesn't mean it can be executed. Why should my copy be the one asked to leave? Why should Sophie's? We'd both had to scrimp and save for every purchase. For Sophie, already burdened with student loans, a $70 textbook was at least ten hours of menial labour. For me, it was one-tenth the price of a trip home. Our books, sepia-steeped in effort and sacrifice, were precious to us.

In any case, the presence of the multiple copies was irritating because they invoked the absence of the one book I knew existed but couldn't find anywhere. I had searched for Memon's book in *Books in Print*, but it didn't list the volume or the author. Google had no mention of it either. My literary friends had never heard of him. The book had never been reviewed, blogged about,

Instagram'd, Facebooked, or sold in remainder lots. Imran Asif Memon seemed to have left no footprint whatsoever in my world. No interviews, no website. Nothing.

So why the hell was I so certain the book existed? The certainty was so intense, at times I feared I was going mad over Memon's phantom volume.

Sophie had been unhelpfully helpful. When I had first mentioned my quest for the book, she'd whipped out her smartphone and made a note of the title. The bookfiend loves nothing more than a good book hunt and Sophie was a ferret par excellence. Plus, she had that generosity of spirit which gains pleasure from giving it. But one morning, over breakfast, she had to admit failure.

'There's no fucking trace! You *sure* the book exists, Chibi?'

Yes, I was *sure*. She wanted to know why I wanted the book, how I had heard of it, where I had heard of it, and whether I had misheard the title. I'd been hoping she would succeed where I had failed, a hope without much faith but enough of a hope for her failure to make me peevish. I sipped my chai in silence. I wished she would stop calling me 'Chibi'. Japanese term for a short, cute, saucer-eyed manga character. I wasn't a short, cute, saucer-eyed manga character.

'You know you can be sure and still be wrong?' she said, smiling. 'Studies show it's a side effect of having balls.'

She swallowed a couple of Tylenol pills with a swig of orange juice. Another headache. These were bimonthly occurrences. Always a three-day affair.

'Sophie, you've got to stop snarfing pills like candy. I know it's part of being American and all but you're half-Cambodian so you should know better. Pills aren't part of a normal healthy breakfast. Something's off balance and we have to find the source of the problem.'

'Love you too, Chibi. And it's Kampuchea, not Cambodia.' I could tell she had liked the use of 'we'.

'I'm serious. Maybe you're allergic to light.'

'I'm not allergic to light.'

'I'm just saying—'

'I'm not fucking allergic to light. I'm not a vampire. Damn, Chibi, what's with you and light?'

She had the American madness for sun, more sun and still more sun. Any empty space was an invitation to drop clothes, stretch out and soak in some high-quality skin cancer. I on the other hand came from a sun-drenched world and had had enough sun to last me this lifetime and seven more. Unfortunately, my office had been designed by an American architect.

It was a long room with angled roofs, two rectangular windows and two skylights. It was situated over the garage and thus got very hot in the summer and very cold in winter. During the day, the sun's glare made it impossible to work; the walls seemed to dissolve and there was a sense of being suspended in a crystal of light. So I had covered the skylights with thick sheets of cardboard and added a layer of blackout fabric to the window curtains. Even so, the sun was hard to keep out. This was partly because Sophie was hard to keep out. Her arrival, which I relished, also meant the drawing of curtains and opening of windows, which I didn't relish.

The long walls of my rectangular office were bordered with

bookshelves. Books were everywhere. Every line of sight ended in a book. Sitting at my desk, the sight of these books, doubled and tripled copies included, became increasingly oppressive. Oppressive, that is, for me. The wife didn't have any qualms in littering the house with idols of our supreme deity, Books.

At one point, Sophie suggested we select a core subset of volumes and get them scanned. Say, four hundred or so of our most essential books.

I looked into it. A number of companies offered cheap high-quality scanning services, costing a few cents per page. Unfortunately, I also had a conscience, and the whole point of having one is to be troubled by it. The scanning process was destructive in that the book's spine had to be broken and the pages separated before they could be fed into a high-volume scanner. I found it hard to contemplate even stepping on a book, never mind permitting it to be torn apart. Then there was the copyrighting skulduggery. The scanning companies hoped to bypass copyright laws by claiming that a copy wasn't considered a copy as long as the original no longer existed. I doubted this argument would hold either philosophically or in a court of law. In any case, I discovered that the total scanning cost, even at a few cents per page, was unaffordable.

'We'll just have to be more careful in the future then,' said Sophie.

'Said the pregnant mother of fifteen children.'

She smiled. 'We both love Books, so what do you want me to say? We're not the first pair of booksluts to face this problem. We sure as hell ain't gonna be the last. Who wrote that book—'

'Anne Fadiman.'

'Yes, Fadiman. In *Ex Libris* she's got a whole chapter on this stuff. Funny as hell. I'm sure we have the book.'

We had four copies of Fadiman's book. I'd bought one, forgotten I'd bought it, bought another copy. Ditto for Sophie.

'Okay, maybe we could donate a copy to Goodwill or something. But only one.' Sophie jovially reminded me of nineteenth-century bookfiend Richard Herber who had held what was true of mistresses was also true of copies: one for the drawing room, one for private consumption and one for lending out to friends. Three was the ideal number. Ha ha.

'I'm sick and tired of Books!'

Sophie and I stared at each other, shocked. There, I had said it. I immediately regretted the confession, but I had meant it and there was no use pretending I hadn't.

'Ok-ay, where did *that* come from?' said Sophie, finally.

'Look around, Sophie. All these tomes. Always about what is and is and is. Never about what isn't. Don't you think we're being systematically led away from a central truth? And to have all these multiple copies—'

'Oh yeah, absolutely! We need to do some serious weeding.' The baffled expression on her face cleared. 'I didn't know you felt so strongly about it.'

'It's not just about multiple copies.' 'Course she knew. If she had disagreed with me, I would have been less irritated. 'Don't you get the feeling sometimes it's the books that don't exist that will tell us who we are? Don't you sense the oppression of being?'

The baffled expression returned. 'The oppression of Being? What do you mean?'

'Let me ask you this: with all this reading, have you found yourself?'

'Jesus... Are you working on a story? Is this the liveaboard situation all over again?'

That stung. But there was more than a grain of truth to her guess. A year earlier, I had begun writing a novella about a character who had shifted to a life on the sea. I had taken seamanship lessons, obtained a Powerboat certification, gone scuba diving, lived off MRE food packs, managed with two pants and three T-shirts, complained endlessly about being a landlocked professor, craved wind, water, the flutter of a sail, and the screeching of gulls overhead. Once the story was done, however, I had returned to being a landlubber with little protestation.

'You *are* working on a story about stories, aren't you?' said Sophie, eyes narrowed in triumph. 'Yes or no?'

'Let's focus on the real—'

'Yes or no, Chibi. Yes or no?'

'Well, yes, but it's not just about—'

'Oh God. I knew it. What's it about this time? Let me read it.'

'THAT'S NOT WHAT THIS IS ABOUT.'

Silence.

'Ok-ay,' she said, in her most reasonable, most infuriating tone. 'What's it about then?'

'A MAN WHO HAS AN IDIOT FOR A WIFE.'

So we didn't speak to each other for the rest of the day. I wanted to apologize for calling her an idiot, but when I opened my mouth, I thought of the sounds taking the shape of words on a page, and then I became small and hateful again. The next morning was chilly. Sophie left early, without so much as a bye. Just a cold glance and a snippy comment about leaving on a quest to find her Being. How callous was that! Didn't she know I was leaving for a conference in Ithaca later in the day? Of course she did. I hoped I would have a terrible accident. I entertained a black fantasy of the airplane falling out of the sky, and all passengers on board charred and mangled beyond recognition, the authorities coming to Sophie to authorize the release of my dental records. Oh, how she would be sorry then. How she would regret her behaviour. But it would be too late; too damn late.

Of course, by the time I got back from Ithaca, we had put the quarrel behind us. It was all so silly. I'd already called and apologized, but she wouldn't hear of it. From her end, she insisted, it was obvious she had been a naughty girl and a good spanking was to be inflicted on said Kampuchean end. Ha ha.

At the house, the first thing I noticed, other than her smiling face, was that my office seemed far more spacious. Half the bookshelves were empty. It's impossible to describe the incredible sunlight that wafted through the windows of my being. I turned to Sophie.

'I got rid of the doppelgänger books,' she said, beaming. 'Don't worry, I only got rid of my copies.'

She'd got rid of her books! My happiness evaporated.

'But you had stuff written all over your books!' I cried. 'In the margins, backflaps, everywhere. They were a part of you and now they're all gone.' I was quite overcome. 'It's not fair to you.'

'Maybe. But it's fair to us. No more of this mine versus yours bullshit. That's why it was so oppressive, wasn't it? We've been together for twelve years, and you're always telling everyone I'm your fucking wife, but I guess I was holding a tiny bit in reserve in case things went south. I know it's stupid – maybe you do have a stupid wife. Maybe it's the fucked-up hood I grew up in; people around me weren't into long-term shit. But it'll be different now. You're stuck with me forever, Chibi. Don't the shelves look creepy? We're gonna need a lot more books.'

Anything! I was so touched by her gesture, I would have been willing to move into the Library of Congress. I'd never had any doubts about her commitment. She had made a huge sacrifice and I felt so terrible about driving her to it, I also knew I would never again complain about having too many books. In any case, my sense of being oppressed had completely vanished. I was also excited by the pleasant task ahead, of rearranging our library, and with it, my office.

When I removed the books from the shelves and systematically stacked them in precarious piles around the room, it became obvious we still had a lot of books to deal with: books in total. I invested – we invested – in a library management system and an ISBN scanner, and I imported my old Access database – our old database – into it and spent a couple of happy weeks enhancing the records with book cover images, publisher metadata and what not. It took me several weeks to re-stack all the volumes and when I was done, my office finally began to resemble one of those beautiful-library photographs that Sophie no longer forwarded to me. I had got rid of several pieces of furniture, including a loveseat and two comfy but space-eating chairs. I now worked standing up; it was much healthier for the back and I lost a couple of inches around my waist. Best of all, it allowed me to get rid of my work-chair, ergonomically designed to be an eyesore. When it was all done, I called Sophie to come take a look.

'I miss our old clusterfuck,' she said wistfully. 'Where do I sit?'

I pointed to the room's sole remaining chair, a Raj-era easy-chair, or the Bombay Fornicator, as it was called in Goa. Comfortable and cosy.

'Then where will you sit?' asked Sophie.

'In your lap, where else?'

'Yeah, yeah. The room is so cold, so formal, so not us. At least let some more light in. A library should be filled with light.'

'And shadows! Everything in proportion. Sophie, imagine you were seeing this room for the first time. Never mind how it used to be or what we supposedly are or what it needs to have. Just see it as it is, the *fact* of it. What does it say?'

'Get lost, Sophie.'

I gave her the Look.

'Okay, I'll try,' said Sophie. She took my suggestion seriously. Way too seriously. Practically De Niro in her seriousness. She examined the room from this corner, then that corner. Much chin stroking. Squinting; left eye, then right eye. She extracted volumes, replaced them. She circumnavigated the entire space, arms locked behind her back. I had never seen a fact sodomized with such thoroughness.

'It does feel like a library,' she finally admitted.

'Exactly! You're welcome.'

'But it doesn't feel like *our* fucking library. This could be a section in any university library. It feels impersonal.'

What nonsense. Every book in the room had been bought because one of us had seen a use for it. It was built from actual use, not potential use. And show me the university library that would stock *Queer Nursery Rhymes for Queer Children* or the flip-book *How the Stick People Became Extinct*. These were our books, our choices, the contents of our minds.

I felt a bit hurt. I had thought we were on the same page. She had been the one who had given away the books. No discussion then. Now she made it sound like she'd only done it to make me happy. As if my happiness was separate from hers. Okay, we had a lot fewer books, but we probably still had more books than all our neighbours put together. We had only subtracted duplicates. Essence wasn't lost when the inessential was removed, and the idea of the original collection had been preserved, plus or minus human error of course.

'Gotta admit, though, the library is much more manageable now,' said Sophie, smiling.

Her smile evaporated all my anger. She was willing herself to like it. My loyal, beloved wife. If she didn't feel like she belonged in this room, neither could I. If I couldn't make her see, at least I could still console her. I went over to the window, drew the curtains to one side. I forced myself to remove the cardboard covers from the skylights. Light flooded the room. I returned to my desk and she took the Bombay Fornicator, stretched out on it with a theatrical sigh. We smiled at each other. Peace at last.

'Definitely more usable,' I said. 'Here, give me the name of a book we own.'

'All right. Wallace Stevens.'

I did a quick search for the book using the book-management software. We didn't have anything by the author.

'Is that the title?' I said.

'What?'

'Wallace Stevens?'

She gave me a strange look. 'Hello? Wallace Stevens!'

'Yes, I heard you. Who's he?' We didn't have any book by that title either. Or keyword.

'Who's Wallace Stevens?' Sophie looked around the room as if she were hoping to spot a psychiatrist. 'Are you messing with me? The poet, of course. *Notes Towards a Supreme Fiction*? Remember? My most favourite poem by an old dead white guy ever?'

'Never heard of him. Do you mean George Wallace?' At her glare, I bent over my laptop, keyed in a Google search. 'There's a number of poets either Stevens or Wallace but no Wallace Stevens. Do you mean Sufjan Stevens? We have his album—'

'Chibi! Not funny. *Wallace Stevens.*' She got up with force, and the Fornicator creaked and shivered in the wake of her agitation. She went over to the stacks.

'Bookshelf B, second shelf,' I said, helpfully. 'That's where we keep the poetry books.'

Glare. I waited quietly as she searched. No point telling her that if the database didn't list it, we didn't have it.

'Fucking A,' said Sophie.

'You must be thinking of someone else. The Academy of American Poets doesn't list any Wallace Stevens. Take a look if you don't believe me.'

'Am I going mad?' Sophie looked at me, completely bewildered. 'I know he exists. Everyone does! I mean – he's a major *major* poet. I have his poems in my head. We talked about Stevens at Professor Novillo's place. Remember? When we first met?'

I did not. Frankly, I was a little worried.

'How can you not remember?' asked Sophie. She moved her head horizontally, almost as if she were scanning lines. She must have been, because she suddenly broke into verse.

Begin, ephebe, by perceiving the idea
Of this invention, this invented world,
The inconceivable idea of the sun.

You must become an ignorant man again
And see the sun again with an ignorant eye
And see it clearly in the idea of it.

Sophie stopped for breath, then something in her turned wary when she saw my expression.

'Either I've gone mad or the whole world has,' she continued. 'I don't remember how we started talking about Stevens, but I laughed when you said that if Stevens had smoked dope like everybody else he wouldn't have needed to write poetry. Later that night, I mentioned that Joan and I were looking for a roomie. You took the hint, finally, after I mentioned it twice.'

'Hmm.' Her force of conviction was beginning to confuse me. 'I don't know, Sophie. I remember the party and all that but I think we talked about Ezra Pound. Right? His Chinese phase was pretty embarrassing. Are you sure you aren't mixing things up? That line – the inconceivable idea of the sun – that's the title of Memon's collection.'

'Who the fuck is Memon?'

'Imran Asif Memon! We have his book. Let me ask The Machine That Never Forgets.' The database pointed to Bookshelf A, shelf 4. I retrieved Memon's slim volume, handed it to her. Sophie flicked desultorily, then lost interest when she couldn't find a reference to the mythical Wallace Stevens, muttered 'must read it' or some such thing, and set the book aside.

'I know this must feel really weird,' I said sympathetically. I told her how I clearly remembered visiting the INS *Vikrant* on a class trip. I remembered the tight passageways, the excess of metal, the smell of engine fuel, the swarm of men in their smart white uniforms. There was only one problem. The ship had been made into a museum ship in 2002, well after I had finished schooling. I must have somehow imagined the whole trip.

'Stevens wrote a poem called *Life on a Battleship*.' Sophie looked frightened. 'I am so certain he existed. What's happening to me? Am I getting Alzy's or something? Jesus, this is crazy.'

'Oh come on.' I tapped my head, more worried than I let on. 'We have a lot of books in there. Bound to get scrambled now and then. Forget about Stevens. Let's talk about how to make this your room as well.'

As the months passed, she persisted in her delusion – I was ready to call it that by then – and during spring vacation, we went down to NYU's School of Medicine to get a neurological examination. A trip to NYC would have been a treat under normal circumstances but now everything was tinged with worry. She was terrified and so was I; there's no place so devoid of worthwhile reading as a hospital.

There was good news and bad news. The bad news was a tiny lesion in Sophie's cingulate gyrus. Hardly a couple of millimetres across. The good news was that it seems to have caused very little damage. She checked out fine on all the tests, plus or minus human variation.

'You may notice other subtle discrepancies,' said Doctor O. 'Keep a diary. It'll come really handy during the biannual checkups.'

'Jesus. Biannual checkups. I'm officially fucking mental now.'

'No, no,' protested the doctor.

'Yes,' I barked. 'You're fine! It could've been ten times worse.'

The doctor calmed us with stories about anonymized patients who were all in much worse condition than Sophie. They all sounded like characters from *Twilight Zone*. People who were convinced their spouses had been replaced by strangers. People who couldn't recognize themselves in the mirror. People who said one word when they wanted to say another.

'But why does it happen, Dr Sacks?' cried Sophie.

'Call me Oliver.' It was clear the good doctor lived to answer the question of why the Brain misbehaved. 'Look, the simple explanation is this. It's not enough to know something; we also need to know that we know. But this metaknowledge isn't conveyed through logic or words or thoughts. It's conveyed through a feeling. We feel sure of what we know. And this feeling is how you know you know. The stronger the feeling, the more certain you are. Unfortunately, for a variety of reasons, in some of us, this feeling of certainty attaches itself to the wrong propositions. Logically, we know what we're claiming is false. Yet we feel absolutely, totally, one hundred per cent certain it's true. Often, we'll twist what we know to match what we feel to be true. It's quite fascinating. And your husband is right, it could have been a lot worse. Fortunately, the damage appears to be very localized.'

'Yeah, just a tiny fascinating rip in my whole fucking universe.' Then she touched the doctor's arm. 'Sorry. I know you're trying to help.'

'It's fine. I deserved that.'

We pondered what we'd learned, in silence. It felt true.

'Well, we'll deal with it,' I said at last. 'It's comforting to have a medical answer, a biological explanation for all this.' I didn't add: even though there's nothing we can do with it.

'He's my rock,' said Sophie, smiling.

Later, as we drove back to the hotel (we were taking the flight back home the next day), Sophie said to me: 'It breaks my heart to think I must lose my faith in Books.'

'Nonsense. Let's not overreact. So you are mixed up about a few authors. Big deal. And don't tell me you buy this lesion business. What's a lesion? What's disease? Remember what Foucault said about the medical gaze? Medicine cures us with fictions. Who cares whether Wallace Stevens existed or not or whether he wrote the books you think he did? Each book contains all the books ever written. Every book is a library of Books, in that sense. Who is Wallace Stevens? You are Wallace Stevens.'

'And you are my Chibi.'

Of course. Encouraged, I went on in this bossy vein at some

length, which earned me a tender kiss from my Wallace Stevens, but whether she felt what I wanted her to feel I could not say. And though I tried to persuade Sophie to claim ownership of her secret library, she wouldn't. She couldn't. Her mind knew it wouldn't be plagiarizing, but if Sacks was correct, her mind didn't know it knew.

Sometimes at night, I would wake to find Sophie gone. I would hear her prowling about the library, searching online used-bookstores, querying rare-book agents, searching, searching for the self that had disappeared into the black emptiness of the lesion. She stopped accompanying me on weekend trips to the bookstore. She'd join me for brunch, pretend to be excited by my purchases, talk about new projects. She began research papers, and though I promised to make sure the world she talked about in her papers actually existed ('just call it a fucking sanity-check, okay Chibi?'), she didn't finish what she started. She got involved with local schools, literacy outreach programmes, drifted from academia into administrative roles. She swore she was happier than ever.

Sometimes, when she couldn't sleep, haunted by nightmares of phantom works, I'd keep her company over her protests. I'd make her hot chocolate, search the world's databases with her, fortify her with my faith, and when the mood was right entreat her to recite a luminous passage or two from inconceivable volumes of the sun.

16

AQUA BIOGRAPHICA

In a village not too far from the rising sun, there once lived a man blessed with the art of telling stories.

Unlike many who find their gifts a burden, the man was as generous with his stories as a cow with her milk; all one had to do was ask.

He was always willing to oblige. He even allowed his listeners to shout out words, random words, and he'd find a way to work them into the story. He wasn't too proud to include trees if his listeners wanted trees, or a great deep slow river with tangled banks if they wanted a bit of water, or emerald-green frogs plopping in and out of the river if they wanted mischief, or a pair of lovers entangled in the hollows of a peepal tree at the great river's edge, blissfully unaware of the emerald-green frogs plopping in and out of the water, if his listeners wanted life itself. Why, he'd even end in the old way: they are there, you are here; they are then, you are now; they have arrived, and you are home.

He hadn't always been a storyteller, but when he was asked the story of his life, he would invariably begin from the time he'd started to tell stories. So listeners got the full history, right from the time the Goddess Saraswati had inscribed the first letter on his tongue to his present state, deeply content with a beloved wife, a passel of jolly kids, and an extended family that grew every year in nephews and nieces.

Perhaps he could have gone on in this manner, growing from one happiness to another, and no one, least of all the storyteller, would have been any the wiser. But, one day, his youngest (or perhaps his eldest, it was hard to tell, they were all so rosy-cheeked and identically happy) asked him for a story. It was nothing out of the ordinary, and the storyteller had already included night and shadows (gracefully cast by a single lamp) and, as if in agreement with his design, his youngest (or maybe his eldest) lay nestled with her head in her mother's ample lap, her large expressive eyes sombre with sleep. The man cleared his throat and began:

A housewife knew a story. She also knew a song. But she wouldn't tell anyone the story, nor did she ever sing the song.

The end, sighed his youngest and eldest.

He had expected there to be more to the story, but now that he had to work the end into the story, it struck him that the story was really quite complete as is. He let himself go silent and, indeed, the silence was as cheerful and heart-warming an ending as any. The quiet breathing of his youngest (his eldest was most likely in another city, working hard at working hard) revealed the night had adopted her. The man gestured to his wife to put out the lamp.

He expected her to protest, but when she complied with a smile, he wondered if he'd stretched the story out longer than necessary. Perhaps all he had needed to say was: *A housewife –* and his audience would have filled out the rest of the tale for themselves with ambitious wives, selfish wives, faithless wives, forgetful wives, happy wives, fat wives, skinny wives, lesson-teaching wives or, more likely, lesson-learning wives. For that matter, why even include those two words: *A housewife*? What was so special about those two words? Surely, his audience didn't need to be goaded with word-prods as if they were ill-trained elephants? Why not just tell the story entirely with silence?

His wife spooned her body next to his, and he felt an overflowing of happiness, almost painful in its intensity, at the perfection of his life.

Now, it is the lot of some to be bound ever more intimately to life by happiness, whereas for others, happiness has the opposite effect. The man discovered, alas, that he was of the second type. As the days went by, he satisfied every request for a story with silence, though his natural generosity of spirit led to many breaches of discipline such as a frown, a nod, or, egregiously, a clearing of the throat. This new mode of storytelling demanded a lot more effort from his listeners. Silence is full of possibility. The man used it only when necessary. But, alas, it is very easy for the listener to hear what is not being said.

One day, lost in silence, in the midst of a most complex tale (it involved a frightened queen, a thousand nights, and many nested levels, quite reminiscent of an ancient stepwell), he heard his wife say, *Don't disturb your father, he has no more stories.*

To use a bit of storytelling jargon, his wife's words threw the man completely 'out of the story'. He had been weighing many possibilities in his head, but this one had never crossed his mind. In one of those unexpected and not always welcome flashes of insight, the man realized the truth of his wife's words.

Many stories say that denial is the first step to recovery in the face of irreversible loss. So it was with this man. That night, as his wife slept by his side, the man tossed and turned. His body burned with the fever of truth. The world rose and fell, keeping time with his rising and falling chest, as if each breath was attempting to build a factual castle from fictional air.

He called out to his wife in terror – make it the way it was, beloved wife. Make everything the way it was. But in the silence, he heard only silence. It was true, it was all too true; he had no more stories, nothing would ever again be the same.

No more stories, no, no, that was impossible, no, no, it wasn't possible. Why, at this very moment, his mind was weaving –

His silence-plagued mind didn't know how to proceed. What should he do next? When the man tried to collect the possibilities, they seemed to dissolve like the mist by the – yes, yes, the river, the peepal tree, the emerald-green frogs, and the lovers eternal. A walk by the river would clear his mind, rid him of this silence, make him whole again. He sat up, got dressed, and stepped out. He wasn't alone; a few of his dearest stories insisted on coming along, and though he pretended to argue he was secretly quite glad.

It was a moonless night, which is always inconvenient for a storyteller. A moonlit night can evoke many fine words and deep connections with other moonlit thoughts. Stories flow along almost effortlessly if there is moonlight to guide things. Perhaps if the man had walked out into a moonlit night things would have turned out differently.

He turned left at the intersection, which was a short distance from the old graveyard, not far from the bus stop that led to the city and all the other cities where his children worked, from the eldest to the youngest. A part of him wanted to turn back, but he consulted his stories, and they told him the river wasn't far, just a few hundred steps away at the most.

Many stories say that the more one walks, the less certain one becomes of origins and destinations. So it was with this man. He walked and walked. He was headed for the river, but the more he walked, the less clear it became where he'd come from and where he was headed. His stories wearied of all the walking. One said it would hitchhike, two waited for the rain to stop, three stopped for some chai ... To make a long story short, he eventually walked alone. He worked when there was work to be had and starved when there wasn't. Everything mattered and nothing mattered.

But something about him still marked him as a storyteller. People would ask him about the weather and somehow the weather would become more than the weather. Or he'd mention knowing a man walking towards water, and somehow it became more than about a man walking towards water. There was no avoiding it. Sooner or later, people would ask him for a story.

Where he had once been silent, now he only loved. But even love, which was only unconditional love, was somehow seen to be other than love. He was asked the secret of happiness, of health, of wealth, of life's meaning, of immortality. He answered as honestly as he could, namely that, as far as he knew, such questions have no answers. But when it frightened some in the crowd, he realized that they'd been asking for the river, the peepal tree, the entangled banks, the emerald-green frogs, and the lovers who would never die. This he could no longer give. Sometimes it made his listeners angry, and then he would have to resume his journey. But at each place he stopped, there were always a few, also ready to let go of their stories.

As the man lay dying, he was pleasantly surprised to see one of his favourite stories approach him, its palms folded. He had believed all his stories had been left behind, and he saw he'd been mistaken. His 'I' had been padding along silently beside him all this time, but now, in these final moments, I sought reassurance. The man embraced his self, his subtlest story, his separation from all, and reminded it that stories are forged as gates, not walls. Open. There is nothing to fear. Let love in. Let love in and live in love.

Behold the river, the peepal tree, the emerald-green frogs plopping in and out of the water, the eternal lovers by the tangled bank. The man could see them now, his beloved wife and each and every one of his little monkeys. O, how he loved them, how he loved life. They were waiting for him, their arms aching to hug, smiles as wide as the universe. He was here, in the now, he had arrived, he was home.

CONTEXTS

Sometimes when a father has an ugly, loutish son, the love he bears him so blindfolds his eyes that he does not see his defects, or, rather, takes them for gifts and charms of mind and body, and talks of them to his friends as wit and grace.

MIGUEL CERVANTES
Don Quixote de la Mancha

01 | The Man without Quintessence

It is almost certain space-faring aliens don't live in India. That's because it is laughably easier to travel from Alpha Centauri to Earth than it is to get the myriad certifications needed to live in this country, where every document depends on at least three other documents, at least one of which must be on stamp paper, each properly witnessed (minimum three, contact numbers to be provided, police verification pending), countersigned by a notary, approved by a gazetted officer, rubber-stamped by his assistant who's having a desultory but passionate affair with

the lady seated next to the photocopy machine, and needless
to say, an infinite supply of photographs whose dimensional
requirements vary from year to year, department to department,
and regime to regime.

This story almost wrote itself. Perhaps because it really
isn't a story. It is simply a contemporary fact without proper
documentation.

02 | As Clear As

'As Clear As' was written for an anthology in honour of Samuel
Delany, credited with popularizing the term 'speculative fiction'.
His stories often play with the faith we have in the persistence of
objects. 'We' as in 'we adults'. Babies are less gullible. They have
just popped out of the quantum-mechanical void and know there
is no such thing as a *thing*. But we soon manage to educate them
into our delusions. We start with games. *Peekaboo, baby!* Oh
no, Mommy's gone. She's gone!! Waaaahhhh ... *Mommy's here!
Ha ha ha. Fooled you!* Whew! Ha ha ha. *Peekaboo!* Eventually
we persuade babies that objects endure, relationships endure,
just relax, things just don't go poof and disappear, just relax,
little quantum-mechanical baby!

The French philosopher Quentin Meillassoux, however,
has managed to hang on to our first grasp of the world. In his
book *After Finitude*, Meillassoux spells out the basic thesis
of Baby-ontology, or 'speculative realism' as it is now called:
'...every world is without reason, and is thereby capable of
actually becoming otherwise without reason... Everything
could actually collapse: from trees to stars, from stars to laws,

from physical laws to logical laws; and this not by virtue of some superior law whereby everything is destined to perish, but by virtue of the absence of any superior law capable of preserving anything, no matter what, from perishing.'

In short, the world is absolutely contingent. I hope he is wrong. *Peekaboo!* Oh God, here we go again.

03 | Invisible Hand

This story hatched from my friend Vivek Balaraman's comment that 'a Shiva in charge of creation and a Vishnu in charge of destruction would lead to a very different world'. Of course, Hindu gods do evolve over time. The fearsome Indra of the Rig Veda transformed into the oafish Indra of the Purānas. But I felt Vivek's comment pointed to something much deeper, about how something once done can never be undone, at least not entirely, not without leaving a mark. Vivek's hypothesis sounded like a fable worth writing and so I wrote it.

Strictly speaking, Lord Shiva and the Goddess Parvati do not entertain themselves with dance. Apocalyptic dice games are more their thing. But that is a different story.

04| Into the Night

We say 'home' when we feel we belong in a space. The English language seems to have no analogous word for how we feel when we belong in time, *a* time. Nor has science-fiction found it necessary to invent a suitable word for this feeling. Science-fiction's interest is in the future, not in time per se, and its heroes are quite at home in the future. Science-fiction's roots lie in boys' adventure fiction, that is, the literature of heroes and honour, and if it does deal with time's exiles at all then it turns events into an awfully good adventure. There isn't much honour for heroes in simply waiting to die.

Kallikulam Ramaswamy Iyer, uprooted and despairing, is close to my heart. I had the misfortune and privilege of sharing this planet with one such soul. He had a dishonourable death. Onwards in peace, old man. In another life, may we travel together again in a happier space-time.

05 | God's Own Country

The story wasn't really working for me until I suddenly realized one day that Helet's real name was actually Tekhelet and that she was a Jew of Indian origin. Or perhaps that should read 'Indian of Jewish origin'. Either way, once I knew her true name, everything fell into place.

The Hebrew word 'tekhelet' refers to a blue dye, extracted from the glands of a particular snail species, the hillazon (*Murex trunculus*). Yahweh had commanded Jewish men to attach a thread of tekhelet to the fringes of their apparel (King James Bible, Numbers 15:37–41), to remind them of the 613 commandments in the Torah. Curiously, a tekhelet dye molecule's colour spectrum has its highest absorption peak centred at exactly 613 nanometers! Tekhelet is God's own molecule, so to speak. Naturally, Tekhelet had to visit God's own country.

This is the sort of origin-myth authors like to construct and it is not realy true. The story came from where stories come from. But I do know that once 'Tekhelet' came to mind, I had no desire to consider any other name.

06 | The Robots of Eden

Ghosts are Air and Water; Robots, Earth and Fire. Ghosts glide; Robots bump around. Ghosts machinate; Robots are machinery incarnate. Ghosts are death unmade; Robots are Made in China. Ghosts speak; Robots execute instructions. Ghosts dream of embodiment; Robots dream of transcendence. Who could have conceived that embedding a Ghost in the Robot would lead to us, the storytelling species?

07 | Seven Questions in a World, Gear-Constructed

Donald Barthelme famously said that 'the writer is one who, embarking upon a task, does not know what to do'. To which I'd like to add, 'nor having completed it, know what they've done'. This story can be seen as evidence of the truth of these two claims, but I like to think there's a deeper and more comforting lesson. It is not a negative capability that this story or any other story points to, but a positive one. If 'mere' stories can transcend their creators, then perhaps, one day, our tragic species will also be able to bring forth a new species, a saner and kinder species, and bequeath this world to their care.

08 | Love in a Hot Climate

In 1955, Milton Friedman was invited by the Indian government to advise the Ministry of Finance on economic planning (which, as Galbraith pointed out, is like asking the Pope to recommend a good contraceptive). During his visit to Delhi, he produced a report. It was ignored at the time, but is now considered something of a classic statement on the post-Independence Indian economy.

I must confess that there is no mention of any time machine in Friedman's original report; indeed, in Professor Gary Dymski's paper, 'Money as a "Time Machine" in the New Financial World', the metaphor is credited to the economist Paul Davidson.

As regards Purushottam: there is a certain character type peculiar to post-colonial nations. He (and it *is* a 'he') haunts government offices, he is forever on the verge of success, he is congenitally optimistic, his entire life is a circus of circumstances, and he can often be spotted holding forth at tea stalls. The Indian novelist G.V. Desani reified this character in his magnum opus, *All About H. Hatterr*.

Desani aficionados will find Purushottam's liberties with the English language rather familiar. Here is how H. Hatterr describes it: 'I write rigmarole English, straining your goodly godly tongue, maybe: but friend, I forsook my Form, School and Head, while you stuck to yours, learning reading, 'riting and 'rithmetic.'

Purushottam's English is Desani-lite. It is not really 'Indian English' (Anurag Mathur's *The Inscrutable Americans* has some great examples of this variant).

I have no doubt that Dr Friedman encountered a Purushottam or two during his trip to India. That's just the way Karma works. Again, H. Hatterr: 'As to *Truth*, the great generalization is, "Dam" mysterious! Mum's the word!" As to *Life*, the locus classicus, "contrast!"'

This story is dedicated to G.V. Desani.

09 | The Mind-Body Problem

Reincarnation is a crazy idea, but as the physicist Enrico Fermi said in a different context, the question is whether it is crazy enough to be true. Ian Stevenson's *20 Cases Suggestive of Reincarnation* credibly argues there is enough evidence that a person's *memories*, their quintessence, so to speak, can survive death (typically, sudden violent death). I have no faith in essences or afterlives of any kind. Fortunately, an author's beliefs don't necessarily reincarnate in their fictions, and hence I was able to write this tale.

10 | The Literature of Change

Bruce Sterling has remarked somewhere that the golden age of SF is fifteen. This has always felt true to me. But I began late, at nineteen, rather than fifteen. My friend Ashok Bhavnani had won the *Mid-Day* crossword prize, a coupon worth fifty rupees redeemable at the Strand Bookstore in Bombay's Fort Area. We went to buy the fattest and largest book fifty rupees could buy. The SF genre understands readers who like to weigh their literature by the kilo, and we chanced upon a satisfyingly thick anthology, edited, I think, by Isaac Asimov. However, we were too cheap to take a chance, and as Ashok browsed for other obese candidates I quickly speed-read the first story. It happened to be Ray Bradbury's *A Sound of Thunder*. A man goes for a time safari, accidentally kills a butterfly, and returns to find history completely altered. It's a poorly written story, but the nineteen-year-old me didn't see it that way. We bought the anthology. I was careful not to step on any butterflies, but I was altered nonetheless. This story is dedicated to that noble savage, the nineteen-year-old me.

11 | The Parrots' Tale

Sometimes we come across a story, fall in love with it, and then it becomes a personal 'best story' in some category. For me, A.K. Ramanujan's *A Story and a Song*, an English translation of a Kannada folk tale, is my favourite short story under 500 words. I have long been inspired by that tale. Since it warns readers of the perils of not telling stories, it seemed fitting that I pay homage by warning readers about the perils of fiction.

12 | God's Own Language

Ever since Galileo claimed that the Book of Nature is written in mathematics, a related idea seems to have taken hold, especially among physicists, that mathematics is God's own language. However, even after 500 odd years of intense study by humanity's greatest physicists, our most sophisticated models can only account for 5 per cent of existence. We wouldn't visit France's British Embassy and jump to the conclusion that the French all speak English. Yet, when it comes to the universe, we do just that. On the other hand, we now know how much we don't yet know. That is a significant achievement.

What lies beyond that small lonely circle of the knowable? Wittgenstein said that 'whereof we cannot speak, thereof we must be silent'. Perhaps that is why we cannot approach the divine through language. The South-Asian philosophers had a different approach. They preferred apophasis, a negative theology. Faced with the indescribable, inexplicable, un-characterizable, they described, explained, they characterized, and then they added: neti, neti. Not this, not this. Or, in the language of mathematics, ¬¬.

13 | Archipelago

John Donne (1572–1631) was a poet and an ex-Catholic in a land that favoured poets and tortured Catholics. For this conflicted apostate, exit must have been an ever-tempting option. He was actively involved in the affairs of the Virginia Company, tasked with colonizing the east coast of North America.

Donne's book *Devotions Upon Emergent Occasions* consists of 23 meditations and describes his struggle with a near-fatal illness (most likely, typhus). Meditation 17 contains the famous lines: 'No man is an island…' and 'Ask not for whom the bells toll…' In the preface, Donne starts by saying, possibly quite sincerely: 'I have had three births; one, natural, when I came into the world; one, supernatural, when I entered into the ministry; and now, a preternatural birth, in returning to life, from this sickness.'

Though we still have no shortage of conflicted souls, one important difference is that the undiscovered country now exists only in the geography of the imagination.

14 | How Not to Tell the Ramayana

Though the Rama of Valmiki's Ramayana was co-opted by the Vaishnavites as an incarnation of Lord Vishnu, I have always seen Rama as more of a Shaivite figure. Like Lord Shiva, he's meditative, serious, invincible, and deeply committed to monogamy. I wondered what a Valmiki Ramayana with Rama as a Shaivite figure would look like. I chose a non-fiction format to discuss this Ramayana, and also set myself the constraint of using actual research papers, not made-up ones. The papers had to be chosen carefully, because they couldn't have any reference to Rama as an incarnation of Lord Vishnu. And these papers could only consider specific aspects of the Valmiki Ramayana, not the whole epic, since that would lead to serious logical inconsistencies. I don't know if I have succeeded entirely in my attempt, but now I do know that such an attempt is feasible.

15 | The Inconceivable Idea of the Sun

Any avid reader knows how invested one gets in the existence of certain works. For me, a world without Dickens's novels or the Hindu epics or Shakespeare or the Bible or any of a dozen other works is a world not really worth living in. Of course with great love comes the fear of losing that love. This story was born from that love and fear.

16 | Aqua Biographica (after Éric Chevillard)

Quintessentially, we have here a writer, a descendant of quill-pushers, an ordinary feather from an ordinary grey goose, a kala-hamsa, *Anser cinerus*, just a swan, question-mark neck, elegant, noble, seen gliding in so many Sanskrit autumn poems, from here to there, as a snake is wont to do, a kala naga, with forked tongue, and fanged bite to match, supple, sinuous, a leap of muscle and bared canines, down Fido, down boy, good boy, this mongrel loves to love, silly fellow, see the wagging tail, fanning rather, a good-natured temple cow, quite learned, stuffed with the Vedas and wit, and bananas of the plantain tree, generous and green, always partly green, as a living tree must be, else it is mere paper, sheets of blank paper, waiting for a writer, perhaps even this writer.

PUBLICATION HISTORY

- **The Man Without Quintessence**
  Avatar – अवतार Contemporary Indian Science Fiction/ Fantascienza contemporanea indiana. Tarun K. Saint and Francesco Verso, eds. Future Fiction. 2020.

- **As Clear As**
  Stories for Chip: A Tribute to Samuel R. Delany. Nisi Shawl and Bill Campbell, eds. Rosarium Publishing. 2015.

- **Invisible Hand**
  Lady Churchill's Rosebud Wristlet. No. 20, 2007.

- **Into the Night**
  Interzone Magazine. Issue 216, June 2008.

- **The Robots of Eden**
  New Suns Anthology. Nisi Shawl, ed. Solaris Books. 2019.

- **Love in a Hot Climate**
  Tel: Stories. Jay Lake, ed. Wheatland Press. 2005.

- **The Literature of Change**
  Muse India. Sami Ahmad Khan, ed. Issue 66. March–April 2016.

- **Archipelago**
  Strange Horizons. 25 April 2005.

- **How Not to Tell the Ramayana**
  Portions of this story appeared in: *Kiski Kahani: The Ramayana Project.* Imran Ali Khan, ed. Open Space Publications. pp. 135–145. 2012.

ACKNOWLEDGEMENTS

Short-story collections aren't easy propositions for publishers. It also doesn't help that speculative fiction is at a nascent stage in India. Poulomi Chatterjee, my editor at Hachette India, has not only helped develop the speculative fiction genre in the country, but was an early champion of this volume. Her insightful suggestions and corrections are reflected on every page. I'm also grateful to Sonali Jindal for taking over from Poulomi, ensuring a seamless transition, and shepherding the manuscript in its final stages.

Before a book can be published, however, it has to be written. The controlled fits of insanity that enable a book to be written are managed more easily when one is surrounded by people who care. I am a lucky bastard in that regard. Saras Sarasvathy was one of my earliest readers. She enabled me to be a writer and these stories have been shaped by the life we shared. I am also indebted to Pervin Saket for not letting me abandon the project, for her brilliant editorial eye, and for just being there, a constant companion.

Suneetha Balakrishnan, Vivek Balaraman, Emma Dawson-Varughese, Rinku Datta, Himanshu Gaur, Suresh Jois, Swapna

Kishore, Abha Iyengar, Manjula Padmanabhan, Geeta Patel, Kavita Philip, Vandana Singh, and Kaushik Vishwanathan suffered through early drafts of these tales. I would have finished the stories sooner without their help, and I am grateful to them for suffocating that possibility. My understanding of how spec-fic does what it does evolved in large measure due to their responses. They gave me their attention and I am grateful for that most generous of gifts.

I also thank the editors who saw fit to publish some of these stories in their magazines and anthologies: John Joseph Adams, Jed Hartman, Jonathan Oliver, Tarun Saint, Brett Savory, Nisi Shawl, Jonathan Strahan, Lavie Tidhar, and Francesco Verso.

The 'Acknowledgement' bears the same burden that Borges ascribed to the translation; namely, that it must perform its duty knowing its performance is also an act of apology. I know I have left out many more generous souls than I have remembered to list. The people who love me; those who loved me; the friends made and unmade; the myriad individuals whose bits and pieces I took without permission to fashion my characters; the kindness of strangers; the writers, living and dead, I learned from; the people whose help went unnoticed: and to all those who touched my life and weighed its curvature: I am in your debt and this book is its inadequate acknowledgement.